Arizona Walls
If Only They Could Speak

Judy Martin

Phoenix, Arizona
1997

Arizona Walls: If Only They Could Speak

Library of Congress Cataloging-in-Publication Data

ISBN: 0-929526-76-7

Limits of Liability and Disclaimer

The author of this book has used her best efforts in its preparation. The author makes no warranty of any kind, expressed or implied, with regard to the suggestions contained herein.

The author shall not be liable in the event of incidental or consequential damages in connection with, or arising out of, the use of instructions.

Production Services By:
Double B Publications
4123 N. Longview
Phoenix, AZ 85014
Phone: 602-274-7236
Fax: 602-996-6928

Typesetting/Layout By:
Running Changes
1307 E. Oregon Avenue
Phoenix, AZ 85014
Phone: 602-285-1834

Foreword

Arizona's wide and diverse history has produced a number of wondrous place names and people, whose stories demand telling...and re-telling. The early pioneers gave their towns picturesquely whimsical names like Two Guns, Canyon Diablo and Tombstone. Those towns were populated in turn, by a litany of folks that ran the wide gamut of frontier society. They ranged from doctors, lawyers, preachers, and teachers, to drifters, con men, outlaws and dance hall girls. On one end of the social spectrum are doctors like Tombstone's George Goodfellow, the famous "gunshot physician," great orators of the bar such as Allen English, and fearless preachers like the Reverend Endicott Peabody. On the other end were colorful characters and obstreperous riff-raff like Gotch-eyed Mary, Bravo Juan and Big Foot Annie. All left a legacy that is today a part of our cherished history.

Judy Martin has come up with a very intriguing premise for a book that is sure to pique the curiosity of anyone interested in the many facets of Arizona history. She's written 55 vignettes centered around a particular building in Arizona. Some, like the bloody massacre at the stagecoach station at Dragoon Springs, and Canyon Diablo, the "Toughest Hellhole in the West," are old tales from the distant past, and others, like Goulding's historic Indian trading post, and the famed Tovrea Castle, "The Wedding Cake House," in east Phoenix are stories of a more recent time.

Arizona Walls takes the reader on a delightful journey to these fascinating places. It's the next best thing to being there. Through Judy Martin's masterful storytelling, you become, like the proverbial fly on the wall, privy to what took place.

Some of the stories from *Arizona Walls* tell of the murder, intrigue, and violence that reflects the wild and woolly side of the past, while others are romantic and poignant. The common thread woven through each is the human drama, humor and courage. Most are about regular, everyday people in common places, dealing with extraordinary events. They appear on the historical stage for only a brief moment, yet each is important.

Judy Martin's purpose for this work was three-fold. She wanted to write an entertaining book; she wanted it to be educational; and perhaps most important, she believes the more people know about a place they will be more willing to respect and take better care of it. I believe she has succeeded on all three fronts with *Arizona Walls*. As her former Arizona history professor, I'm very proud of her and the work she's done.

Marshall Trimble
Arizona State Historian

Introduction and Acknowledgments

The concept of this book grew in the back of my mind as I was conducting city tours of Phoenix when I worked as an Arizona Tour Guide. As I led tourists around the city in a large motorcoach, I would point out the various buildings of the area and tell the "people stories" behind the buildings. From city tours, to a slide show presented in Territorial costume, to a book was a normal progression. The material quickly outgrew Phoenix and soon took in the entire state.

The stories are all true. At least, they are as true as research and memories can make them. Marshall Trimble, the Official Historian of the State of Arizona, remarks that "History is the story you choose to believe." Often there are several versions of the same true event. To enliven the telling I have added apocryphal quotes or conversations to some of the stories. These quotes are what the people probably said, although no one actually wrote down their exact words.

My three goals in writing this book were to entertain, to educate, and to preserve. What we choose to do with what we know about the past—ignore it, destroy it, preserve it , cherish it—dictates how much of our past history we will have to show future generations. Just a heap of rocks, all that is left of Dragoon Springs Stage Station, comes alive only after hearing about the life and death struggle that took place there so many years ago. That heap of rocks becomes an important site to maintain, now that we know the human drama. We have an enormous obligation to educate ourselves and forthcoming generations so they, too, will understand our past and take part in the preservation of our history. The stories of our predecessors, be they courageous pioneer or scoundrel, enrich our lives in a special way. To leave the record blank and allow some of our historical sites to be destroyed through neglect or ignorance is unconscionable and im-poverishes us all.

Many friends have been supportive of my writing and to each of them I am grateful. A special thanks to Fayly Cothern, Dale Harvey, and Diana Weeks who have been such a faithful cheering section. You, especially, have always been so encouraging. A large bouquet of thanks goes to Esther Stewart who helped with the book far beyond the call of friendship.

The writing of this book would never have happened without the encouragement and enthusiasm of my best friend and husband, Dick Martin. He has, with unending good nature, endured creeping our mini-van along rocky, washed-out dirt roads (which resulted in costly car repairs), searching along river banks for ruins during snake season, and coming home from work anticipating a good meal only to find a dark kitchen and the ticketey-tick of the computer keyboard awaiting him. Loving Arizona and finding these out-of-the-way haunts and stories as much as I do, he is always excited about the next trip to the hinterlands.

Judy Martin
Phoenix, 1997

I am indebted to the following people:

Bernard L. Fontana—personal letter - historian - San Xavier
Terry Luke—*telephone interview - Frank Luke, Jr.*
John Thompson—telephone interview - Phoenix police - Miranda
Jerry Mitchell and Jennifer Tuzzolino—*tour of Camelback Castle
    and personal interview*
Mason Coggin—telephone interview - Southeastern Arizona
Jim Farris—*telephone interview - Southeastern Arizona*
Walter Cox—tour of Fort Grant with permission to take photos
Linda Van Tilborg—telephone interview - member of the Evans
    family - Evans house
Bill Jacobson—telephone interview - Tovrea Castle

All photographs were taken by the author except the following:

Dr. Corbusier, Pg. 37—Courtesy of Fort Verde State Park

   Charleston (#96-3179) Pg. 75
   Dr. George Goodfellow (#97-2735) Pg. 84
   Apache May (#97-7888) Pg. 93
   Lynching of John Heath (#97-2648.) Pg. 107
   Burt Alvord (#97-6452) Pg. 120
   Gov. Hunt (#96-365) Pg. 137
   Frank Luke, Jr. (#97-4401) Pg. 154
   Ernesto Miranda (97-7386) Pg. 220
   Texas John Slaughter (#97-7876) Pg. 94

Courtesy of the Research Division, Arizona Department of Library,
    Archives & Public Records, Phoenix

Cane Ranch, North Kaibab, Pg. 147—Courtesy of Yvonne Magnuson

Alissio Carraro & Leo, Pg. 158/ German POW's, Pg. 196—Courtesy of
    Arizona State Historical Society - Central Arizona Division

Wrigley Mansion, Pg. 173—Courtesy of Western Savings Brochure

Goulding's Trading Post, Pg. 189 / the *Gouldings*, Pg. 190 / *John Ford, Pg. 193*
    —*Courtesy of Ronnie Biard of Goulding's Lodge and Trading Post*

Rex Allen, Pg. 206—Courtesy of Douglass Dunn, Rex Allen Museum

Paolo Soleri, Pg. 234—Courtesy of Cosanti Foundation

Pueblo Villages, Pg. 240—Courtesy of Greg Schaefer - Private Collection

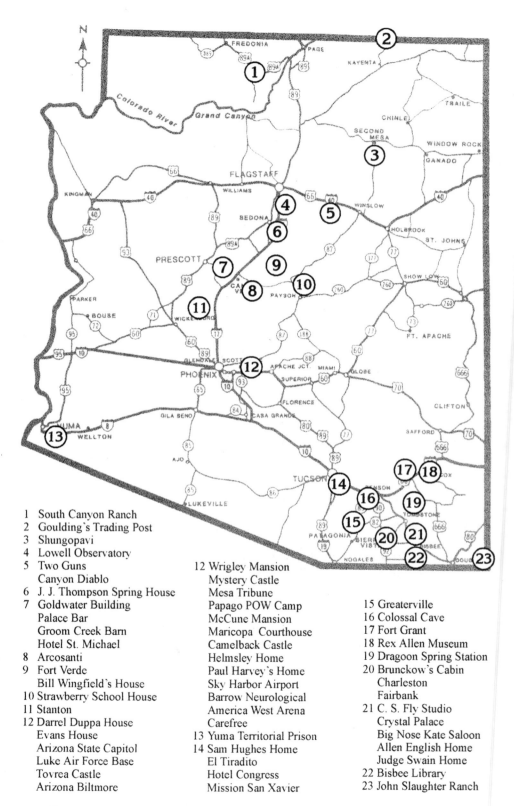

STATE MILEAGE MAP

	AJO	ASH FORK	BENSON	BISBEE	CASA GRANDE	CHANDLER	CLIFTON	COOLIDGE	COTTONWOOD	DOUGLAS	DUNCAN	FLAGSTAFF	FLORENCE	FREDONIA	GILA BEND	GLENDALE	GLOBE	GRAND CANYON	HOLBROOK	HOOVER DAM	KINGMAN	LK HAVASU CITY	LAS VEGAS, NV	MESA
AJO	★	262	185	233	99	129	309	121	215	284	305	256	130	452	42	116	197	341	331	357	295	304	387	125
ASH FORK	262	★	307	357	197	170	349	204	82	381	355	49	213	246	220	155	239	76	140	167	94	155	187	167
BENSON	185	307	★	49	113	142	115	112	261	74	121	302	115	498	170	170	152	382	286	414	342	362	444	153
BISBEE	233	357	49	★	161	192	164	161	311	24	170	351	163	547	221	219	200	431	335	464	390	409	494	201
CASA GRANDE	99	197	113	161	★	31	198	21	150	185	204	191	34	387	59	59	89	276	207	303	230	249	333	32
CHANDLER	129	170	142	192	31	★	190	34	124	216	196	165	43	365	88	32	79	249	183	277	209	223	307	8
CLIFTON	309	349	115	164	198	190	★	179	303	156	29	302	166	498	259	208	111	383	213	466	383	401	496	183
COOLIDGE	121	204	112	161	21	34	179	★	157	185	183	198	9	394	80	65	68	283	204	311	237	256	341	41
COTTONWOOD	215	82	261	311	150	124	303	157	★	335	308	48	166	243	173	103	172	129	139	248	175	236	278	121
DOUGLAS	284	381	74	24	185	216	156	185	335	★	162	374	188	571	242	242	200	460	333	487	414	433	517	226
DUNCAN	305	355	121	170	204	196	29	183	308	162	★	333	172	500	264	213	117	388	242	462	386	407	492	188
FLAGSTAFF	256	49	302	351	191	165	302	198	48	374	333	★	207	197	209	144	173	81	91	217	143	204	247	161
FLORENCE	130	213	115	163	34	43	166	9	166	188	172	207	★	403	93	75	56	291	191	318	246	265	348	49
FREDONIA	452	246	498	547	387	365	498	394	243	571	500	197	403	★	404	340	370	197	288	413	339	361	443	357
GILA BEND	42	220	170	221	59	88	259	80	173	242	264	209	93	404	★	75	146	293	286	317	247	203	347	83
GLENDALE	116	155	170	219	59	32	208	65	103	242	213	144	75	340	75	★	98	225	231	245	171	190	275	25
GLOBE	197	239	152	200	89	79	111	68	172	200	117	173	56	370	146	98	★	254	135	341	273	291	371	72
GRAND CANYON	341	76	382	431	276	249	383	283	129	460	388	81	291	197	293	225	254	★	172	240	170	231	270	246
HOLBROOK	331	140	286	335	207	183	213	204	139	333	242	91	191	288	286	231	135	172	★	308	234	296	338	175
HOOVER DAM	357	167	414	464	303	277	466	311	248	487	462	217	318	413	317	245	341	240	308	★	73	135	30	269
KINGMAN	295	94	342	390	230	209	383	237	175	414	386	143	246	339	247	171	273	170	234	73	★	61	103	196
LK HAVASU CITY	304	155	362	409	249	223	401	256	236	433	407	204	265	361	203	190	291	231	296	135	61	★	165	219
LAS VEGAS, NV	387	197	444	494	333	307	496	341	278	517	492	247	348	443	347	275	371	270	338	30	103	165	★	299
MESA	125	167	153	201	32	8	183	41	121	226	188	161	49	357	83	25	72	246	175	269	196	219	299	★
MIAMI	190	232	158	206	82	73	117	61	175	231	123	194	48	377	148	90	7	275	142	342	265	284	372	65
NOGALES	191	327	73	89	131	162	198	131	280	113	193	321	134	517	189	189	171	406	303	434	360	381	464	169
PAGE	378	182	433	482	322	296	465	330	179	507	444	132	337	106	336	276	365	107	212	349	275	340	379	293
PARKER	207	193	321	321	210	184	373	218	207	394	369	254	227	444	165	154	251	280	345	167	100	38	197	178
PAYSON	203	140	228	276	117	86	190	119	72	282	198	91	127	288	161	103	82	172	98	307	234	297	337	78
PHOENIX	110	152	156	205	45	19	207	52	105	229	203	146	61	342	68	14	87	231	221	259	185	204	289	15
PRESCOTT	212	50	258	307	147	121	299	154	41	331	305	87	163	286	163	101	189	131	174	213	144	192	243	117
SAFFORD	266	316	82	131	165	157	43	144	250	123	39	250	133	447	232	174	77	349	212	418	349	368	448	149
ST. JOHNS	329	198	283	332	220	212	155	201	196	321	184	149	188	340	287	229	132	230	58	366	292	353	396	204
SEDONA	229	77	275	324	164	138	297	171	19	349	302	28	180	224	180	117	142	108	120	244	171	232	275	135
SHOW LOW	284	187	238	287	175	167	169	156	163	285	204	139	143	336	242	184	87	220	48	355	282	343	385	159
SIERRA VISTA	215	343	35	33	148	177	150	147	296	57	156	337	150	534	205	205	187	422	320	450	376	397	480	188
SPRINGERVILLE	318	230	287	334	217	213	123	196	218	328	152	182	185	359	276	227	130	228	84	390	323	380	420	202
SUPERIOR	173	215	147	195	68	56	135	44	167	219	141	209	31	405	131	73	24	294	159	317	246	267	347	48
TEMPE	119	161	156	205	45	14	188	47	114	225	194	155	55	351	78	19	78	240	211	263	194	213	293	6
TOMBSTONE	211	333	26	24	138	168	141	137	286	48	147	327	140	523	195	195	177	412	310	439	366	387	469	178
TUBA CITY	336	128	377	426	266	244	381	281	127	455	387	80	285	138	278	219	254	79	162	441	222	284	480	236
TUCSON	140	263	45	93	68	98	169	67	216	118	166	257	70	453	125	125	107	342	240	370	296	317	400	108
WICKENBURG	168	111	214	263	103	77	256	110	101	287	261	150	119	347	119	43	145	186	279	200	128	148	230	73
WILLCOX	221	344	36	86	149	179	82	148	297	77	88	338	151	534	206	206	126	398	261	450	377	398	481	189
WILLIAMS	279	17	333	383	203	197	334	228	80	406	321	32	238	229	236	175	205	59	123	185	111	172	215	193
WINKELMAN	200	242	115	165	95	83	145	71	196	189	151	209	58	423	158	100	36	307	170	349	275	294	379	75
WINSLOW	214	107	318	368	201	175	246	208	105	367	275	58	208	255	272	214	168	139	33	275	201	262	305	189
YUMA	156	267	282	331	172	201	380	193	287	355	403	316	204	512	114	186	269	400	404	283	215	155	313	197

Mileage information compiled by the Travel and Facilities Branch of the Arizona Department of Transportation & Planning.

	MIAMI	NOGALES	PAGE	PARKER	PAYSON	PHOENIX	PRESCOTT	SAFFORD	ST. JOHNS	SEDONA	SHOW LOW	SIERRA VISTA	SPRINGERVILLE	SUPERIOR	TEMPE	TOMBSTONE	TUBA CITY	TUCSON	WICKENBURG	WILLCOX	WILLIAMS	WINKELMAN	WINSLOW	YUMA
AJO	190	191	378	207	203		212	266	329	229	284	215	318	173	119	211	336	140	168	221	279	200	214	156
ASH FORK	232	327	182	193	140	152	50	316	198	77	187	343	230	215	161	333	128	263	111	344	17	242	107	267
BENSON	158	73	433	321	228	156	258	82	283	275	238	35	287	147	156	26	377	45	214	36	333	115	318	282
BISBEE	206	89	482	321	276	205	307	131	332	324	287	33	334	195	205	24	426	93	263	86	383	165	368	331
CASA GRANDE	82	131	322	210	117	45	147	165	220	164	175	148	217	68	45	138	266	68	103	149	203	95	201	172
CHANDLER	73	162	296	184	86	19	121	157	212	138	167	177	213	56	14	168	244	98	77	179	197	83	175	201
CLIFTON	117	198	465	373	190	207	299	43	155	297	169	150	123	135	188	141	381	169	256	82	334	145	246	380
COOLIDGE	61	131	330	218	119	52	154	144	201	171	156	147	196	44	47	137	281	67	110	148	228	71	208	193
COTTONWOOD	175	280	179	207	72	105	41	250	196	19	163	296	218	167	114	286	127	216	101	297	80	196	105	287
DOUGLAS	231	113	507	394	282	229	331	123	321	349	285	57	328	219	225	48	455	118	287	77	406	189	367	355
DUNCAN	123	193	444	369	198	203	305	39	184	302	204	156	152	141	194	147	387	166	261	88	321	151	275	403
FLAGSTAFF	194	321	132	254	91	146	87	250	149	28	139	337	182	209	155	327	80	257	150	338	32	209	58	316
FLORENCE	48	134	337	227	127	61	163	133	188	180	143	150	185	31	55	140	285	70	119	151	238	58	208	204
FREDONIA	377	517	106	444	288	342	286	447	340	224	336	534	359	405	351	523	138	453	347	534	229	423	255	512
GILA BEND	148	189	336	165	161	68	163	232	287	180	242	205	276	131	78	195	278	125	119	206	236	158	272	114
GLENDALE	90	189	276	154	103	14	101	174	229	117	184	205	227	73	19	195	219	125	43	206	175	100	214	186
GLOBE	7	171	365	251	82	87	189	77	132	142	87	187	130	24	78	177	254	107	145	126	205	36	168	269
GRAND CANYON	275	406	107	280	172	231	131	349	230	108	220	422	228	294	240	412	79	342	186	398	59	307	139	400
HOLBROOK	142	303	212	345	98	221	174	212	58	120	48	320	84	159	211	310	162	240	279	261	123	170	33	404
HOOVER DAM	342	434	349	167	307	259	213	418	366	244	355	450	390	317	263	439	441	370	200	450	185	349	275	283
KINGMAN	265	360	275	100	234	185	144	349	292	171	282	376	323	248	194	366	222	296	128	377	111	275	201	215
LK HAVASU CITY	284	381	340	38	297	204	192	368	353	232	343	397	380	267	213	387	284	317	148	398	172	294	262	155
LAS VEGAS, NV	372	464	379	197	337	289	243	448	396	275	385	480	420	347	293	469	480	400	230	480	215	379	305	313
MESA	65	169	293	178	78	15	117	149	204	135	159	188	202	48	6	178	236	108	73	189	193	75	189	197
MIAMI	★	177	358	243	83	80	182	84	139	193	94	193	137	18	72	183	225	113	138	134	228	43	175	262
NOGALES	177	★	453	341	247	175	277	154	301	294	255	65	299	166	175	71	396	64	233	109	353	135	336	302
PAGE	358	453	★	375	223	278	231	421	269	160	259	469	295	341	287	459	77	389	288	470	164	358	179	448
PARKER	243	341	375	★	261	166	154	327	382	226	337	357	380	226	175	346	328	277	110	358	211	256	360	115
PAYSON	83	247	223	261	★	93	178	159	135	119	90	263	136	106	84	253	171	183	151	208	123	118	91	275
PHOENIX	80	175	278	166	93	★	102	164	219	119	174	191	217	63	9	181	221	111	58	192	169	90	204	182
PRESCOTT	182	277	231	154	178	102	★	266	236	60	226	293	273	165	111	283	162	213	61	294	67	192	145	216
SAFFORD	84	154	421	327	159	164	266	★	198	283	164	117	205	101	155	108	329	126	222	49	282	112	245	364
ST. JOHNS	139	301	269	382	135	219	236	198	★	177	45	317	26	156	210	309	222	237	277	247	181	167	91	401
SEDONA	193	294	160	226	119	119	60	283	177	★	175	310	220	182	128	300	108	230	120	311	60	204	86	301
SHOW LOW	94	255	259	337	90	174	226	164	45	175	★	274	43	111	165	264	219	192	232	213	171	122	81	346
SIERRA VISTA	193	65	469	357	263	191	293	117	317	310	274	★	317	182	193	33	415	80	249	71	368	150	353	318
SPRINGERVILLE	137	299	295	380	136	217	273	205	26	220	43	317	★	154	207	310	254	235	275	251	206	166	116	399
SUPERIOR	18	166	341	226	106	63	165	101	156	182	111	182	154	★	54	172	288	102	121	150	233	31	192	235
TEMPE	72	175	287	175	84	9	111	155	210	128	165	193	207	54	★	182	234	112	63	193	179	81	175	190
TOMBSTONE	183	71	459	346	253	181	283	108	309	300	264	33	310	172	182	★	405	70	239	62	350	141	343	307
TUBA CITY	225	396	77	328	171	221	162	329	222	108	219	415	254	288	234	405	★	335	222	417	112	290	129	403
TUCSON	113	64	389	277	183	111	213	126	237	230	192	80	235	102	112	70	335	★	169	81	280	71	273	238
WICKENBURG	138	233	288	110	151	58	61	222	277	120	232	249	275	121	63	239	222	169	★	250	128	148	208	172
WILLCOX	134	109	470	358	208	192	294	49	247	311	213	71	251	150	193	62	417	81	250	★	362	152	394	318
WILLIAMS	228	353	164	211	123	169	67	282	181	60	171	368	206	233	179	350	112	280	128	362	★	241	90	283
WINKELMAN	43	135	358	256	118	90	192	112	167	204	122	150	166	31	81	141	290	71	148	152	241	★	201	268
WINSLOW	175	336	179	360	91	204	145	245	91	86	81	353	116	192	175	343	129	273	208	294	90	201	★	376
YUMA	262	302	448	115	275	182	216	364	401	301	301	318	399	235	190	307	403	238	172	318	283	268	376	★

Mileage information compiled by the Travel and Facilities Branch of the Arizona Department of Transportation & Planning.

TABLE OF CONTENTS

TABLE OF CONTENTS (Cont.)

Dragoon Spring Station

A Grim Murder Scene
1858

*On a still warm day in September, 1858, the walls of the Dragoon
Spring Station would have heard the moans of dying men.*

When the Butterfield Overland stage route was laid out from St. Louis
to San Francisco in 1857, the surveyors looked for sights with an
adjacent stream or spring to supply water. Wells were dug only where
necessary. The spring in the Dragoon Mountains, north of present
day Tombstone, had been a source of water for the Apache for
hundreds of years and was in the center of their homeland. In
addition, it was a well-known watering spot for earlier visitors to the
Arizona Territory.

At the time the Dragoon Springs Station was built, a temporary peace
had settled over southeastern Arizona Territory. Thanks mostly to the
efforts of Indian agent Tom Jeffords, Cochise was at peace with the
Americans. Cochise, Indian war chief of the fierce Apache, had come

to see the Americans as allies in his traditional and ongoing battles with an older enemy, the Mexicans. Travelers to California and its gold fields moved through the area with comparative safety and freely made use of the few waterholes. Butterfield Stage agents made agreements with Cochise, supplying him with blankets and other goods, and paid the Chiricahua Apache for furnishing the stations with firewood.

To avoid encroaching on the Indians, the stage stations were built from one-half mile to one mile from the springs. Construction crews worked from east to west across the Arizona Territory building stations as they went. As each stage station neared completion, the main crew headed west, leaving a small group of men to finish the building.

By August, 1858, the work crew arrived at Dragoon Spring. They built solid walls of rugged mountain rock, 45 feet long on one side and 55 feet on the other, reaching a height of ten feet. The rock walls were held in place with local clay. The building had one gate with an eight-foot-square office just inside and an iron safe built into the rock wall. The remaining space was used for storage, living quarters and a stock corral.

By late August, the construction crew moved westward to build the San Pedro Station and left Butterfield agent Silas St. John in charge at Dragoon Springs. With him were three other Butterfield men, a blacksmith, James Hughes of New York, James Laing of Kentucky and William Cunningham of Iowa. Three Mexican laborers, then called peons, remained to finish the building: Guadalupe and Pablo "El Chino" Ramirez of Sonora and Bonifacio Mirando of Chihuahua.

The night of September 8th, 1858, after Laing had taken the first watch, agent St. John posted Guadalupe Ramirez to the second watch. Even though an uneasy peace was keeping the Apache at bay, not all Indians had joined Cochise in the peace agreement. In addition, the country was still filled with bandits and marauders who would be happy to relieve the station of it's remuda of horses and stock.

St. John slept in the office, Cunningham bedded down in the store room, and Laing took the center room with the stock. Hughes and

2   Arizona Walls

the two Mexican laborers slept outside. An hour later St. John awoke to the stir of the animals shuffling uneasily. Suddenly he was startled to hear the screams and sounds of fighting from his men outside. He leapt from his bed and reached for his rifle. The three attacking Mexican laborers, armed with a chopping axe, a broad axe and a sledge hammer got to him first.

St. John vainly fought the Mexicans off with his fists, still trying to reach his rifle from the saddle he'd been using for a pillow. He ducked a blow to his head, but took a deep axe gash to his hip. Knocking down Mirando, he was cut badly on the palm of his hand. As he was finally jerking the rifle from the scabbard, he was slashed on his forearm. While swinging the rifle like a club to keep the Mexicans away, he received a blow with an axe that severed his left arm below the shoulder. His courage in continuing to swing the rifle viciously at the men drove them back for a moment. Unable to fire the rifle with just one hand, he dropped it in order to pick up a pistol. As soon as the rifle dropped, the Mexicans attacked him again. He managed to fire one wild shot from the pistol. The cowardly killers dropped their weapons and ran into the night.

St. John realized he was rapidly bleeding to death. He managed to stop some of the flow of blood by tying, one handed, a tourniquet. Using a handkerchief and stick, he painfully twisted them around what remained of his severed arm. He was still bleeding profusely from the deep axe wound in his hip. Hearing the moans of his companions, he dragged himself to each of them to see how he could help.

Hughes, the blacksmith, was lying dead outside the enclosure, his skull crushed by a blow from the sledge hammer. James Laing was momentarily alive and conscious though his brains could be seen through the massive wound to his skull. William Cunningham had three deep gashes in his skull and moaned continually for water.

There was no water in the station, and the spring was a half mile away. St. John was able to drag himself to the top of a stack of sacked grain where he would be in the best defensive position in case of another attack. Morning brought the horror of clearly seeing the devastation. All day Thursday, St. John watched over his still moaning companions, tortured by thirst and swatting at hungry insects.

After sunset St. John used his pistol to drive away skulking coyotes from Hughes' body which still lay outside the walls. At midnight Cunningham died. St. John spent another horror-filled day, bleeding, thirsty, but rousing himself enough to drive away ravens and buzzards from his friends' bodies. Half conscious, he heard the coyotes return, fighting among themselves over the body of Hughes. On Saturday the raptors returned, drawn by the smell of blood and death. By Saturday night St. John lapsed into a coma.

Sunday morning, four days after the vicious attack, a reporter for the *Memphis Avalanche* named Archibald, along with a guide, arrived at the station. They had been traveling eastward on their way to El Paso. They suspected something was amiss, not seeing any sign of activity or a flag flying. They soon discovered the ghoulish scene and hurried to the spring for water. As Arichibald returned from the spring, a road building crew with three wagons arrived. St. John revived as they dressed his wounds, and he related the gruesome tale. Hughes and Cunningham were buried in the same grave. The next day, Monday, Laing died and was buried beside them.

Two riders were sent to Fort Buchanan, west of Tombstone, for a doctor. Since a direct route was considered unsafe, they made the trip by way of Tucson, going completely around the Santa Rita Mountains. They reached Fort Buchanan on Wednesday. The assistant surgeon, Dr. B. J. D. Irwin, left immediately with an escort of cavalry. The courageous surgeon rode sixty hard miles through Indian territory to reach the Dragoon Springs station by Friday. Sturdy St. John was still alive. Dr. Irwin cleaned his wounds and surgically completed the amputation of his left arm. Without the rapid arrival of Dr. Irwin, combined with his surgical skills, St. John would not have survived.

After recuperating at the Dragoon Springs station for six days, St. John was moved to the hospital at Fort Buchanan. Three weeks later, St. John rode a horse to Tucson and went back to work for the Butterfield Stage. St. John, only twenty-three years old at the time of the attack, lived a long and useful life in Arizona, dying at the age of eighty-four.

The three Mexican murderers fled across the border and disappeared. In spite of a large reward offered for their capture, they were never apprehended. In 1887 an earthquake soundly shook southern Arizona and Dragoon Spring ceased to flow.

The ruins of Dragoon Springs Stage Stop are located approximately three miles from present day Dragoon, Arizona.

Dragoon Springs.

Sign at Dragoon Springs Station.

Sam Hughes House

"My hobby was making a town."
1858

"Wear black at my own wedding? How could he make me do that? I'll look like such a sinner, and I'm not," tiny Atanacia wailed.

Putting his arms around her small shoulders, Sam replied calmly, "It'll be all right, Darlin', you'll see."

Sam Hughes had immigrated from Wales to Pennsylvania in 1837. Sam's first experience with formal education was at a small country school. He was 12 years old. The other kids made fun of him because of his inability to speak English. Sam gritted his teeth and took three days of their hectoring and teasing. At the end of the third day Sam slammed down his book and said that if this was what getting an education meant, he wanted nothing more to do with it.

With that he walked out of school never to return. The remainder of Sam's education was self taught.

In 1850 Sam heard about the gold rush in California and joined a party of immigrants who were headed for the west coast. The group of wagons to which young Sam was assigned didn't have enough horses so he had to walk the entire distance.

Upon arrival in California, Sam got a job as a chef at a large hotel. Soon he was earning eight dollars in gold per day. This was a dizzying amount for a boy used to making less than fifteen dollars a month. While in California, he learned a hard lesson about handling money. In just a few months he managed to save $3,000. Sam decided to travel to Sacramento and left his money buried in the sand, trusting a friend to bring his hard-earned money later. The friend gambled Sam's money away, leaving him with nothing more than a harsh lesson learned.

Continuing to earn good money cooking at a hotel, Sam began investing his money. Soon he had an interest in three of the leading hotels of California. In the early 1850's Sam was either injured or contracted tuberculosis (accounts differ). His doctors told him that he would probably die, but if he moved to a warmer climate, he might live a little longer.

Sam caught a stage headed for Texas, but by the time they had reached Maricopa, Arizona, about 30 miles south of present day Phoenix, Sam was so ill the driver thought he was going to die on the stagecoach. The driver told Sam to get off at Maricopa since he didn't want to bother with a dying man.

Sam pleaded with the driver, "There's no one in Maricopa who speaks English. Please don't leave me here to die among strangers!"

Softening to his plight, the driver reluctantly agreed to take Sam as far as Tucson. The driver also told Sam that if he died on the stagecoach, he would just shove him off the seat and not even stop to bury him. He insisted Sam absolutely had to get off in Tucson. "Don't worry," the driver assured Sam, "there's at least four gents who speak English there."

Having no other options, Sam gratefully agreed and arrived at the village of Tucson at dawn on March 12, 1858. Sam Hughes is considered to be the first man to move to Tucson for his health. He was the first of many.

Sam's health improved rapidly. At the time of his arrival, Tucson was an adobe Mexican community with a large garrison to which the residents returned each evening. At sunset a sentry was posted at the one entrance. Across the river was a small Indian village. Sam could see great potential in this barren, desolate land.

When Sam was twenty-eight years old he fell in love with dark-eyed Atanacia Santa Cruz. Atanacia was the younger sister of Petra Santa Cruz Stevens who married Hiram Stevens. Hiram and Sam had become business partners, and the sisters were often together. It was only a matter of time before Sam realized that Atanacia was the young lady with whom he wanted to share his life. It was said that he fell in love with Atanacia after seeing her dance at a public fiesta when she was a mere eight years old. He waited four years before he asked for her hand in marriage. Twelve year olds were not considered too young for marriage on the western frontier.

Atanacia wore a black dress and long black veil to marry 32 year-old Sam Hughes. One source stated that the priest at Mission San Xavier del Bac insisted on black. It is not known whether he disapproved of the age difference, or that Sam was not Catholic. One source stated that black was a common color for brides in the territorial days. However, pictures of the era rarely show brides in black. In contrast to the black bridal attire, there were many flowers to liven the festivities.

Sam was active in politics all of his life and he helped to build churches. In addition, Sam Hughes, the man who had given up on formal education after three days, was most active in seeing that schools were built and that laws helpful to schools were enacted. A Tucson elementary school is named in honor of Sam Hughes.

Sam and his bride purchased a small adobe home which still stands at the corner of Washington and Main in the old Presidio section of Tucson. Sam and Atanacia enlarged the home from time to time as needed—which was fairly often, as they went on to have fifteen children. Sam and his child bride lived a long life together and celebrated their 50th wedding anniversary in their adobe home.

∽∽∽∽∽∽∽∽∽∽∽

The Sam Hughes home is presently a series of garden apartments in the Old Town section of Tucson at 223 N. Main Ave. The old adobe building is difficult to see because of all the heavy growth of shrubbery around it.

Brunckow's Cabin

The Bloodiest Cabin in Arizona
1860

"We have nothing against you, Señor. You are a good Catholic."

Brunckow's Cabin, situated on a knoll just off the Tombstone-Huachuca road, is one of the oldest ruins in Arizona not built by Indians, Spaniards, or Mexicans. Its ground is also perhaps the bloodiest. The walls of this cabin, if only they could speak, would tell of more murders than possibly any other location during the territorial days of Arizona.

Frederick Bru,ckow, born in Berlin about 1830, received a classical education at the University of Westphalia. He graduated from the School of Mines at Freiburg, Saxony, before immigrating to the United States. He traveled westward, working his way across the continent, arriving in Tucson in August, 1856. He was soon employed by the Sonora Exploring and Mining Company which was headquartered in Tubac where he planned mining explorations in the surrounding hills.

In 1859, having found a rich vein, Brunckow built an adobe cabin for himself and a store to service his Mexican laborers. He began mining in the area some twenty years before Ed Schieffelin was to discover his fortune at the Lucky Cuss Mine, just nine miles away.

July 23, 1860, dawned hot and dry as William Williams, a mining employee, saddled his horse and left the Brunckow cabin. He headed for Fort Buchanan, 35 miles away, where he planned to purchase a wagonload of flour. Remaining at the cabin were James Williams, cousin of William and a mining engineer from Virginia; Mr. Morse, a former professor of chemistry at a St. Louis high school; Frederick Brunckow; and David Brontrager, a German cook who had arrived just two days previous.

Williams had difficulty procuring a wagon and teamster at the fort to haul the flour back, so he was delayed returning until the morning of July 26. Along with him were two young boys, sons of Mr. Acke, a Sonoita Valley rancher, who were hired to return the team and empty wagon to Fort Buchanan.

The trip took all day and well into the night to cover the rough terrain. At midnight, as they approached Brunckow's cabin, they were puzzled by the eerie silence. The mining area was usually overrun by a noisy pack of mongrel dogs owned by the eleven Mexican laborers who worked the mine. Williams thought it strange that their arrival hadn't set off the usual bedlam of barking and howling. As the wagon drew closer to the buildings, they were overcome by a horrible stench which became unbearable as they entered the deep night darkness of the store.

Williams, striking one of his last two matches, looked around the store and surveyed complete chaos. Food and other merchandise had been ripped from the shelves and thrown about the store and counter tops. Williams lit a lantern and it's flickering light revealed the bloated, fly-blown body of his cousin, James. Staggering and gagging, Williams and the boys ran from the store to the wagon. Not knowing who had done the killing or whether the killers were still lurking about, they decided to return to the fort for help.

Wearily arriving back at Fort Buchanan, after traveling the remainder of the night, Williams told what he knew of the grisly scene. Capt. Ewell, commanding officer, immediately sent Sergeant Henderson and a contingent of soldiers to investigate.

Late in the evening of July 27, David Brontrager, the German cook and lone survivor, staggered into Camp Jecker, the headquarters for the Sonora Survey Commission. Brontrager, barefoot and exhausted, was covered with bruises and scratches. As quickly as he could, he told what had happened just a few hours after Williams had left to get the flour.

Brontrager said that about two or three o'clock in the afternoon he had been sitting in the kitchen of Brunckow's cabin reading a book when two of the Mexican miners came in and asked for a light for their small hand-rolled cigars. As he lit their smokes, gunfire erupted outside. Brontrager started for the door, but the two Mexicans blocked him, growling that he must remain inside the building and no harm would come to him. Quickly a few other Mexicans joined them in the cabin. They told Brontrager that he wouldn't be hurt because he had once lived in Sonora and that he was known as a good Catholic. Also none of the Mexican miners had anything against him. They told him that he would have to go with them and give his word that he wouldn't try to escape.

After the shooting stopped, Brontrager was allowed to look around the area. In the store he found James Williams lying on the floor, dead from several gunshot wounds and bloody from a deep gash on his head. Just outside the store was the body of Mr. Morse, also shot several times. He was told that Frederick Brunckow had been stabbed to death near the mine.

Greed motivated the bloody crimes. A shipment of some $2,000 worth of goods had just arrived at the store. In addition to money, the Mexican workers took jewelry, several horses and mules. Immediately after the massacre, the killers and their families began looting the store and loading everything they could carry onto the mules. They left immediately for Sonora with Brontrager as hostage.

They traveled about 30 miles without stopping, but sometime in the night arrived at the San Pedro Ranch where they let Brontrager go free. Brontrager somehow survived four days alone in the wilderness before he stumbled into the camp of the Sonora Survey Commission. After hearing Brontrager's account of the murders, a messenger was quickly sent to Fort Buchanan. Brontrager was fed, treated for his wounds and taken to the fort the next morning.

Meanwhile, William Williams, Sergeant Henderson and the soldiers from Fort Buchanan were busy with the gruesome task of burying the dead. The body of Mr. Morse, having lain outside the building, had been torn apart by wild animals. Frederick Brunckow's body, also torn apart by animals and almost completely eaten away, was found next to the mine shaft a half mile from the cabin. The body of James Williams had badly decayed in the summer heat of the store.

"The stench was so great that all hands were made sick, but by the help of whiskey and camphor they gave the deceased a good burial, although they could not put them (back) together," stated the San Francisco *Bulletin*.

The murderers escaped into Mexico and were never made to pay for their grisly crime.

The Brunckow mine and property lay idle for several years after the slayings until they were purchased by Major Milton B. Duffield, the first United States Marshal of Arizona Territory. To say that Major Duffield was disliked by most who met him would be a kindness. His slaying at the Brunckow cabin in 1874 was no surprise to anyone.

After his slaying, the *Citizen* (June 13, 1874) had this to say about Major Duffield:

He (Major Duffield) very frequently marched through the streets like an insane person, threatening violence to all those who had offended him. It is claimed by some good men that he had redeeming qualities. Such may be the case, but we are free to confess that we could never find them.... But his stormy life has ended and he has gone to that unknown land whence none return. May his ashes rest in peace, and may his Maker deal more kindly and gently with him than he was disposed to deal with his fellow men.

His killer, Joseph T. Holmes, surrendered himself to the authorities and pleaded self defense. He was found guilty of manslaughter and sentenced to three years in the Yuma Territorial Prison.

After Duffield's death, Brunckow's cabin seemed cursed, bringing bad luck to everyone who crossed its shadow. One outstanding exception, however, was Ed Schieffelin.

Fond of prospecting in the San Pedro Valley, Ed had a hunch that there was ore in the area. He had wandered up to Brunckow's cabin and temporarily joined forces with Bill Griffith and Ira Smith who were doing assessment work on the old San Pedro mine. The pair hired Ed to stand guard for them against the marauding Indians while they completed their work. Ed used the cabin often while he was prospecting in the area. He went on to find the Mother Lode and the town of Tombstone grew up around the Tombstone Mining District.

Being located so close to the rough mining town of Charleston, center for most of the rustlers and hooligans of the area, it is no surprise that Brunckow's cabin continued to be the site of several more killings.

The May 20, 1881, issue of the *Arizona Democrat*, Prescott, stated that the "dark and bloody history" of the Brunckow cabin with its "uninterrupted series of violence and murder" had created a reputation known all over southern Arizona.

"Bronkow (sic) and three companions were the first victims, assasinated by Mexicans. Since then, no less than 17 men have been killed on this property. The graves lie thick around the old adobe house. Prospectors and miners avoid the spot as they would the plague, and many of them will tell you that the unquiet spirits of the departed are wont to revisit...and wander

about the scene which witnessed their untimely taking off. The gloomy old building is unoccupied. The present owners of the mine, not caring to reside there, have put up a house some distance away. Although much blood has been spilt and many lives lost over this claim. It has not proven of much value. It is still in dispute and as I passed I noticed two men standing behind a low adobe wall, armed with Henry rifles..."

The ruins of Brunckow's Cabin are now all but melted back into the desert. What remains is located on a knoll eight miles southwest of Tombstone before you get to the second cattle guard on the road to Sierra Vista. Compared to pictures taken in the 1980's which show 6 foot high walls and the wooden frames of windows and doors still intact, it could be estimated that only a few years remain before all trace of bloody Brunckow's Cabin will be erased by the slow erosion of the desert forces.

Brunkow's cabin near Charleston.

Stanton

Murder at the Base of Rich Hill
1863

"Gold! GOLD! Chunks as big as my thumb! ...as big as your foot!
Come see! Hurry up!" The prospector was fairly dancing at
what he had seen at the top of a nearby hill.

Pauline Weaver, the famous western explorer and scout with a curiously feminine name, lead a prospecting group organized by Abraham Harlow Peeples in 1863. They prospected along a stream at the foothills of the mountains north of present day Wickenburg.

One evening the party killed three antelope. After dinner they camped along a stream at the base of a rock-strewn hill. The next morning a mule was missing, so while one of the Mexican workers looked for it, the others searched for placer gold along the creek. The Mexican, Alvaro, climbed the nearby hill and found a one-acre basin containing gold nuggets shining in the sun. The Peeples Party later reported that they nudged the gold out of the ground with penknives and the toe of their boot, retrieving as much as $7,000 before breakfast.

The stream became Antelope Creek, the canyon on the east side of the mountain was named Weaver Gulch, and the hill that made them rich was appropriately named Rich Hill. A small mining town originally named Antelope Station grew up along Antelope Creek. Most of the residents were miners, but the usual variety of merchants arrived with their supplies. A shady character named Charles P. Stanton had immigrated from Europe. Rumors at the time reported he had been expelled from a monastery on a charge of immorality. Stanton opened his own dry-goods store in direct competition with G. H. "Yaqui" Wilson who owned the other general store. Stanton began plotting a method to eliminate the competition.

Stanton's chance to dispose of his competitors occurred when some pigs belonging to "Yaqui" Wilson got loose. The pigs broke into the property of William Partridge, an Englishman, who owned the stagecoach station. Wilson stated before several witnesses that he would pay for any damage the hogs had done. However, the hog incident had created hard feelings between the two men. Stanton allegedly bribed a Mexican to tell Partridge that Wilson was "out to get him." When Wilson approached Partridge's residence, Partridge shot him dead. He claimed self-defense, but the jury didn't agree, and poor Bill Partridge, Stanton's fall guy, was sent to the Yuma Territorial Prison. While there, he claimed he was haunted by the ghost of "Yaqui" Wilson.

With one down, Stanton began to connive to eliminate the rest of his competition. Wilson had a silent partner named Timmerman. Locals believed that Stanton hired a gang of *bandidos* headed by a man named Francisco Vega to get rid of Timmerman. They promptly filled Timmerman full of lead.

Stanton became Postmaster in 1875 and renamed Antelope Station after himself. He rerouted the stagecoach so it rode directly past his store instead of the former Wilson and Timmerman store. Stanton soon reaped the monetary rewards of the advantageous stage route.

With Partridge in prison, his creditors sold his stage station to Barney Martin. Martin and his wife ran the nice red-brick station in the center of town with honesty and integrity, something often missing in frontier mining towns. The Martins were good, honest folk, well-liked and never in trouble. Even if they hadn't been competition, this would have been enough to bring on the enmity of Charlie Stanton.

After repeated warnings that the outlaw gangs of the Stanton area were out to get him, Barney Martin sold his store and decided to move his family to the safer, new farming community of Phoenix. In July, 1886, he loaded his belongings and his family into a wagon and set out across the desert. Sensing that his trip might be dangerous, Martin notified his friend, Capt. Calderwood, that he was on his way and should arrive at Calderwood's home on a certain date.

When the Martin family failed to arrive on time, Calderwood organized a search party. Backtracking along the stage road, the group found fresh tracks where a wagon had turned off the road and headed into the hills. At the end of the tracks was a grim sight. Calderwood found the still smoldering, burnt remains of the Martin wagon and belongings, along with the dead bodies of Martin, his wife and children.

Responsibility was charged to the Valenzuela gang with Stanton accused as an accessory. As often happened in frontier Arizona, no one was convicted.

Stanton didn't have long to enjoy the power which he so brutally had achieved. In November of that same year, a young Mexican member of the Vega gang, Cristero Lucero, rode through town and aimed one bullet at Stanton who was leaning back in a chair at the saloon. The deadly bullet found its mark. Stanton had made the mistake of insulting Lucero's sister—a fatal mistake to a hot-blooded young Mexican.

As he galloped out of town, Lucero passed Tom Pierson, another Stanton adversary. Lucero quickly told Tom that he was fleeing to Mexico because he had just killed Charlie Stanton. Pierson replied, "You don't have to pull out. If you stick around, you'll get a reward."

The mining town of Stanton was abandoned within four years of the killing of Charlie Stanton. After changing hands several times, the property was purchased by the Lost Dutchman Mining Association. This group of gold-mining, card-playing, tale-swapping retirees convenes every winter, pulling up RV's and mobile homes near the three remaining buildings of Stanton. From there, they go out with metal detectors and shovels and find "a little color", when they're lucky. They seem to enjoy visitors and proudly show off the old buildings.

The turn off to Stanton, along with two more ghost towns, Weaver and Octave, is 3 miles north of Congress on U. S. 89. Stanton is 6.3 miles east on a wash-boarded dirt road. Weaver and Octave are a short distance further east, but the road is very rough and demands a high clearance sports utility vehicle.

Stanton ghost town.

Darrell Duppa House

Pumpkinville or Phoenix?
1865

"Yep, if you could only hear me, I could tell you all about the beginnings of Phoenix and how its grown up to be the big, lively city it is today. I've seen it all. Gosh, dang, I'm about the only old timer left to tell the old stories."

If the walls of the Duppa House could speak, they would be able to tell us of the earliest beginnings of the city of Phoenix.

Lt. John Y. T. Smith mustered out of the army in 1865. He decided to stay in the Valley of the Salt River when he was awarded a contract to provide hay for Fort McDowell, east of present day Phoenix. John Smith had noticed that there was an abundance of wild grass growing along the Salt River. All he needed to do was harvest the crop.

Smith set up a hay camp at what is now 40th Street and Washington. He also started a general dry goods store, called a suttler's store, to provide for the needs of both Fort McDowell and the rip-roaring mining camp of Wickenburg, 40 miles to the northwest. He called his place Smith's Station. Other than his store, there were only some small, peaceful Pima Indian villages scattered along the Salt River.

John Smith and the Pima were not the first people to live in the Salt River Valley. Nomadic Indian tribes, hunters and gatherers, had wandered through the area at least 15,000 years ago. They hunted mastodon and woolly mammoth. Not much is known of them, and they left little besides a few arrow points.

Approximately 2,000 years ago a new group of Indians arrived from Mexico. They built complex villages throughout the Salt River Valley. Archeologists estimate that as many as 100,000 lived along the river. Since they had no written language, we have no name for them other than the Pima word *Hohokam* which means "all used up" or "vanished ones."

The Hohokam were master engineers and built a complex network of canals to water crops. They knew that if a canal is built too wide, it would eventually silt up because the water would run too sluggish. If they built it too narrow, it would overflow during a rainy season. They even changed the size and shape of the canal to help move the water along. Miles and miles of canals were built without metal tools, without a wheel for a cart, and without draft animals. They lived in the Salt River Valley for 1400 years and then abruptly left. Many theories abound to explain the Great Migration, but they remain theories.

September, 1867, tall, lanky Jack Swilling rode into Smith's Station. Dressed in buckskins, with his long, dark red hair flowing down his back, he was a true frontiersman. He had fought in both the Mexican and Civil wars—actually, he fought on both sides of the Civil war. He'd fought both the Apache and Comanche. Swilling had been with the Peeples prospecting party when they discovered the fortune at Rich Hill. Once during a fight his skull was split open with a gun barrel. He was shot a couple of times and he carried one bullet in his side all his life. His old wounds pained him almost constantly. Sometimes he'd drink too much to dull the pain, and when liquor wasn't enough he took morphine.

Swilling sensed that one way to get rich was to figure out where everybody wanted to live, then get there first and secure the water rights. Swilling took one look at the old Hohokam canals and thought he could make a profitable enterprise out of them. He formed the Swilling Ditch Company and, with a crew of sixteen strong-backed men, he began cleaning out the old Hohokam canals. By March, 1868, the wheat and barley crops had been planted and there were fifty hearty souls making a living in the Salt River Valley.

The main canal became know as the Town Ditch and served every purpose water could be used for. People would bathe in it, drink it, irrigate with it and do their laundry in it. A rumor went around that the saloon keepers washed their spittoons in the ditch when nobody was looking which caused a great public outcry. That was too much.

The federal census taken in 1870 reported a population of sixty-one women and 164 men. The ages of this sturdy group of pioneers ranged from twenty-one to thirty. Ninety-six said they were farmers. There wasn't a single doctor, banker, teacher or lawyer in the whole group. They used to say, "Heck, we didn't need laws until the lawyers came."

By October of that same year, a group of citizens was selected to pick the townsite. Among the group was Bryan Philip Darrell Duppa, better known as "Lord" Duppa. He wasn't royalty, but he talked so proper, having immigrated from England, that his friends took delight in dubbing him with a title. The oft told story has it that Duppa was booted out of a wealthy family in England, his family actually paying him to stay away. He had a very good, classical education and could speak five languages. The problem was that whenever he drank, he tended to speak all five languages at once — and he was rarely sober.

After much heated discussion, the site selection committee decided that the area along present day Van Buren, between 7th Avenue and 7th Street, would be the center of town. Jack Swilling, who wanted the town located nearer his Ditch Company, was so hot under the collar at losing he shot off his shotgun as he left the meeting, filling an opponent's tender parts with birdshot.

The next job was selecting a name for the new town. After considering Stonewall, Salinas, Millville and Pumpkinville, they turned to Lord Duppa. He later said that he sat up on the buttes east of town and

looked out over the old Hohokam canals. "I foresee a new and grander civilization arising from the ashes of the old," Duppa thought to himself. "Let's name our new town Phoenix after the mythical Greek bird that is consumed in flames and arises ever more beautiful."

Lord Duppa had a farm in Phoenix and built a two-roomed adobe structure just before moving away to other adventures. The Duppa House is one of the last buildings in Phoenix that would have heard the voices of those early pioneers, Duppa, Swilling and Smith.

Detail of Duppa House.

ഗ‌ഗ‌ഗ‌ഗ‌ഗ‌ഗ‌ഗ‌ഗ

The Duppa house is located at 116 W. Sherman, three blocks south of the Central Avenue underpass. While not open, it can be seen from the outside.

El Tiradito

The Shrine to "The Little Castaway."
1870's

"Holy Mother, hear my prayer...It's my son..."

The soft-spoken Mexican women come at dawn or just after twilight, as though the hours of transition from dark to light might hold a special power for hearing prayers. They come with their candles to the adobe shrine of *El Tiradito*, "the little castaway." A small shrine as shrines go, it is located at the edge of the *barrio* near downtown Tucson. Here the faithful women kneel to pray and light candles before the soot-stained statue of the Virgin of Guadalupe.

The story of *El Tiradito* has been handed down from family to family in the *barrio*. Like many folk traditions, it has several variations. The most commonly accepted version takes place in the 1870's. A young shepherd named Juan Oliveras was working at the Goodwin Ranch where he lived with his wife and father-in-law. Juan is said to have fallen in love with his beautiful mother-in-law who lived in nearby

Tucson. Unable to stay away from her, Juan would slip into town whenever he could. One day the father-in-law became suspicious and followed Juan. Surprising the two lovers, the older man became enraged. He seized an axe from the woodpile and slaughtered his son-in-law. The killer fled across the border into Mexico. Without even a coffin, young Juan was buried where he fell.

The devout Mexican women, perhaps thinking of their own wayward sons, felt sorry for Juan. After dark, they would slip through the desert bushes to light candles beside the grave and pray for his soul. Gradually, they would add prayers for their own families. Among the women grew a strong belief that if their candle would burn all night, their prayer, if pure, would be answered.

The shrine remains a powerful reminder, a symbol of faithfulness in the community. In 1971 a freeway was proposed which would have divided three historic inner-city neighborhoods: Armory Park, the Barrio Historico and El Hoyo. In addition, it would have destroyed *El Tiradito*. Characteristic of the thinking of bureaucrats, no alternate routes could be considered. Refusing to accept the destruction of their shrine, *Barrio* residents initiated an intense campaign. Through their efforts the shrine was placed on the National Register of Historic Places, thus protecting it from destruction by a federally-funded highway. In 1978 the entire Barrio Historico was placed on the National Register.

The newspapers of the day called *El Tiradito* "the shrine that stopped a freeway." It is believed to be the only shrine known to exist in the United States dedicated to the soul of a sinner buried in unconsecrated ground.

You can visit the open-air shrine of El Tiradito located in Tucson, on Main Avenue just south of Cushing Street. Local residents request that you be respectful and not disturb the candles or any other objects placed at the shrine.

Greaterville

I said, "She's MY girl!"
1874

"Those doors won't stay locked for very long," the cowboy bragged as he climbed on the roof.

All the jealous miner could think of was, "She's MY girl!" as he watched her being swung around the dance floor by the lithe cowboy. Jealousy and revenge were frequent guests at the Greaterville Saturday night dance. This night was no exception.

The small town of Greaterville had sprung up at the site of a placer gold strike in the Santa Rita Mountains south of Tucson in 1874. The peak population was about five hundred, mostly Mexican miners, with only about one fifth of the population Anglo. Like most mining towns, it had its share of dance halls, saloons and mercantile shops. The local jail was a deep hole in the ground. The law breakers were simply let into the jail by a rope which was then pulled back up. Usually an overnight sobering up was all that was needed.

The Saturday night dances drew cowboys and miners from all over the surrounding area, eager to court the pretty, dark-eyed *señoritas* of Greaterville. One night the miners decided not to share the ladies, so they locked the doors before the cowboys arrived. Not to be denied, one resourceful cowboy simply climbed up on the roof and dropped a handful of live ammunition down the chimney. Moments later all hell broke loose. The doors burst open as miners and *señoritas* screamed their way out of the building, headed for cover. The cowboys quickly grabbed their favorite fleeing *senorita* and took back the dance floor.

One jealous miner, seeing his girlfriend in the arms of a cowboy, followed the pair around the dance floor with his knife drawn, lest the cowboy try something ungentlemanly. To keep the situation even, a friend of the wrangler shadowed the knife-toting miner all around the floor with his six-shooter drawn and cocked. It was a stand-off.

When the gold played out, most of the residents left Greaterville. The town lives on, mostly in name only on a map. Greaterville, what's left of it, is a private ranch. Locals say that there were a number of out-buildings on the ranch which were the remnants of Greaterville. The county assessor told the owner of the ranch that she would have to pay taxes on all the old buildings. She tried to explain to him that they weren't being used, but they did have historic value as they could be considered a ghost town. No exceptions could be made, and unable to afford to pay taxes on unused old buildings, the owner had no other choice than to hire a bulldozer to destroy the memory filled buildings of Greaterville.

∽∽∽∽∽∽∽∽∽∽∽

Greaterville is a private ranch on a dirt road north of Sonoita.

Fort Verde

Hunt Them Down as Wild Animals.
1874

"I believe the hostile Indians of Arizona should be destroyed, and I encourage troops to capture and route out Indians by every means, and hunt them down as wild animals."

- Gen. O. C. Ord
- Arizona Territory, 1870

"Greed and avarice on the part of the whites - in other words, the almighty dollar was at the bottom of nine-tenths of all our Indian troubles."

- Gen. George Crook
- Arizona Territory, 1890

"Our Indian policy, or rather the lack of a sane one, marked by broken treaties, dishonest, ignorant, and tactless handling of the entire subject and the infliction of untold misery on our Indian wards, has been such that an army man who has had to stand by with hands tied, can hardly keep within the bounds when writing or speaking about it."

- Brig. Gen. Wm. C. Brown
1875

General Order #10 stated that all roving bands of Indians were to be on reservations by February 15, 1872, or be considered hostiles. By 1873, most of the members of two different tribes, Tonto Apache and the Yavapai, had been gathered onto a reservation near Fort Verde. In spite of the fact that these two tribes had historically been roving bands of hunters, they were now told to create irrigation ditches and to farm. Without tools other than their own digging sticks, they did the best they could. Used to roaming over large stretches of northern and eastern Arizona, they felt crowded on the small plot of land allotted to them. They went hungry during the first year before they could harvest a crop. Malaria killed so many that the remaining Indians had difficulty gathering enough wood to fuel the funeral pyres.

Even with the hardships they endured the first year, their first harvest was bountiful. Afraid the federal government might establish water rights for the Indians, the surrounding settlers requested that the Indians be sent to another reservation. The white settlers sent delegations to Washington to convince the government the Indians were all Apache and that all the Apache would be happier together on one reservation.

By the fall of 1874 the Indians began to wonder why the promised seeds and farm equipment had been delayed so many times. Even Dr. Corbusier, attending physician at the Rio Verde Indian Agency, noticed a strange disinterest on the part of Indian agent Oliver Chapman toward the Indians' eagerness to plow and to enlarge their cultivated fields which had just brought in such a full harvest.

"Somebody make bad medicine," Pa-ka-ki-va, son-in-law of old war chief Delshay murmured. Why was Chapman evasive when asked about plowing the fields? Why did issuing day come and go with only a small portion of the promised goods delivered? Chapman's excuse was that the supply train had broken down. None of the chiefs believed him.

One night two Apache runners from the San Carlos Reservation who had relatives at Rio Verde sneaked into the reservation and their curiosity turned to rage. The runners warned the chiefs that the San

Carlos Indian agent was preparing to receive more Indians. The Rio Verde Yavapai and Apache who had been prepared to settle into a peaceful, farming lifestyle exploded into pandemonium and hysteria.

All night the torches and campfires flickered across the valley camps. The chanting and wailing echoed from the nearby cliffs. Dr. Corbusier and his wife, Fanny, trusted and loved by the Indians, were barraged with questions which were difficult to answer. A band of Tontos dressed in war paint arrived at agent Chapman's tent and made war-like gestures. In a panic, agent Chapman sent a courier to Fort Apache requesting help from General Crook. Crook alerted the nearby army posts to be prepared for action.

Several days later the reason for the supply delays became clear when special agent Edwin Dudley arrived with his assistants. He informed agent Chapman that General Grant was requiring all Indians on the Rio Verde reservation be moved to San Carlos immediately. Word of this order shot through the reservation like a cannon, nearly causing a revolt.

Dudley announced his intention to move the Indians across the mountains instead of on the roads, thus eliminating the possibility of using wagons. The route would take them along old Indian trails from Camp Verde south to East Verde, then through the valley to Rye. From Rye they would travel the rough back country to the meeting of the Salt River and Tonto Creek, up the mountain to Globe and then on to San Carlos.

Both Dr. Corbusier and agent Schuyler tried to reason with Dudley. They asked him to wait until spring when the snow would melt in the mountains. They asked him to take the roads so the Indians could build wagons and take their goods, and allow people to ride. But Dudley wanted to get the affair over with as quickly as possible. His attitude was, "They were only Indians."

Small groups of Indians gathered together with the intent of killing agent Dudley. Dr. Corbusier and his wife spoke to them and calmed them down. Agent Dudley ordered the chiefs to meet with him the next day. Each one refused. Once again, Dr. Corbusier circulated among the Indians and persuaded the chiefs to meet with Dudley the next morning.

On a cold February morning the young men of each tribe along with their chiefs arrived at Dudley's tent stripped down and painted for war. Agent Schuyler and his troops watched warily. After the Indians had waited about a half hour, Dudley came out of his tent. Instead of giving the chiefs the honor they deserved, Dudley brought a buffalo robe from the tent, sprawled on it, and leaning back on his elbow, began to speak to the crowd.

Dr. Corbusier had stayed to the back of the crowd so he could hear the comments around him. As Dudley spoke in low, garbled tones an interpreter translated. Dr. Corbusier heard one Indian remark, "He is drunk." He turned and looked Corbusier in the eye and said again, "He is drunk." Corbusier merely pointed back to Dudley and told the Indian to listen.

Through the interpreter, Dudley read the orders to remove the Indians to San Carlos. He promised they would be going to a much better place where they could be with the rest of their tribe. Suddenly Dudley got up from the buffalo hide and walked back into his tent.

One of the chiefs murmured, "He went to get another drink." Further low grunts could be heard in the crowd about Dudley's drinking. In a few moments Dudley returned and once again flopped down on the buffalo robe. The crowd was ominously silent. Two rifles clicked. Dr. Corbusier leaned against the two young Indians who had cocked their rifles. Slowly, with hooded eyes, they let the hammers down. Dudley continued talking, his English incoherent even to Dr. Corbusier.

When Dudley had finished, Captain Snooks, spokesman for the chiefs, addressed Dudley and the group.

"We will not go where we will be outnumbered by our enemies," he said. "Our fathers and grandfathers were born here and died here. Our wives and children were born here. The father in Washington promised that the country along the river and ten miles on each side would be ours forever. This is little enough land for people who are accustomed to roaming for many miles before the white man came and stole our land from us."

Dudley yawned in his face. Captain Snooks moved closer and asked Dudley not to drink any more whiskey so that he might know and understand what was being said to him. Other chiefs stepped forward to plead with Dudley to understand what was being asked by the Indians. Abruptly Dudley waved them away, gathered up his buffalo robe and returned to his tent.

February 27, 1875, grey and snowy, saw 1500 Indians, all on foot, begin their journey of 180 rough miles. The non-Indians who accompanied the group were Indian agent Chapman and his two assistants; Commissioner Dudley and two assistants; Chief of Scouts, Al Sieber and a small group of his Indian scouts; Harry Hawes, chief packer and four mule-skinners; and Lt. George Eaton commanding a troop of 15 cavalrymen from Fort Verde. Dr. Corbusier was not ordered to accompany the group but agreed to go along to help these people whom he had loved and befriended. He had been asked to come, not by the United States government, but by the chiefs of the tribes.

The long, silent, tragic procession slowly passed Fanny Corbusier who stood in speechless anguish watching them leave. What belongings they could carry were on their backs. Old and young were burdened with as much as they could carry. One old man tenderly placed his ancient wife into a V shaped back basket with her feet hanging out. He gently lifted the basket to his back and adjusted the band which held the basket to his forehead. Except when forced to cross a raging river, when he allowed a cavalryman who volunteered to carry her, the old man uncomplainingly carried his precious bundle the entire trip.

Dr. Corbusier reported that many babies were born on this miserable migration, later called the March of Tears. He stated that the mother, when feeling the birth was imminent, would go off from the trail, unattended. She would emerge later with her newborn. There was seldom even a blanket to wrap the baby in, so the babies were carried naked. Many of them froze to death in their mothers arms. The new mothers, in their weakened condition, could no longer carry as much of the burden as they had when they set out from Rio Verde. When a baby sickened, the weak mother, having to chose between the needed possessions and a baby who was dying, would hang the baby in its cradle board in a cedar tree. As she left her baby, her wails of grief could be heard throughout the group, now united in their misery and sorrow.

The March of Tears continued uninterrupted.

Going through the rocky terrain, their leather moccasins wore out. They would tear the only blanket they had and wrap their feet with the shreds.

The medicine men saw evil omens at every turn. They chanted and wailed. They appealed to Dudley, reminding him of the broken promises made to their people. As the first week wore on, Dudley and his two assistants grew ever more revolted and sickened at the job which had been thrust upon them. Dudley's two assistants deserted and were never seen or heard from again.

Hunger and rage increased as the march continued. The cavalrymen increasingly found the job distasteful, driving the wretched, foot-sore Indians up steep, rugged, snowy trails. When the group reached Strawberry Creek, five miles south of the present day town of Childs, they found the usually gentle stream a raging torrent. There had been a huge storm the day before, filling the creek with foaming water and debris. Al Sieber and Lt. Eaton suggested to Dudley that he delay crossing the river a few days to allow the waters to subside.

Later, in his official report, Dudley would write, "We fortunately found the stream could be forded...sad duty to compel men, women and children, to wade through cold water...even though they were Indians." He reported that the water was about waist deep to a tall man. He also reported that the crossing was a "pitiful sight."

Dr. Corbusier remembered it differently. Strawberry was a rushing white-water deluge. Rock and debris would pile up forming dams which would suddenly break lose, crushing and pounding human victims in its path. Some soldiers with a sympathetic heart offered to carry babies, small children and the old across on their horses. Some passed ropes to those who looked like they might be carried away in the torrent. But there were others who followed Dudley's cruel commands and bull-whipped the people into the icy water.

For days after the crossing of Strawberry Creek, Dr. Corbusier kept busy ministering to the injured, sick and dying. He applied splints to broken bones and treated other injuries the best he could.

By the second week, the beef and flour were gone. The half-starved Indians were left to forage for food from what grew along the trail. According to Dr. Corbusier there was plenty of game, but the Indians were not allowed to hunt. They had no weapons. One night a deer wandered into the camp and Al Seiber shot it. The Yavapais from above the camp and the Tontos who were camped below rushed toward the fresh killed meat. There was a frantic, furious dive for the food. The Tontos emerged with the entire deer and drove the others back to their camp, still hungry.

Although bonded together in their suffering, old animosities between the Yavapai and Tonto Apache soon resurfaced and war dances were heard in the night. Never friendly, the real feud had begun several years previous when the Yavapai joined with the cavalry and became scouts against the Tontos.

Dudley became increasingly uneasy with the growing anger. On the twelfth day of the march he reported that a fight broke out between the two tribes. Agent Dudley wrote in his report, "A difficulty occurred, which resulted in a general fight between the two tribes.... The escort under direction of Mr. Al Sieber, Chief of General Crook's scouts, at once took a position between two contending parties and made every effort to send them to their respective camps, and success attended their efforts. When the loss came to be counted, we knew of five dead, the Indians said seven, and ten wounded. Not a great loss when so much lead was expended."

The Indian survivors passed down a different story to their children and grandchildren. The Indians claim that present day Bloody Basin is the place where the Indians finally said, "No, we will go no further," and the soldiers opened fire on them.

The Indians also reported that all guns and knives, anything which could be used as a weapon, had been taken away from them at the beginning of the march. If they'd had weapons, they would have been able to hunt and feed themselves.

Dr. Corbusier reported that after the "fight," he climbed to the top of the mesa and found 25 Indians sprawled out in various positions. He said that he treated the ten worst wounded. He wrote that he found four dead, although others estimated that up to 30 had died. All agree that none of the Anglos were shot.

The ten Indians Dr. Corbusier treated were carried by younger Indians, and the march continued. The unearthly, mysterious wails of the medicine men continued hour after hour.

The last dangerous river crossing lay ahead. The group faced crossing the huge Salt River before they would have to climb the steep, narrow footpath now known as Apache Trail. Facing the rushing water before them, the elderly members of the tribes sat down on the trail, unable to go further. The crippled and injured joined them. The soldiers bull-whipped them to their feet.

After the river crossing, they faced the steep, rocky trail, so narrow that the horses had to be led. The terrified children screamed until some sympathetic soldiers picked them up and carried them. Their parents were already too burdened down with their own heavy possessions to carry their frightened children. A sturdy mule lost its footing, bounced off the rocky sides of the drop-off and plummeted into the raging river far below. Lost with the mule were the last of the critically needed supplies.

The next day the Yavapai men were prepared for war. Their faces were painted the colors and patterns of death, and beneath the paint was the look of death. Agent Dudley decided this was a good time for him to leave the group and go ahead to San Carlos. He promised to bring back food and fresh supplies.

San Carlos Indian agent, John Clum, accompanied by Dudley and some troops from San Carlos, met the group at the next camp. The

Yavapai claim that the food was poisoned. The people were so hungry that many cooked the food and ate it right away. They remember that many died. There were others who remembered being given tainted food by the government authorities before, so they merely held the food in their hands but refused to eat it.

1500 Indians traveled the six week March of Tears to the San Carlos Apache Indian Reservation. Various reports indicate that approximately 375 either escaped or did not survive the journey. Not counted are the un-numbered babies who were born and died along the way.

Dr. Corbusier.

Fort Verde is located one block off main street in the town of Camp Verde, 90 miles north of Phoenix. Open to the public are several well restored buildings as well as a very nice visitors' center. Open 8:00 a.m. to 4:30 p.m. every day except Christmas. Nominal entry fee.

Address: Fort Verde State Historic Park, PO Box 397, Camp Verde, AZ, 86322. Call (520) 567-3275 for more information.

Fort Verde.

J. J. Thompson Spring House

First Anglo in the Red Rocks
1876

*"Abraham, you must bring your family to Arizona.
I believe that I have found a paradise."*

John James (J. J.) Thompson was eleven years old when he ran away from home in Londonderry, Ireland. The year was 1853. He said he never looked back.

Although J. J. rarely spoke of his early years, he did admit he ran away because he got tired of going to school six days a week and spending Sunday in church. He managed to get to Liverpool, England. This is where most eleven year old runaways' stories would end—with discouragement and no funds, most children would see the impossibility of their situation and return home. But J. J. was adventuresome and determined and he was intent on getting to America. However, J. J. Thompson had no money at all. Even if he had the money for the voyage, no one would allow such a young child to travel by himself.

Undaunted, J. J. hung around the seedy docks in Liverpool hoping for a lucky break. Luck smiled on him when he made friends with a young man in his twenties. J. J. was a winning young kid, and soon his new friend offered to pay J. J.'s passage. In addition, he offered to assume guardianship for J. J. until they reached New York.

Once in New York, J. J. was on his own. There the luck of the Irish beamed upon him once more. He met another lad, close to his own age, whose father was a ship captain. His ship was bound for Galveston, Texas. J. J.'s new friend convinced him that once they were in Texas they would be able to get jobs fighting the Comanche. The two young boys stowed away on the ship and managed to hide for two days. When hunger drove them out and they were discovered, they were given a stern lecture by the ship's captain and made to work the rest of the voyage.

Bidding goodbye to his young partner in crime, J. J. was once again all alone and pennyless when he departed ship in Galveston. Wandering around lonesome and friendless, he met an old man and struck up a conversation with him. Once again, J. J. was befriended. Soft-hearted and generous, the man named Finley took the likeable young Irish lad home to Refugio, Texas. The Finleys were childless so they gave the boy a home and brought him up as if he were their own son.

J. J., now called Jim, turned 19 as Texas seceded from the Union in 1861. He enlisted in the Southern army. During the four years of the Civil War, he spent some time in prison as a POW in Illinois. He came home with a musket ball wound in his arm and shoulder.

He returned home to Refugio, and after a short visit with his adoptive parents, he went to Mexico where he worked on a ranch learning the skills of a cowboy. Returning to Refugio, he was offered a job leading a large herd of cattle to California. The former trail boss had let the herd stampede a few days out from the ranch. J. J. managed to round up almost all of the scattered herd and headed west. The year was 1868.

The cattle were sold to Mormons in Utah, so they never did make it to California. Jim, now 26, took his money and headed for northern Arizona Territory. He had heard of gold nuggets the size of potatoes being found at the western edge of the Grand Canyon along the Colorado River.

Stopping near present-day Lake Mead, he found that the tales of gold were greatly exaggerated. For a short time he went into the ferry business, hauling people, animals and goods across the Colorado River. During this time he lived with the Abraham James family.

Margrett James, Abraham's daughter, was only six years old when the handsome, tall, adventuresome Jim Thompson arrived at her family home on the Muddy River. Jim lived with the family for six years, becoming the best of friends with Abraham. By the time Jim left, pretty little Margrett was twelve years old, and had already caught his eye.

In 1875 Jim Thompson's itch to move on had to be scratched, so he sold his ferry business. He purchased two wagons and eight pair of oxen. He dug rock salt from a cliff near the Colorado River and hauled it to the frontier mining town of Prescott. Needing the salt for meat preservation as well as a spice, Prescott's Fort Whipple Army Post was happy to purchase his load.

From the sale of his salt, J. J. bought a wagon load of wood shingles and took it to Phoenix to sell. His Irish luck failed him this time. In the 1870's Phoenix was a small grouping of adobe homes. Shingles were useless on the flat-roofed adobes. Undaunted, J. J. stored the shingles and butchered one of his oxen. With the meat he made jerky and sold enough of it to make his way back to Prescott. Disgusted, he said he'd never visit Phoenix again. And he never did.

In Prescott he sold his wagons and oxen, using the money to purchase a horse, pack mule and supplies. He headed into the Verde Valley looking for a place to settle down.

During the first year, Jim farmed with a friend, Ed Conway, near what is now Page Springs. One day in the summer of 1876 he was out hunting with B. F. Copple, and they both began to talk about the red-rocked canyon they could see to the northeast. Curious, they rode over and saw for the first time the lush, sweet-smelling, verdant canyon of Oak Creek.

Conway and Thompson arrived just weeks after Al Seiber, famed army scout for General Crook and Agent Edwin Dudley, had forced the last of the Apache from their home to the San Carlos reservation.

Picking their way up the canyon, tangled with wild growth, they came upon a level spot near the clear creek which had until recently been home to the Apache families. There were their carefully tended gardens of beans, corn and squash. Thompson claimed Squatter's Rights to the place and named it Indian Gardens. Thompson became the first Anglo man to settle in Oak Creek Canyon.

As Jim built his cabin on his land, he wrote to the Abraham James family encouraging them to move to the area. Describing a paradise, he told James that the area had abundant game, a clear cold creek, moderate weather, wild berries, fertile soil and nearby grazing land. Abraham James loaded up all his possessions and his family and prepared to move. Herding his cattle through several hundred miles of trackless desert, high plains and forests, the James family arrived in 1878. They settled first near Page Springs and later moved to land just below the present King's Ransom Motel off Hwy. 179, known today as Copper Cliffs. Abraham built Sedona's first irrigation ditch.

J. J. Thompson had not forgotten pretty Margrett. She was fourteen years old when she moved to Oak Creek Canyon, old enough for J. J. to court her. A patient man, J. J. waited two more years until Margrett was sixteen years old before marrying her. J. J. was 38. J. J.'s farm at Indian Gardens was too wild and remote for a family so he built a cabin for her at the mouth of the canyon where the Sedona Arts Center is located today.

Margrett and Jim Thompson had a large family which they raised in Oak Creek Canyon, seven boys and two girls. The last boy, Guy, was born when Margrett was 47 years old and Jim was 69.

Eventually the road through the wild brambles of Oak Creek Canyon was improved and other families joined the Thompsons and the

James family. The Purtymun family, with six sons and two daughters, soon joined these early pioneers. Eventually two of the Purtymun boys married two of the Thompson girls. The weddings each lasted three days and three nights.

After moving the family to the Indian Gardens area, J. J. built a sturdy stone spring house for Margrett. The rock house was built over a cold, bubbling spring and had a ledge around the outer wall to keep the eggs, butter, cheese and milk cold. It was a very efficient natural refrigerator for Margrett and the family.

Laura Purtymun McBride, J. J.'s granddaughter, in a conversation with this author, reminisced about how she used to sneak into the spring house and dip her finger into the top of the milk and lick off the cream. She thought she was the only one doing it until years later other grandchildren "'fessed up to doing the same." Laughing, she said it was a wonder that Grandma Thompson had any cream left at all, with all those sneaky grandchildren licking it up!

The Thompson Spring House is on private land near the Indian Gardens area of Oak Creek Canyon.

J.J. Thompson spring house.

Fort Grant

Billy the Kid in Arizona
1875

No blowhard like "Windy" would get the best of Billy the Kid.

Most of the notorious years of Billy the Kid's life were spent in New Mexico. However, in 1875 he ventured into Arizona Territory using the name Henry McCarty. Some sources regard Henry McCarty as Billy's real name, and William Bonney as an alias. It is thought he was probably about fourteen years old at the time.

J. W. "Sorghum" Smith, a hay contractor for Camp Thomas, recalled a short waif who walked up to him and asked for work. "He said he was seventeen," Smith remembered, "though he didn't look to be fourteen."

The Kids' previous brushes with the law had been for stealing butter and then later for receiving stolen property—clothes taken from a Chinese laundry. For the clothes stealing he was held in a cabin that had been converted into a makeshift jail. During the night, Billy the Kid found an easy escape by squirming up the chimney.

Known as Henry McCarty, Billy the Kid spent about two years in Arizona. Most of his visit is undocumented so legend, folklore and the handed down stories of old-timers have to fill in the gaps.

While in the Camp Grant area, he got a job cooking and busing tables at the Hotel de Luna. There he made the acquaintance of an ex-soldier named John R. Mackie. Together they began stealing horses and saddles, especially cavalry horses.

One story goes that a lieutenant and a doctor came down from the camp one day. They had an idea which they said would prevent anyone from stealing their horses. They had long ropes tied to their horses and when they went into the bar, they carried the other end of the ropes with them. Mackie struck up a conversation with the lieutenant and the doctor, and they talked for quite a while. When they came out of the bar they found the loose end of the rope draped over the horse rail and their horses gone.

The victims didn't see much humor in the situation and filed a complaint with Justice of the Peace Miles Wood. A warrant was issued and a peace officer went out to arrest the daring duo. Wood recalls, "He came back and said he could not find them. I knew he did not want to find them."

Not long after that, Miles Wood saw the Kid and Mackie boldly enter the hotel for breakfast. "I told the waiter that I would wait on them," Woods wrote. "I took a large serving tray and took it in and slipped it on the table in front of them. Pulled a six-gun from under it and told them, 'Hands up.'"

With his gun pointed at their backs, Wood walked the two horse thieves out of the hotel and marched them the two and one-half miles to the guardhouse at Camp Grant. About an hour after he was locked up, the Kid asked the sergeant of the guard to take him outside. Just outside of the guardhouse and in sight of several soldiers, the Kid turned and threw a handful of salt in the guard's eyes and attempted to grab his gun. The guard yelled for help and the nearby soldiers disarmed the Kid. He was returned to the guardhouse.

Wood had no sooner walked back to his hotel when he was summoned back the two and one-half miles to the camp. There he had the black-smith fit the Kid with a pair of iron shackles riveted around his ankles.

That night, while Wood and his wife were at a reception at the colonel's house, a sergeant of the guard came to the door and asked to see the colonel. In a few moments the colonel returned shaking his head. The Kid was gone, shackles and all.

McCarty (the Kid) was seen in Globe City, now known simply as Globe, where he went to see his step-father, William Antrim. One historian believes that it may have been Antrim himself who alerted the officials. At any rate, he was arrested twice more and twice more he was able to escape.

Foolishly, McCarty returned to the Camp Grant area and began hanging around George Aikin's saloon. There he would sometimes get into trouble with the local blacksmith, Francis P. "Windy" Cahill. Cahill was called "Windy" because he was always blowin' about first one thing and then another,...kind of a blow-hard.

On the night of August 17, 1877, the big bully once again began wrestling around with McCarty. He would throw the Kid to the floor, ruffle his hair, slap his face and generally try to humiliate him before the other men in the saloon. The Kid decided that was the last time old "Windy" would blow on him. The Kid pulled his gun from his pants belt and fired. "Windy" staggered backward, fell to the floor hard, and died the next day.

Henry McCarty left Arizona and chose the name of William Bonney for his new life in New Mexico. He was to live three years and eleven months longer before meeting with the wrong end of Sheriff Pat Garrett's gun.

∾∾∾∾∾∾∾∾∾∾∾

Brown's Folly is the last remaining structure at Fort Grant which would have heard the voice of Henry McCarty. Built in 1882 of 26" thick stone walls, it is now a part of Fort Grant State Prison.

The building now called Brown's Folly was built under the direction of Capt. William Brown in 1882. The US Government was billed $28,000 for the construction. The actual costs were $20,000. After an investigation, Brown was court martialed. While he was in the guardhouse (the same one which had housed Billy the Kid), some friends snuck a gun in to Capt. Brown. He used the gun to commit suicide rather than face further disgrace. It is not known how the friends intended Capt. Brown to use the gun.

The fort was abandoned by the cavalry in 1905, leaving behind a single care-taker. By 1908 the cavalry had a cantankerous old colonel whom they were trying to force to retire. Col. Stewart was put in charge of several hundred acres with no livestock, empty buildings, a Chinese cook and the one care-taker. It wasn't long before Stewart got the message and retired.

In 1912 Fort Grant became Arizona State Industrial School. Until 1973 the facility was used to house youthful offenders as well as children who became wards of the court due to being orphans. Some of the boys were as young as eight years old. In 1973 Fort Grant became an adult prison.

Brown's Folly as it looked to Billy the Kid.

Two Guns

Murders, Gunfights, Massacres, Train Robberies, a Zoo, Buried Treasure and a Cave with a Curse

1878

The Navajo warrior cocked his head to one side.
"I hear voices, and yet we are alone. How can this be?"

The Navajo warriors stopped their horses and paused on the wind-swept high desert, puzzled at the sound of muffled voices. The Apache marauders from the White Mountains who they had been pursuing for several hours seemed to have vanished. Sweeping down on scattered hogans around the Newberry and Garces mesas, the Apache had slaughtered more than 50 Navajo men, women and children in their surprise raid. They took with them three young Navajo girls as captives. The enraged Navajo men, on swift horses, split into two groups with one riding ahead in an effort to cut off the Apache from their favorite escape routes. Now the Apache seemed to have vanished—except for the voices.

One young Navajo, Bahe, got off his horse, listened, and silently motioned for the others to listen as well. Soon they smelled smoke from cooking fires rising from a crack in the ground. Navajo chief scouts, remembered as Natani, B'ugoettin Begay and Redshirt, had lost the trail in the rocky soil near present day Two Guns. Now they began to understand why the Apache seemed to have vanished into thin air.

The scouts sent for help and soon a large group of Navajo men arrived. While tracing the numerous cracks in the earth, they came to a great cave with an entrance large enough for horses to enter. Trapping the Apache in the cave, they opened fire. The Apache returned the fire, but quickly realized they were trapped. The Navajo gathered wood and built a large fire at the entrance to the cave. They kept feeding the fire until they could see smoke rising from the many cracks in the earth around the cave.

In an effort to block off the smoke, the Apache killed their horses and stacked their carcasses at the entrance to the cave.

The Apache were desperate. A spokesman came stumbling out of the smoke filled cave begging for terms to save their lives. Although speaking only "pidgin" Navajo, he managed to make the Navajo warriors understand that the Apache wanted to strike a bargain if they would be allowed to live. This proposal was an old custom among southwestern Indians. It was not unusual for Indians to pay in goods and stock to evade corporal punishment for murder.

Natani told the Apache to send out the three captured girls and they would talk further. When the Apache spokesman hesitated overly long, the Navajo knew that their worst fears were confirmed. The girls had been slaughtered by the Apache attackers.

In a wild rage the Navajo rained bullets into the cave and once again built the fire to a ferocious level. They watched and fed the fire until first wisps and then more and more smoke began to pour out of the crevices near the entrance. The Apache's last desperate attempt to escape death had failed.

Long after dark the Navajo fed the fire until the last of the wailing Apache death chants finally stopped. The fire was allowed to burn out, but it was noon the next day before the rocks had cooled enough to permit the Navajo to cautiously enter the blackened depths of the cave. Burnt horses nearly blocked the entrance. Dragging those aside, they were met with the nightmare vision of 42 dead Apache who lost their lives struggling for air in the death cave. They lay in grotesquely twisted positions, frozen in death as they had choked for a final breath of fresh air that never came.

The Navajo stripped the bodies of valuables and reclaimed the loot taken by the Apache raiders. The Navajo warriors retreated from the cave quietly, fearing the revenge of the evil spirits of the dead, the Chindi. They were not joyous over a victory, but felt that the cruelty of the deaths of their three young girls had been avenged.

This incident put an end to further use of the cave at Two Guns by the Apache. In fact, no raid in that direction was ever undertaken against the Navajo again. The Indians of the area considered the cave an evil site, inhabited by the Chindi.

Years later the construction of the railroad, as it moved from east to west across the rocky high desert, was stopped for a time at a steep gorge known as Canyon Diablo just three miles north of present day Two Guns. Without enough money to build a bridge, the rails stopped at the precipice. The wildest and most lawless of towns, also called Canyon Diablo, sprang up at the rail end. After a short reign of terror, it died a natural death when the gorge of Canyon Diablo was bridged and the railroad built further west to California.

After the rails were completed, robbing passenger trains became a popular pastime. It appealed to young cowboys as a quick and sure means to grab a small fortune. Trains going through Canyon Diablo station were held up on a regular basis. One of the biggest of the robberies in terms of loot occurred on the blustery cold night of March 21, 1889.

Four cowboys from the Hashknife outfit, John Smith, "Long" John Ford, Daniel M. Havrick and William D. Starin, planned the daring robbery.

On a freezing, sleet-filled night the eastbound Atlantic and Pacific Express No. 7 stopped at Canyon Diablo for water. Two of the robbers grabbed the engineer and fireman, taking them out of the cab. Then they blew the express safe, looted it and took several packages of money. They also took watches and jewelry which were not locked up.

Later one of the bandits said they had buried the silver watches, their rifles and the jewelry near present day Two Guns on the rim of Canyon Diablo. Before the jewelry was buried, Smith removed some of the diamonds from the ring settings, putting them in a shirt pocket in which he carried smoking tobacco. Emptying the sack sometime during his flight from the posse, he soon began rolling his cigarettes from the loose tobacco at the bottom of the pocket. Thinking about it later, he realized that he must have rolled the diamonds into his last few cigarettes, and then thrown them away with the butt of the cigarette.

On the canyon rim the loot had been divided into four piles of equal value. Havrick was then blind-folded. Another cowboy held his hand over a pile of stolen goods, one at a time, Havrick was asked to name whose pile of loot it would be. Each man claimed his plunder. It was generally known that the bandits obtained $100,000 in currency contained in a small metal box, $40,000 in gold coins and 2,500 new silver dollars besides a considerable amount of jewelry.

After a feeble attempt to throw off the posse by riding around in circles, two robbers rode off together for Black Falls downstream on the Little Colorado. The other pair, after starting north across the Navajo reservation, changed their minds and swung west. All four crossed the Colorado River at Lee's Ferry in the dark of night and galloped on into Utah.

Sheriff Buckey O'Neill pursued the robbers with a couple of deputies, several express company detectives and railroad officers. By the time the posse reached Utah following the tracks of the four robbers, the bandits had escaped capture by several Utah settlers, shot up the town of Cannonville and turned back into Arizona. Hungry and exhausted, Sheriff Buckey O'Neill and his posse finally captured the four errant cowboys in the Arizona Strip north of the Grand Canyon.

The prisoners were taken to the Prescott jail. Managing to part his leg-iron chains, Smith tied them to his boot tops. That same night he escaped, stole a settler's horse and headed for Texas. Before reaching the border the gentleman bandit rescued a school teacher lost in a blowing snow storm. After delivering her to the country home where she boarded, he rode on. When the teacher told how chains and irons had been tied to his legs, the settlers promptly mounted up and pursued the helpful bandit. Well ahead of the posse and clearing the snow storm, Smith ran into Texas lawmen who had been alerted. He soon rejoined his bandit buddies in jail.

They were tried in the Prescott court and convicted of robbery and sentenced to 25 years in the territorial prison at Yuma. None served their full term, being pardoned out as the years went by.

When the cowboy robbers were captured less than $100 was found on all four of them together. What happened to the fortune in stolen money and jewels? It was buried in four different locations somewhere on the canyon rim or down in the gorge near Two Guns where the descent could be made by foot. Treasure seekers have been actively looking for the riches for years, but none have been found.

Earl and Louise Cundiff reached Arizona in 1922 from Arkansas and filed a range claim of 320 acres, encompassing that part of the canyon now called Two Guns. Earl constructed a large stone building complete with living quarters on the west side of the canyon where the dirt road turned down into the crossing. Near the foot of the driveway he put in a concrete dam to impound water, such development being necessary to improve the homestead and keep the land.

Earl created a trading post on his land. As more and more automobiles came into use, the earliest tourists began using the transcontinental highway, eventually Route 66, across northern Arizona. The trading post enjoyed a brisk business both from the Indians as well as the tourists. Cundiff soon added gas pumps, oil service and a restaurant.

Harry E. Miller, claiming to be a full-blooded Apache, as well as part Mohawk, saw possibilities in the area, too, and leased a business site from Cundiff in 1925. Miller, with a flair for gaudy publicity, let his hair grow long and wore it in a braid. He advertised himself as "Chief Crazy Thunder."

Miller and his wife began an extensive building program. With Indian labor, he constructed a long stone structure, in the rear of which and facing the main canyon, were wild animal cages and pens. He called this a lion farm. The center of the building and entrance into the zoo contained a small store and living quarters.

Miller investigated the Apache Death Cave and cleaned out the first two caverns. Ignoring the warnings of the Navajo not to go into the caves, he threw out all the human and horse bones and other remaining evidence of the massacre. He kept the Indian skulls for decorations to scare tourists. It is believed that he also destroyed evidence of prehistoric Indian occupation of the cave as well. He then hired the Hopi to build phony "cliff dwellings" in the cave's grottoes and he strung electric lights inside so tourists could see the fake ruins.

Miller and Cundiff had never gotten along and argued regularly over the details of the lease, which had been worded in rather broad terms. Finally, the anger came to a crisis on March 3, 1926, when Miller shot Cundiff to death. Despite the fact that Cundiff had been unarmed, Miller was acquitted of the charge of murder.

Miller's life at Two Guns was not easy. The Navajo felt he should have heeded their warnings of the Chindi in the cavern. Miller continued building a series of stone-walled buildings along a side canyon and also a circular building over the cave entrance. At the circular building, he kept a zoo of sorts. He said that his zoo contained every beast and bird native to Arizona. One day one of the mountain lions clawed him almost to death. A year later a small Canada lynx very nearly disemboweled him, almost cutting him in two.

When Miller's beautiful teen-age daughter was killed in a highway accident, Miller finally called it quits and moved away. The various buildings of Two Guns passed through a number of hands as the years went by. Eventually, many of the stone buildings were abandoned.

In 1971, when Two Guns consisted of a trading post, gas station, cafe and small motel, a fire started in the motel. Unchecked, it quickly spread to the underground gasoline tank at the gas station. The resulting fire and explosion nearly pulverized all of Two Guns.

Two Guns.

The stone buildings are now ruins, but Two Guns continues to live. Hopefully, the curse of the Apache Death Cave has dissipated since the explosion which virtually destroyed the little town. The newest owners of Two Guns, John and Kathy Morrison, run a gas station, mini-mart and KOA campground on the old, historic location. John leads tours down into the caverns for the curious and brave.

Two Guns is about 30 miles east of Flagstaff. Take Interstate 40 east from Flagstaff to the Two Guns exit. The ruins of the town are south of I-40. Go into the mini-mart and ask about seeing the ruins. There is a small charge to drive close to the ruins which are on private property by a dirt road. For more information call (520) 527-2784.

Another view of Two Guns.

C. S. Fly
Photography Studio

Site of the "Gun Fight at O. K. Corral"
1879

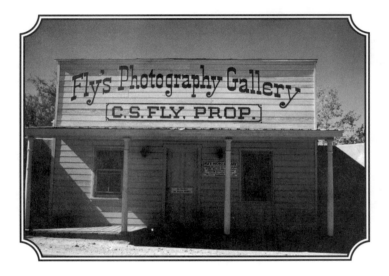

"You men are under arrest," Virgil Earp warned. "Throw up your hands."

The famous gunfight in Tombstone between the Earp brothers and the Clantons and McLaurys actually took place next to C. S. Fly's Boarding House and Photography Studio, spilling out into Fremont Street. The gunfight was near a back entrance to the O.K. Corral which faced the next street over. Locals would never have labeled it the "Gun Fight at the O.K. Corral." That was for Hollywood to invent about 40 years later. Somehow "The Gunfight in Front of C. S. Fly's Photography Studio" just doesn't have the same magical ring. Tombstone now happily lives with the inaccuracy.

On that fateful day, October 26, 1881, the Earps and Doc Holliday roughly pushed aside Sheriff Behan who tried to stop them from the coming tragedy. Sheriff Behan then took refuge in Fly's studio. With the first shots fired, Billy Claibourne passed through the studio at high speed, saving his own skin. Ike Clanton, who had no gun, ran from the fight through Fly's front door. Slipping out a side door, he ran along the passage between Fly's studio and the Fly home and then on down the street, living to fight and die another day.

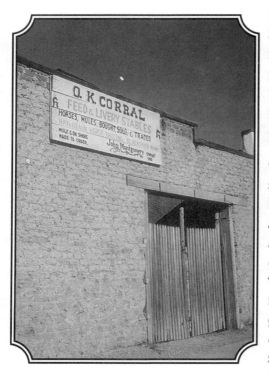

Entrance to the O.K. Corral.

Camillus Sidney Fly was a man of action, a one-term Sheriff, an unsuccessful miner, but a prolific and greatly successful photographer. He was more than a photographer; he was more of a documenter of history.

Camillus Sidney was one of six sons and three daughters born to Boone and Mary Fly in Andrews County, Missouri. Mary had read a great deal about the Roman Empire and was quite impressed with many of the famous Roman generals. She named Camillus after the great general and savior of the Roman Empire, Marcus Flavius Camillus. For reasons known only to herself, Mary gave some of her children names from ancient Rome, and others (luckily for them) she did not. She named the girls Camelia, Alice and Mary; the boys were tagged with Quintus, Flavius, Leonidas, Webster, Camillus, and Robert. Calling the children to supper must have sounded like the role call at the Roman Senate.

With a name like Camillus Sidney, it is no wonder that he preferred to be known as "C. S." His friends called him "Buck," taken from the buckboard in which he traveled with his bulky equipment.

At the age of thirty, Camillus married Mollie E. Goodrich. Unsuccessful at the photography business in San Francisco, he and Mollie set out for the silver rich southwest territory. They arrived in Tombstone in December, 1879, when the silver camp was still a rough tent and shanty town. Apache controlled the surrounding countryside. Saloons, dance halls and houses of ill repute were jammed with noisy patrons 24 hours a day. Bloody arguments seemed to be a part of the everyday scene.

The Flys built a boarding house and an adjoining photo gallery. A sign out front read:

COLORED WORK
AND INSTANTANEOUS PHOTOGRAPHS
COPIES MAY BE HAD AT ANY TIME

With the new riches, the citizens of Tombstone enjoyed having their families' images recorded by the recently arrived photographer. Even the rough miners and cowboys as well as some of the shooters and gamblers arrived at Fly's studio to have their likeness captured. By the end of 1881, Fly's Photography Studio was the largest photographic studio between San Francisco and El Paso.

Fly recorded the normal everyday scenes of Tombstone, providing an invaluable history of the early days of the mining camp. He photographed miners at work in the mines, the working of the stamp mills, merchants and businessmen posing for photos for relatives back east, and graduates of the Tombstone schools. In addition he photographed parties, picnics, parades, and organizational gatherings. Several times Fly took pictures of Tombstone as it burned, including the time his own business went up in flames.

While C. S. was taking pictures, Mollie ran the boarding house. One of her first boarders was "Big Nose" Kate, Doc Holliday's girlfriend.

It has been said that Fly was the only man who was able to photograph hostile Apache Indians who were still fighting with Federal troops. During the talks between General George Crook and Geronimo in March, 1886, which led up to Geronimo's final surrender, Fly was in the camp with them taking pictures. He photographed the fierce Geronimo with his warriors, going right up to them and requesting them to change poses, in addition to remaining still to ensure clear pictures. He took several thousand pictures of the primitive Apache during this time.

In 1893 a large fire destroyed the water pumps in the Tombstone mines and the mines began to fill with water. The boomtown faded quickly and the need for photographs dried up as well. Fly tried being Cochise County Sheriff for a term but did not run for re-election. By 1899 Fly was deeply in debt, and no longer able to support himself with photography. He moved to a ranch in the Chiracahua Mountains, leaving Mollie who chose to remain in Tombstone to run the boarding house.

By 1900 Fly had contracted erysipelas, an acute, painful inflammation of the skin caused by streptococcus. He grew weaker and lost any desire to live. Camillus S. Fly died in Bisbee on October 12, 1901, separated from Mollie, aged and penniless. He was 52 years old.

Since his death C. S. Fly has been recognized as one of the premier frontier photographers who recorded the unique events and lifestyle of the rugged western frontier.

∾∾∾∾∾∾∾∾∾∾∾∾

The Fly's Photography Gallery stands as
one of the old, cherished buildings in Tombstone.
It is still a photography gallery featuring C. S. Fly's photography.

Goldwater Building

Arizona's First Lottery
1879

"We must build a new capitol building," the city fathers agreed.

Prescott had just taken the location of the state capitol away from Tucson, and the city fathers wanted very much to build a grand building so the capitol wouldn't be moved again. The elated citizens had already selected the site for Prescott's majestic, domed capitol building: one block east of the present courthouse square. From that hill the government would be able to look out over a grand vista stretching seventy miles northward to the snow-capped San Francisco peaks, as well as across the nearby forest and rocky prominences of Prescott.

Several leading citizens banded together forming the Arizona Development Company with a plan to bring huge amounts of money into the state funds which could be used for the capitol building and then for Arizona schools. The leaders of the group were Charles P.

Dake, the new U.S. Marshal for Arizona; George Curtis, a local politician; W. C. Bashford, member of a wealthy pioneer Prescott family; Joseph C. Crane, a popular saloon owner; and Michael Goldwater, a prominent merchant. Their goals were not only to raise money for the capitol and schools, but they also planned toll roads, electric lighting companies and much more.

Their plan called for the initiation of Arizona's first lottery. Territorial Governor John C. Fremont, the acclaimed "Pathfinder" of the West and first man to run for U. S. President on the Republican ticket, thought it was a sensational plan. He issued a proclamation encouraging all Arizonans to participate and designated Michael Goldwater, grandfather of Senator Barry Goldwater, the President of the Arizona Development Company which would operate the lottery.

The Arizona Development Company was required to post a $20,000 bond with the Territorial Treasurer. The Bank of Arizona agreed to serve as custodian of all lottery funds. The new company was officially incorporated on January 3, 1879. It was to be financed for the staggering sum of five million dollars with 100,000 shares to be sold at fifty dollars each.

A bill before the Legislative Assembly to place the company in charge of the Arizona Lottery passed with ease. Governor Fremont signed the bill into law on February 5th, 1879. By late February the first tickets were on sale at Goldwater's store in Prescott. The Arizona Lottery Commission placed ads in newspapers across the territory announcing the new lottery.

ARIZONA LOTTERY
Under the direction of
GOVERNOR J. C. FREMONT
Territorial Commissioner
M. Goldwater, President
Bank of Arizona, Treasure

The ads also stated that the drawing would be held in Prescott on Wednesday, June 4th, 1879.

Tickets were priced at five dollars each. This was the first of several bad decisions that the Development Company made. In 1879, five dollars was about a full day's wage. Most who bought tickets had to pool their money just to buy one.

The second bad decision was in allocation of funds. The capitol building and public education funds were to receive only ten per cent of the lottery prize money. Gross proceeds were estimated to be $60,000 (12,000 tickets at five dollars each) and $32,000 would be given as prize money. Ten percent of the remaining funds would be designated toward the new capitol building and education. It didn't take long for the citizens to realize that there was a large amount of money unaccounted for. They demanded to know who was spending the $23,400 and on what.

Michael Goldwater protested that he and the Lottery Commission members would not personally make a dime on the deal, but that the $23,400 would be used to run the lottery.

Michel knew he was not making any money on the lottery, but he had a hard time convincing the skeptical citizens, which included some of his best friends.

Charley Beach, publisher of the *Arizona Miner* of Prescott and an old friend of Goldwater's, publicly expressed his doubts in his newspaper. Michael answered the criticism with a letter to Prescott in the competing *Arizona Enterprise*:

> *Charley Beach hints that I am getting richer and the people poorer by this lottery. The profits which I have made or may make out of the Arizona Lottery I am ready at any moment to turn over to any benevolent institution in Yavapai County...*

This was a very low blow for Michael Goldwater. For twenty years he had been esteemed as a pioneer and a major influence in the building of the Arizona Territory. He had fought off Apache attacks and had braved the hardships of living on the primitive frontier. He had earned a reputation as a man of integrity, and now his good reputation was being attacked, even by his own friends.

The storm of protest came from church and community leaders as well as the press. They complained that only Prescott would benefit from the profits of the lottery. John P. Clum, editor of the *Tucson Citizen,* publicly warned Goldwater to disentangle himself from the impending debacle:

> *We are assured by many that Mr. Goldwater is an honorable man; yet if he gets into an unpleasant and unprofitable controversy over the miserable and wrongly conceived lottery business, he will, we feel sure, admit that punishment is not altogether undeserved.*

The first drawing was planned for June 4, 1879, at the theater in Prescott. The lucky winner would go home with $10,000, with subsequent prizes from $2,000 to ten dollars. Each of the 12,000 numbers would be inscribed on a strip of leather and dropped into a huge glass container. The governor, having been appointed "territorial lottery commissioner", would seal the container himself to prevent any "hanky panky." Then the leather tickets would be rotated in the glass container over and over in front of the audience until everyone was convinced that the tickets were thoroughly mixed up.

With just one month to go before the planned drawing, the officers of the Arizona Development Company should have seen the obvious disaster that was looming ahead. Expenses had been higher than expected and ticket sales, after the first flush, had been sluggish. The wise thing would have been to cut bait and run, admitting failure.

It is difficult to know if it was giddy optimism or bull-headedness which prompted them to continue onward. Hoping for some last minute miracle to salvage the situation, the leaders placed new advertisements into the newspapers around the Territory:

The Lottery heretofore advertised to take place
June 4th, 1879
is hereby postponed until
August 4th, 1879
To be then held at the same place and drawn in the
same manner heretofore announced.
ALL TICKET HOLDERS
desiring to do so may surrender their tickets to
J. GOLDWATER & BRO., Prescott, Arizona Territory,
and will thereupon receive full cash value for the same.

Michael Goldwater hoped that his generous offer to refund any tickets would end the barrage of criticism. It didn't work. In fact, the editors smelled a rat.

The editor of the *Expositor* attacked Goldwater like a Gila Monster on a tender ankle:

THE SECRET OUT

So that frantic rush for lottery tickets, reported in nearly all the 'respectable' newspapers of the territory, was all a fiction—we might say a deliberate falsehood. We will bet our last shirt and longest Faber pencil that the ticket sale didn't amount to 600 dollars...

M. Goldwater offers to pay back the money for all tickets...Well done, friend Michael; got a good name, even if it does cost you...You need some sort of purification to keep you from stinking...

Poor Michael was left swinging in the breeze to take the harshest criticism. Legislator Fitch who had introduced the bill to the Territorial Legislature found this to be a convenient time to be out of town. Governor Fremont, as usual, was on an extended visit to Washington, D. C., New York and New England.

Governor Fremont's reaction to an official investigation was to shrug his shoulders and point to someone else:

I was not informed of this (his own prominent role in the administration of the lottery) or any other provision of the bill until it was presented to me for approval, and I did not think this objection sufficient to justify refusing my signature.

Ever optimistic, the Arizona Lottery officials frantically looked for ways to salvage the plan. The death knell came when the U. S. Postmaster General ruled that no communication about the Arizona Lottery could be sent through the mails. Pointing out that the lotteries of Cuba, Ireland and several states were publicized through the mails only brought Goldwater more criticism from the angry Arizona press.

Finally whipped, Goldwater sent out an announcement in late July that the lottery was called off and buyers could have their lottery ticket money refunded. During the next legislative session, a bill was quietly passed which repealed the lottery.

In addition to the loss of reputation and friendships, the records of the Goldwater family, now in the archives of the Arizona Historical Foundation at the ASU Library, show that more than $8,000 was spent on lottery advertising, ticket printing and other overhead expenses.

The exact figures of the ticket sales were kept secret for many years in order to let the whole debacle die a quiet death. The Goldwater records, however, reveal that only 138 tickets were sold, bringing in a total of $690. Nearly one hundred years passed before Arizona was ready to attempt another lottery.

∽∽∽∽∽∽∽∽∽∽∽

The original Goldwater Mercantile store building still stands in Prescott on the east side of the courthouse square.
It now houses a travel agency.

Canyon Diablo

The Canyon of the Devil –
Toughest Hellhole in the West
1880

"Slow-go" Duckin needed holes in his pockets to stay alive.

The low group of buildings which formed the town of Canyon Diablo stretched a mile along a dusty road between present day Flagstaff and Winslow. The town took its name from the chasm to the west. The steep rock walls of the impassable canyon stopped all westward traffic for several years.

Lieutenant Whipple, on his historic thirty-fifth parallel survey in 1853, gave the canyon its name, Canyon Diablo, meaning Devil's Canyon. Searching for a good railroad route through northern Arizona Territory, his party was stopped unexpectedly by the chasm. Two hundred fifty feet deep with perpendicular sides of solid limestone, the rough gorge was impossible to pass. His party had to travel twenty-five miles north to find a suitable crossing for the mules and wagons.

In 1880, as the railroad expanded westward, it, too, stopped at the brink of the gorge to await the construction of a bridge. Financial constraints held up construction and a small town sprung up at the end of the rail line.

Honky-tonks, sleazy restaurants, and a few supply stores completed the picture for the town of Canyon Diablo. Aptly named, the town seemed to attract the roughest lowlifes of the area. It was said that no sheriff survived more than three weeks. They pinned a badge on the first peace officer at three in the afternoon and buried him that evening. He had worked five hours.

One sheriff made the town record by lasting three weeks. After the first week, a considerable amount of money changed hands every day that he lived. Whether he met his appointment on Boothill from an unexpected swirl of dust blinding him at the moment of decision or whether it was the rotgut whiskey in his stomach which caused him to shoot wild, he met his fate like so many before him, with his boots on.

Another sheriff, a tobacco-chewing ex-preacher from Texas, wandered into town needing a job. The lanky new-comer was hesitant about giving his name and finally settled on Bill Duckin. The name sounded good enough to him, and besides, few of the citizens of Canyon Diablo used their real names anyway.

Apparently unaccustomed to doing any work, the locals soon renamed the sheriff "Slow-go Bill." Allergic to work, his guns still moved fast enough to keep him alive. Just moments after pinning on the badge, two would-be robbers ran across his path at the end of a dusty town trail. They unwisely decided to shoot their way out, but merely earned their place in the local Boothill.

Sheriff Duckin had to collect his own salary. Soon the locals noticed that he collected his monthly salary every week. He spent most of it on the city's finest cuisine—ham-and- eggs and steak.

Being in Canyon Diablo in the icy winter, "Slow-go" bought himself two long-tailed coats. He cut the pockets out of the first coat before he wore it, the better to get to his guns in a hurry. One day "Slow-go" realized too late he had forgotten to cut the pockets out of his second coat. Caught in a gunfight, he reached into his coat expecting to pull out his guns, and all he could grab was cloth. There was a quick end for "Slow-go."

Ruins of Canyon Diablo.

Old timers remember when an outlaw robbed the payroll intended for the railroad construction crew. A posse formed and rode out in hot pursuit. They chased the robber over the rough, rocky plateau. Sometime during the chase the outlaw's saddlebags containing the loot slipped off of his horse unnoticed. After he was captured, an exhaustive search of the rough area failed to turn up the money.

Twice as angry now because their payroll was gone, the group decided on a "suspended" sentence. The story goes that the group placed a noose around the outlaw's neck· and threw the other end around the branch of a huge pine tree. (They must have chased him a substantial distance, as there are no trees within a fair number of miles of Canyon Diablo.) Watching the stormy sky, they pulled tighter on the rope. Just as they were about to slap his horse out from under him, a huge lightening bolt struck the tree.

Feeling perhaps this was divine intervention, the group, unhurt, decided to turn the robber over to the proper authorities. He was convicted and sent to the Yuma Territorial Prison. The incident passed and was pretty much forgotten until a lucky cowboy, some years later, happened upon the weather-beaten leather saddlebags with the loot still inside.

The transient residents of Canyon Diablo consisted of railroad construction workers, cowboys, prospectors, hunters, Indians, sheepherders, ex-Civil War soldiers and rough men just passing through. Most stayed a few days and drifted on. Besides those who found permanent residence in Boothill, only a small, hardened core remained for any length of time.

Attracting the most violent brutes of the area, Canyon Diablo soon had a reputation for daily stabbings, shootings, bludgeonings, hackings, knifings, horsewhippings, gougings and general mayhem.

The women of Canyon Diablo were always referred to as the "girls" and were, without exception, not the kind to take home to mother. They were controlled by such madams as Gotch-eyed Mary, California Lil and Big-foot Annie.

Annie and Mary feuded. Their fight was mostly verbal until Annie "lost her temper complete" one evening. Big-foot Annie took her sawed-off shotgun and decided to end the fight once and for all. She entered Gotch-eyed Mary's place and not only took out Mary, but a gentlemen caller and two of Mary's girls as well. Big-foot Annie didn't have much time to gloat over her revenge as later that same evening someone entered Annie's residence and slit her throat with a razor.

The town residents at the time suspected that Annie's killer was a gambler who had been fond of one of the dead "soiled doves." It didn't make too much difference, since he was killed in a gunfight the next day.

A macabre event, but not all that unusual considering the era and the lawlessness of the time, is told with several variations. One old timer says that the Wigwam Saloon was robbed in nearby Winslow by two young cowboys, John Shaw and Bill Smith. They relieved the dice

70

table of a heavy load of six hundred shiny silver dollars. A posse set out immediately. Some rode the rough countryside, others took the train, planning to search as far as Flagstaff. They caught up with the two miscreants at Canyon Diablo. Guns were pulled and when the smoke cleared Shaw was dead and Smith lay in the dirt wounded. The posse dug a shallow grave in the rocky desert and buried Shaw that night.

Meanwhile, back at the Wigwam Saloon, word was out about the gunfight. One wrangler, who had bent his elbow at the bar all evening had a great idea. Thinking that it would be a shame to just bury a feller like that without a ceremony, he suggested they should all go to Diablo and give Shaw his last drink. His cronies, being drunk enough to see the brilliance of the scheme, all clambered aboard the next westbound train.

Once at Canyon Diablo, they found the freshly dug grave and promptly dug up Shaw's bullet-riddled body. They held it upright and poured a straight shot of whiskey between his stiff, white lips. The group, now sobering, solemnly reburied Shaw in his rough pine coffin and reverently said a prayer over him, feeling that they had now done right by him.

The other robber, Bill Smith, AKA William Evans, was sentenced on October 12, 1905, to nine years in the Yuma Territorial Prison.

Not long afterward the bridge spanning the Canyon of the Devil was completed and the railroad continued on west toward Flagstaff. Canyon Diablo, "the shooter's town," began to empty out as the gamblers, saloon keepers and girls followed on west with the railroad. Now nothing much is left but heaps of silent stones to mark what was once a town named after and ruled by the devil.

The ruins of Canyon Diablo can be reached by driving
three rough, rocky miles north of Two Guns from
Route 40, between Flagstaff and Winslow.

Ruins of Canyon Diablo.

Big Nose Kate's Saloon

1800's

The Swamper and the Grand Hotel

Over one hundred years ago in the 1880's, the saloon now known as Big Nose Kate's, was one of the finest hotels in the Southwest—the Grand Hotel of Tombstone. It was the largest and tallest building located between St. Louis, Missouri, and San Francisco, California. Its hotel rooms could accommodate 50 guests and the upstairs dining room could seat 150 people. This luxurious hotel hosted such infamous residents of Tombstone as Wyatt, Virgil and Morgan Earp; Doc Holliday; the Clantons; and the McLaurys.

In this hotel lived a janitor and odd-job man known as "the swamper." He was a trusted and honest worker who was given his room as part of his hard- earned pay.

"The swamper" had his own special bedroom located in the dark basement of The Grand Hotel. This was his solitary, private haven where he could enjoy peace and seclusion away from the busy coming and going of the many hotel guests. The room was his exclusive domain where no guest was invited. In addition to his private room, he had a private passion—silver.

The basement was deep enough below the surface of the ground to allow entrance into one of the catacomb-like mine shafts. The mines ran underground beneath the hotel as well as most of Tombstone.

"The swamper" spent many painstaking hours over a period of years tunneling an entrance into the shaft. When the digging was completed, he had gained access to a thick vein of silver. There he extracted, ounce by ounce, precious silver nuggets.

It is still unknown if "the swamper" spent his silver or if he hoarded it in an unknown niche somewhere on the premises of The Grand Hotel. However, several workers of the now Big Nose Kate's Saloon swear they have seen a ghost wandering the halls and stairs. Photographers have caught the ghostly image of an unknown being in a photo. There is even a postcard of the saloon's interior with a mystery image on it.

The locals will tell you that the ghost is perhaps "the swamper" and that his afterlife is being spent protecting the silver that may still be buried somewhere in this legendary building.

Big Nose Kate's Saloon is located on Allen Street in Tombstone. In addition to alcoholic and non-alcoholic beverages, it serves light meals and snacks. You can also enjoy the rinky-tink piano player and join a game of poker with an old time gambler. The mine entrance is still a prominent feature of the bar's basement.

Arizona Walls

Charleston

"Lord, Rescue Me From These Evil Men and Save Me From These Murderers!" 1880's

Charleston, approx. 1930's

"Don't drink that, Shorty, it's piezen."

T he wind whistling through the low, silent adobe foundations is all that is left of the once rip-roaring town of Charleston.

Great amounts of water were required to pound the tightly bound silver from the rock in which it was found. Since Tombstone was dry, the rough ore was carted nine miles away to the mill town of Charleston, located on the banks of the San Pedro River. The mills ran 24 hours a day pounding silver from the hard rock. The men who worked the mills and ran the Charleston businesses became just as hard as the rock that they worked.

When the Earp brothers arrived in Tombstone and began to put teeth into the law, the local cattle rustlers, horse thieves, and other nefarious crooks changed their base of operation to nearby Charleston.

In Charleston, custom decreed that every man was given a fighting chance, but nothing more. Killing a man was tolerated as long as the dead man had been armed and was shot from the front. Each man generally defined what was legal by his own standards. If one man considered cattle rustling his just reward for his hard work, and another disagreed, well, that was what shoot-outs were for. In addition, the judges generally applied their own twist to the law. Charleston's first justice of the peace, Judge James Burnett, once ended a trial by stating, "It served the victim right for getting in front of the gun."

In the early 1880's an Irishman named Durkee was awarded the contract to freight the raw ore from Tombstone to Charleston's mills. Happy that his first year was profitable, he hired a hall in Charleston and threw a party to honor the men of the district. Only working men, disarmed at the door, were welcome. Liquor was free and in unlimited amounts. An orchestra played in the background as the working girls tantalized the men.

The party was huge and boisterous even by Charleston standards. Each man felt a sincere obligation to get enormously drunk. To do less would be an insult to the host. As the evening wore on, some of the teamsters, who revered Texas, began to extoll the wonders of their native state. The miners and mill men decided they hated Texas.

The voices rose and violence looked inevitable; the women fled and the orchestra quit playing in order to take sides. The party erupted into a massive brawl, one that would do honor to a John Wayne movie. Bottles were broken over heads, chairs were thrown, and tables were turned over as the fight grew larger. The wobbly combatants eventually spilled out into the nearby streets. When the dust settled and the party sobered up, they discovered they had completely destroyed the hall and damaged several buildings in the surrounding blocks. The next morning, Durkee, figuring the damages were just part of a good party, paid the considerable bill for repairs. The various party goers were seen limping toward the cool water of the San Pedro where they soaked their heads and discovered their wounds.

Judge James Burnett, the first justice of the peace in Charleston, was born in New York in 1832. Upon arriving in Charleston he listed his occupation as "butcher," but a closer description would be that of both judge and extortionist—closely related fields at that time. James Wolf, a pioneer rancher of the area, remembers, "He could use a .45 with speed and precision. Hence, there was a vast amount of order and some semblance of law in his particular vicinity at all times."

Judge Burnett was expected to collect fines and fees and turn them over to the county commissioners. The commissioners were then to return to him what they felt was an appropriate amount for his salary. Judge Burnett, feeling he was short-changed, decided to keep all of the money. He determined that he had built the court up and didn't need the outside help or interference of the county officials. Burnett held court wherever it was convenient and never let the decision of a jury interfere with his own interpretation of the case before the court.

One Sunday morning, Curly Bill Brocius got religion, at least temporarily, and led his outlaw friends to the little adobe church of Charleston. The church going citizens rapidly left the church to Curly and his gang, abandoning the quaking pastor at his pulpit. Dumping a large amount of bills and coins into the collection plate, Curly demanded a sermon. The minister gulped and quickly changed his sermon topic. Lost to history is his exact text, but perhaps he chose Psalm 6 and read,"Depart from me, all ye workers of iniquity; for the Lord hath heard the voice of my weeping. Let all mine enemies be ashamed and sore vexed: let them return and be ashamed suddenly." His application of the scripture came out more like, "Lord, rescue me from these evil men, save me from these murderers!"

Relaxing and warming up to his theme once he realized he wasn't going to be shot, the preacher roared out with his best hour's worth of hell-fire and damnation. A foot stomping version of a favorite hymn ended the Sunday services and Curly Bill and his gang clumped out, satisfied that they had gotten their money's worth of religion that morning.

Word got around town of the disruption of the Sunday services. The next day, Judge Burnett caught Curly Bill loitering under a tree. The judge convened court then and there and fined Curly $25 on the spot. As he paid the judge, Curly Bill grumbled, "That's the last time I'm goin' to church. It's too damn expensive."

ᘡᘡᘡᘡᘡᘡᘡᘡᘡᘡ

During WWII the United States Army selected Charleston as a "practice location." Using live ammunition, the 93rd Infantry Division from nearby Fort Huachuca practiced street fighting under what they thought were conditions simulating those they might later encounter in the bombed-out cities of Europe. Most of Charleston was destroyed. Time and the harsh desert elements have almost completed the job. What's left of Charleston is on the north side of the paved road which connects Sierra Vista and Tombstone.

Crystal Palace

Doc Goodfellow of Tombstone
1880's

"Send for Doc Goodfellow... I'm... I'm... shot"—a man's first thought after being gunned down on the mean, dusty streets of Tombstone.

Still proudly preserved in the window of the Crystal Palace in Tombstone is the advertisement for Doc Goodfellow, where he kept his upstairs office. Doc spent only eleven years in Tombstone, but it was there he made his reputation. Too often pictured as a featureless, one dimensional person who slides in after all the gunfighting is over, Doc was far more complicated than Hollywood portrayed him. Volumes of novels, movies and television series have been inspired by the Doctor's more infamous friends—the Earp brothers, Doc Holliday, Bat Masterson, Curly Bill Brocius and the Clantons. Almost nothing has been written about Doc Goodfellow, one of the West's most colorful, adventurous and courageous men.

In addition to his impressive professional and scholarly accomplishments, Doc was a man of action, as daring and robust as his more disreputable contemporaries. He entered smoke-filled mine shafts and carried out unconscious men. Rushing to a bleeding patient, he drove a locomotive at breakneck speed. He rode with the men who captured Geronimo. He endeared himself to the Mexican town of Bavispe by lovingly caring for the wounded after a devastating earthquake leveled the area.

A complex man, he was a tireless physician, a great dry wit, a published scholar, and a man of great courage. Doc, however, was no saint. Doc's office was conveniently located above the Crystal Palace where he spent most of his evenings drinking. Although married, he spent a goodly sum of his earnings on the more famous and fashionable prostitutes. One night on Allen Street he stuck a knife into a man named Frank White. Many of his colleagues considered him tough, arrogant and cocky. In addition, he was a racist.

Doc Goodfellow's advertisement still can be seen from the window of the Crystal Palace Saloon.

George Goodfellow was born on December 23, 1855, in Downieville, California. He was a member of the 1871 freshman class at the University of California at Berkeley. While there he received an appointment to West Point. He promptly and angrily refused it when he found out the Academy had recently enrolled its first black cadets. Some time later he accepted a commission to the United States Naval Academy.

Much to his displeasure, Goodfellow arrived that fall at Annapolis at the same time as a young man from South Carolina named Conyers. Conyers was the first black midshipman to be appointed to the Academy. Suppressing his anger, Goodfellow ignored Conyers and concentrated on his studies and boxing. Goodfellow did very well in boxing, defeating every opponent and becoming Academy champion.

One afternoon during the winter term, Conyers and Goodfellow bumped together on the stairway. Goodfellow felt that Conyers had bumped into him deliberately as an act of aggression. Using his well trained fists, he smashed Conyers in the face, knocking him back down the flight of stairs.

The incident caused a big uproar. With Post-Civil-War feelings still running high, Reconstructionists bombarded the Eastern newspapers with letters accusing the Naval Academy of allowing racial bias among their midshipmen. The newspapers howled for Goodfellow's immediate dismissal.

Rear Admiral Robley Evans, on staff at Annapolis at the time, blamed the Academy's administration for the problem. Evans wrote, "In our efforts to protect the colored boy, we ran into the error of paying him too much attention and he gave himself undue importance... the boy was really unbearable." The pressure continued, however, and Goodfellow was expelled. A few months later, Conyers got into a fight with his white roommate and was dismissed from the Academy.

Abandoning his hopes for a military career, Goodfellow enrolled in medical school at Wooster University in Cleveland, Ohio. He earned his medical degree in 1876 and married his girlfriend, Katherine Colt. After short stays in Oakland, California, Prescott and Fort Lowell, the couple arrived in Tombstone in 1880.

Ed Schieffelin had filed his five mining claims only two years before and the new mining town of Tombstone was rough, rich, and roaring. The previous year, 1879, 600 people lived in tents clustered around Tombstone's only saloon. A visiting newspaperman from Chicago described the saloon as "dirty and abominable but they dance away nevertheless—the men inanely grinning, the women evidently dancing as a matter of business…two women are white and two are Mexican. One of the white women looks old and worn, dancing with evident effort. All are homely; and with the evidence of worthlessness and probable disease stamped on their faces, they form a ghastly picture of the Low Type of Immorality."

When Doctor and Mrs. Goodfellow arrived a year later, the population had grown to over 10,000. In just two years Tombstone had become the largest and richest town between El Paso and San Francisco. It now sported a dozen garishly decorated saloons where white-jacketed bartenders worked behind ornate mahogany bars serving mixed drinks in stemmed glassware. The millinery shops featured dresses for the newly rich ladies of Tombstone costing as much as $500. Nine-course dinners featuring such delicacies as oysters, lamb, buffalo tongue, suckling pig and elaborate desserts were served in the fancy restaurants. Replacing those four tired dancers of the year before, the ladies of the night were now imported from Paris. The "high class" prostitutes had arrived.

The excess of money, drinking, gambling and womanizing bred nightly violence. Doc Goodfellow responded to one crisis after the next. In medical school he had been taught to avoid surgery in the abdominal and peritoneal cavity—invasion there would surely lead to poisoning and death. Most gunslingers "shot for the gut," knowing that a gunshot to the belly would produce an agonizing, but sure death. Faced with two choices, either watch a man die or operate, Goodfellow stated, "It is inexcusable and criminal to neglect to operate."

Goodfellow determined his treatment by the size of the bullet. If the victim was shot by a .32 caliber gun or less, Goodfellow stabilized the patient and waited to see if he would recover. However, any ball larger than .32 caliber inflicted enough damage to make surgery a necessity. By his courage to operate, Goodfellow saved the lives of many men when another doctor would have shaken his head, administered a sedative, and quietly left the room. Modern physicians who have studied Goodfellow's techniques stated that it is amazing so many of his patients recovered.

On June 22, 1881, a fire raged down Allen Street destroying 65 businesses. The only man injured in the blaze was George W. Parsons who was under the balcony of the San Jose House when it collapsed. In his diary Parsons wrote that his "face caught it all."

> ...the worst wound was caused by a stick going through my under lip cutting a round hole and going thence through everything up through the left side of my face. Piercing the nasal cavity by bridge of the nose. My upper lip was torn loose from its holdings so that one could run a finger up into the nasal cavity.

One month later, Dr. Goodfellow performed plastic surgery.

> The doctor inserted the knife just to left of bottom end of the bridge and cut across and down nearly to end of the nose...After cutting sufficiently—the cartilage was seized and raised to its proper place when a needle with silver wire was forced through the nose from one side to the other and this wire held the cartilage in place after being fastened to the splint on my nose.

Doc Goodfellow refused any payment from Parsons because he was injured while trying to defend the town during the fire.

After several further operations, Parsons reported that he felt "quite elated as nose is hardening into good shape..."

After the gunfight between the Earps and the "cowboys" on October 26, 1881, Billy Clanton was taken to a room across Fremont Street and Goodfellow was quickly called. Clanton was so badly wounded that Goodfellow could do nothing but remove his boots. The 19-year old rustler had promised his mother he wouldn't die with his boots on.

The following December Goodfellow was called to operate on Virgil Earp whose arm was shattered when he was ambushed at night on his rounds of Tombstone. Goodfellow was able to save the arm by removing four inches of bone, leaving the arm and hand useless.

In March, 1882, Morgan Earp was killed while playing billiards in the back of the Campbell & Hatch Saloon. One of the bullets passed through Earp's body and struck George Berry who had been watching the billiard game. Although he was only shot in the thigh, Berry slumped to the floor in a faint and never regained consciousness. He died a short while later. Doc Goodfellow stated that, "Berry's injury was inconsequential and hardly more than an abrasion. Technically, he died from shock. The simple fact was, the man was scared to death."

Often in his coroner's reports, Doc Goodfellow showed his gallows humor. When a man named McIntire was shot to death in a saloon brawl, Goodfellow wrote that he "found the body rich in lead but too badly punctured to hold whiskey."

Dr. George Goodfellow.

Goodfellow wrote an article for the *Southern California Practitioner* regarding the impenetrability of silk to bullets. He reported that a notorious cattle-rustler was shot in the neck with a Colt .45 at point-blank range. Goodfellow examined the wound and discovered that the man's silk neckerchief had been driven far into his neck by the bullet. When Goodfellow carefully extracted the neckerchief, the bullet came out with it. The patient was back in the saddle in two weeks. Goodfellow concluded, "He is now, I presume, pursuing his trade on the border, if not in peace, at least in prosperity."

Goodfellow, like most men on the frontier, was tough. On one of his journeys his saddle-strap broke, tossing him to the hard-packed earth. His fall broke his arm. Alone in the desert, he set it himself.

Another time he was called across the border to help deliver a baby. The new father was a wealthy rancher and gave Doc a sack of gold coins in payment for his services. When Doc got back to Tombstone, he headed straight to this favorite hang-out, the Crystal Palace, and bought drinks for the house. The party ended when the last gold coin clinked from the sack.

In May, 1887, news reached Tombstone of a devastating earthquake in Bavispe, Sonora, Mexico. Doc loaded a wagon full of medical supplies and struck out for the border. After two bumpy weeks in the wagon, Doc finally arrived and found people still painfully holding broken arms and hobbling on unset broken legs. He immediately set up a make-shift hospital and a seemingly endless line of moaning injured formed. Goodfellow worked for weeks from sunrise to sunset. The Mexicans called him *"el santo doctor."*

News of the "saint doctor" reached President Diaz in Mexico City. In gratitude, he presented Goodfellow with a pure-bred Kentucky stallion as well as the silver double-headed eagle of Austria, which was supposed to have been found among the treasures Maximilian ordered buried before he attempted to flee Mexico. The people of Bavispe never forgot the kindness of the doctor who was a saint.

∽∾∽∾∽∾∽∾∽∾∽∾∽

Goodfellow's window advertisement can still be seen on the upper floor of the Crystal Palace Saloon in Tombstone. The Crystal Palace is located at the corner of 5th and Allen, open from 10:00 a.m. to 9:00 p.m. Closing times vary depending on how busy they are. Phone 520 - 457-3611.

Allen English Home

The Shakespeare of "Rotten Row"
1880's

"He was never out-spoken."

Of all the flamboyant lawyers who hung their shingles on the adobe walls of "Rotten Row" in Tombstone, Allen R. English was probably the most capable. A popular man, English stood well over six feet tall and sported a sprangly, outswept mustache which appeared to hover over his scraggly, long Van Dyke beard. He dressed his tall, solid body in a formal cutaway coat and striped trousers. Handsome, with thick, dark hair, he was blessed with a lawyer's most coveted instrument—a deep, sonorous, powerful voice. In addition, he was witty and intelligent. He made friends easily, had a great sense of humor and was one of the most popular lawyers in the Arizona Territory of his time.

English was born into a wealthy Eastern family. Precocious and bright, he earned a law degree while still a teenager. He was twenty years old when he arrived in Tombstone. Oddly, he didn't immediately go into a law practice but worked as a hardrock miner. During his nightly rounds of the honky-tonks of Tombstone he met Marcus Aurelius Smith. Smith was cut from the same cloth as English. He, too, was a handsome, gregarious lawyer as well as a consummate politician, gambler, heavy-drinker and general good-ole-boy.

Smith took a liking to young English and persuaded him to join the Smith law practice. Together they practiced law by day and prowled the noisy saloons along Allen Street each night.

Soon English's reputation for brilliant lawyering and chronic imbibing was wide spread. Phelps Dodge kept him on a retainer. Every time a case was pending, they'd lock him up in the Copper Queen Hotel in Bisbee and post a guard outside the door in an effort to keep him sober during the trial. Inevitably, some crony of English would figure out a way to smuggle a bottle or two up to his room and English would appear before the magistrate in his usual state—grandly inebriated.

English was at his best when performing before a jury. The large, graceful man used his rich, resonant voice to its fullest, roaring with indignation one moment and whispering with a plea the next. He could mold the jury like a sculptor before a soft mound of clay. He was a symphony conductor before the orchestra. He was the supreme actor standing in the spotlight. He could force genuine tears at will, both from himself and the jury. His bombastic plea to the jury would be embroidered with Shakespeare, English poetry, the Bible and Greek philosophers. He would ring every emotion from the courtroom. In the space of a few moments he would be somber, derisive, indignant, outraged, compassionate, misty-eyed, sarcastic, or sympathetic—all for the jury held captivated by his oratory. Then, just as he had convinced the jury he was a towering colossus of the bench, he would turn to a friend on the jury and leaning on the rail say, "Got a chew, Jim?" with a homespun wink. All of this while fully besotted.

Sometimes it appeared that strong drink even improved his ability to win cases. Once when he was defending a gunslinger named Wily Morgen who was charged with murder, he arrived at the courthouse with a painful hangover. The court recessed for lunch just prior to the closing arguments, so English found his way to Billy King's Saloon where he proceeded to clear his throat with liquid fire. By the time court was to reconvene, English was passed out on the barroom floor. Several of Morgen's friends hurriedly got a wagon, laid English out in the back and rushed him to the courthouse. They hauled English up the back stairs, arriving just in time for closing arguments. Drunk as a lord, English opened his eyes, slowly stood up and focused his bleary eyes on the jury. History was made that day as Allen English gave one of the most masterful pieces of courtroom oratory ever given in a territorial court of law. When he sat down, the jury found his client innocent of all charges.

Once during a break in a trial someone was overheard to remark, "My, that Mr. English is certainly an outspoken man."

The weary prosecutor answered, "Mr. English may be out-smarted, out-fought, out-thought, and out-maneuvered, but he will never be out-spoken."

Once the Santa Fe Railroad offered him the unheard of sum of $25,000 a year to work for them, on one condition—that he stop drinking. This was at a time when the miners in Tombstone were making about $25 to $30 per month.

"What," he roared indignantly, "give up my inalienable rights to a bloodless corporation? Hell no!"

As both a lawyer and investor in the local mines, English made fantastic sums of money, but he didn't have much talent in keeping it. With the profits from two mining ventures, he and his wife took a trip East. They returned after several months of unlimited spending and high living, dead broke.

Allen English was married three times, each marriage failing because of his excessive drinking. His first wife gave him two sons and his second wife gave him one son. The third wife stuck around only long enough to give him a piece of her mind.

On one occasion English appeared in the courtroom so inebriated that he was staggering and could hardly stand up. Judge George Davis, angered at such a disrespectful display by a member of the bar, fined him twenty-five dollars for contempt of court.

Gripping a sturdy chair for support, English rose and bellowed back to the judge, "Your honor, twenty-five dollars won't pay for half the contempt I have for this court!"

ᔕᔕᔕᔕᔕᔕᔕᔕᔕᔕᔕᔕ

The restored Allen English home is a private residence in Tombstone.

John Slaughter Ranch

"Hit the Road"
1880's

"Hit the road!" "Leave town or die!"

These words, uttered by fearless lawman Texas John Slaughter, were enough to make most of the thieves and rustlers he went after high-tail it out of the territory.

The popular history of the West portrayed by Hollywood is filled with smoking six-guns, unshaven, tobacco-spitting bad guys and steel-jawed lawmen. The more prosaic story, but more accurate, would also include men whose days were filled with just plain hard work—farmers, ranchers and miners. Texas John Slaughter belongs to both histories.

John Slaughter drove the first herd of Texas longhorns into the lush San Bernardino Valley of southeastern Arizona in the late 1870's. Left a widower with two small children, he had been both a rancher and a Texas ranger before he purchased the immense acreage. The ranch, which

John enlarged over the years until it comprised in his words "100,000 acres, bought and leased," was part of the old Ignacio Perez land grant which spread over both sides of the border and deep into Mexico.

Before his move to Arizona, Slaughter had married his second wife, Viola Howell, who was his junior by nineteen years. Viola loved Slaughter's two children and raised them as her own. Addie was about twelve and Willie was about six when they arrived in the Arizona Territory. Also with them was Jimmie Howell, Viola's younger brother, who was also about twelve. Slaughter built two adobe houses on the ranch, one for his in-laws, Amazon and Mary Ann Howell who had driven cattle from Texas with him, and one for himself, his ranch foreman, and the cowboys. He and Viola maintained a home in Tombstone so the children could be properly schooled. John and Viola did not have the benefit of much formal training and they were both adamant that their children would be educated.

Over the years John and Viola took in a number of foster children—orphans, semi-orphans, the children of relatives and friends—whom they raised and educated. They both loved children and believed they could help give them a chance at a better life through education. At one point, around 1896, they had living with them a Negro child, an Anglo child, an Indian child and a Mexican child. The children worked at whatever tasks their age permitted along with the rest of the family on the ranch. None of the children were ever officially adopted, but each remained a friend of the family after they grew to adulthood.

A little Indian girl, who Slaughter named Apache May, was one of the children who really stole Slaughter's heart. In 1896 Slaughter heard there was a small band of Apache with stolen horses camped in the Sierra Madres. He formed a group of his men along with Lieutenant N. K. Averill, 7th Cavalry, and a small military force.

Just before dawn they descended upon the camp, scattering the Indians into the nearby rock formations. As the men were searching the campsite to see if there were any more Indians, one brave stuck his head out from around a rock, evidently to see what was going on in the camp. He was shot dead. The cowboys later wondered if he was the father of the baby girl found moments later hidden beneath blankets.

Apache May.

Slaughter was poking around the bedding when his rifle butt touched something soft. Lifting the blankets he saw a small baby girl with large, frightened brown eyes. As he picked her up, she immediately put her arms around Slaughter's neck. After identifying the horses they started back to the ranch. During the rough 75 mile trip home this little Apache baby, only about 15 months old, rode in the saddle in front of Slaughter. She didn't cry once.

Apache May was a delight to John Slaughter for just four short years. When "Patchey," as John called her, was about five years old, she and some of the children were playing with the dying embers of a fire when little Apache May's dress caught on fire. She lived for several painful days, but in spite of all the loving care and natural nursing given to her by the Slaughters, she died from pneumonia caused by the inhaled smoke. It was said that a light went out of John Slaughter's eyes that never returned.

The Earp brothers left the Tombstone area in 1882 after the gun battle near the back entrance to the O.K. Corral. The citizens of Tombstone wanted an end to the continuing crime and lawlessness. In 1887 they elected John Slaughter Sheriff of Cochise County. Although a short man, some records say just five-foot three, he was not to be trifled with. Most accounts describe him as "flinty-eyed" although Viola was fond of saying that he had a twinkle of humor in his eyes. It was apparent that he reserved his humor, what there was of it, only for family and friends.

"No one on whom Slaughter bestowed the most casual glance ever forgot his eyes," wrote one of his acquaintances. "They were the blackest, brightest, most penetrating eyes I ever saw…If someone had held a newspaper at the back of my head, it wouldn't have surprised me if Slaughter, looking straight through my skull, had read the want ads."

Texas John Slaughter.

Incredibly fearless, Sheriff Slaughter let it be known that horse-thieves and cattle-rustlers would no longer be tolerated in the area. Quickly word got around that Slaughter would go out alone after a horse-thief and return days later, grim faced, with the stolen horses. Often a horse with an empty saddle trailed after him. No one asked any questions. He was doing his job to the tacit satisfaction of the honest citizenry of Cochise County.

If a clever lawyer got an obviously guilty man acquitted, Slaughter set things right. He would either chase him out of town or bury him. "Leave town or die," was the choice Slaughter gave them. He brought many crooks to justice in a court of law. *The Tombstone Prospector* of October 7, 1887, dubbed the Tombstone jail, "Hotel de Slaughter."

By the time Slaughter had served two terms as sheriff, the territory had become a much safer place to live. Tombstone citizens asked him to run for a third term, but Viola just wouldn't have it. "Mr. Slaughter, I do not think I could stand another term," she told her husband. Feeling that he had done the job he set out to do, he moved his family to the San Bernardino Ranch and settled down to build an empire.

The ranch was remote—65 miles from Tombstone and 45 from Bisbee. The town of Douglas, now 18 miles to the west was not founded until 1901. Viola Slaughter presided graciously over the organization and management of the domestic responsibilities at the large ranch. For convenience of the ranch employees and neighbors, the Slaughters maintained a postoffice and small store. The house was always filled. In addition to family members, she offered hospitality for lengthy stays to foster children, elderly relatives, relatives visiting for their health, ranch schoolteachers, and grandchildren. Wandering through and staying for a few nights or a few weeks would be visiting friends, neighbors, surveyors, outfitters, lawmen, military officers, passersby and boarders.

Viola and Slaughter.

Certainly not all of the problems with rustlers had been solved by the time Slaughter left office. On one occasion Slaughter was riding along the Mexican part of his range when he saw a large number of calves in a corral. The mothers, who stood about bawling for their babies, all showed the Slaughter brand. The thieves had separated the calves, trying to wean them. Slaughter went back to the ranch to sleep the night and decide what to do. The next day he left before dawn, went to the corral on the Mexican side and simply let down the corral bars. He drove the sixty calves and their satisfied mothers back to the home ranch on the American side, all the while risking a bullet in the back for his efforts.

One of the workers on the Slaughter ranch was Mormon. To satisfy the local bureaucrats, he built his three room house straddling the Mexican/American border. On the Mexican side lived one wife, and on the American side lived the second wife. Each maintained citizenship in her own country. Each had her own stove and cooked an evening meal in her own "home."

Once when Slaughter was bringing his large herd up from Mexico to graze on the American side of the range, he was confronted with an officious border inspector who decided that Slaughter's cattle were diseased. He began turning back about every fourth or fifth cow, telling Slaughter that they couldn't come across the border. Slaughter just calmly waited him out, knowing that his wranglers were at the other end catching the returned cows and herding them back in. By the end of the day all of the cattle were on American soil.

For the Slaughters there was a great deal of difference between being hospitable and being robbed. Just a few days after being badly beaten at the conflict at Agua Prieta, Pancho Villa's revolutionaries straggled back to the San Bernardino Valley. They swarmed the countryside, injured, hungry and ragged, needing clothes and begging for food. One of the officers, leaving his horse and guns near the barn, approached the ranch house on foot. The Slaughters invited him in, fed him, and gave him a room for the night. Although the officer pulled out a large roll of cash the next day and offered to pay for their help, the Slaughters refused to accept any money. The code of the west prevailed. When the officer left, he gave Viola "a great hilted sword and silver mounted saddle and rifle." The sword is part of the John H. Slaughter Memorial Collection at the Arizona Historical Society in Tucson.

Just days before however, in late October of 1915, on their way to attack federal forces at Agua Prieta, Pancho Villa and his army of eight to ten thousand men arrived at the San Bernardino Ranch. They were hungry, thirsty and exhausted. They had crossed the Sierra Madres with little or no food and water. At the lush Slaughter ranch they helped themselves to the abundant ripe corn and slaughtered fifty head of cattle. John Slaughter sat in his rocking chair on his front porch glowering. Not one to take this insult lightly, he finally stood up and strapped on his six-shooter. As he called for his saddle horse and shotgun, he was asked what he planned to do. Squinting his eyes in anger, he replied, "I'm going down and jump old Pancho Villa." He rode the half mile to where Pancho Villa had set up his camp and sat down for a talk. No one knows what transpired, but the results say a lot about the man—John Slaughter, alone, faced down a known cold-blooded killer with ten thousand men backing him up, and came back with a pocket full of United States twenty-dollar gold pieces to compensate for the lost cattle. Slaughter was seventy-four years old at the time.

~~~~~~~~~~~~

The Texas John Slaughter ranch is restored to reflect what the ranch looked like when John and Viola lived there. It is open to the public. The rooms are semi -furnished with a nice collection of photos of the Slaughter family and ranch happenings. Part of the ranch property has become the 2,330-acre San Bernardino National Wildlife Refuge.

Among the existing out-buildings is the six-car garage Slaughter built to house his cars. Although he was always more at home in the saddle and never learned to drive, he was fascinated with cars and owned at least six, including a 1912 Cadillac.

From Douglas, take 15th Street (which becomes Geronimo Trail) east for 16 miles to the ranch gate. There is a nominal admission charge. The ranch exhibits are open Wednesday through Sunday 10:00 a.m. to 3:00 p.m. It is best to call first to reconfirm the times that the ranch is open. Phone (520) 558-2474.

Texas John Slaughter Ranch.

Yuma Territorial Prison

Killed Because of a Joke?
1883

"I have no intentions of marrying Mae Woodman,"
Bill Kinsman angrily declared.

Prisons hold a certain morbid fascination for law-abiding citizens. Like the neck craning that is common at the scene of a horrible accident, we look but hope not to see the worst. Prisoners flaunt the laws upon which our society is based. Without the laws we would have anarchy. Law-abiding citizens look at disbelief at the repeat criminal and ask, "Why did you do that?" Prisoners bring to the front larger issues than trespassing the law. Sin, violence, revenge, jealousy, hatred, greed, poverty, ignorance and perhaps penance and redemption are all bound up in the prisoners' stories.

At the Yuma Territorial Prison the worst of the criminals in the Arizona Territory sweated out their sentences behind the strap iron cage doors of their cells. Each spent his time with the gnawing discontent common to all confined humans.

Prisons built to house the longer term outlaws during the late 1800's were different than those built today. Prison officials gave little thought to reform, retraining or rehabilitation. Rather, a prison was built to punish the offender. It was hoped that if the prison was a bad enough experience, the criminal would mend his ways upon release and decide never to do anything bad enough to have to return. Territorial prisons were intended to be tough on the meanest *desperado* that the devil ever made—and they were.

The men who designed the Yuma Territorial Prison, open from 1876 to 1909, never considered that women might be held within the walls of the prison, so they made no provision for them. However, in the 33 years that the prison was open, 29 women spent time behind the bars. Mae Woodman, a murderer, was one of them. Her story has been told wrong so many times that she seems to cry out from the past for someone to set the record straight.

Mae Woodman arrived in Tombstone with an itinerant gambler named Bill Kinsman sometime in the early 1880's. Handsome and well-liked, Bill made his living at the gambling tables in the local saloons. In February of 1883 a friend, playing a practical joke, placed a notice in the *Tombstone Epitaph* that Bill Kinsman was announcing his marriage to Mae Woodman. The next day Bill answered by placing his own notice that he had no intentions of marrying Mae. That morning Mae took a revolver and, finding Bill Kinsman in front of the Oriental Saloon, raised the gun and fired at close range.

Mae made an attempt to fire a second shot, but her arm was knocked down by a nearby peace officer. Kinsman lived only a few agonizing hours. He was 25 years old. Mae was immediately arrested and taken to jail.

As she was being led to jail, she asked the sheriff if she had hit Bill. He replied, "You have not only hit him, but probably killed him." The newspaper reported that she seemed perfectly satisfied at this reply. Her attitude was to come back to haunt her. Tucson's *Arizona Daily Star* also reported that she "claimed she was driven to it by abuse received from Kinsman, with whom she had been living for some time." Ignoring that, the newspaper went on to say that "the supposition is that jealousy caused her to commit the deed."

Mae was tried, convicted and sentenced to five years in the Yuma Territorial Prison, the harshest sentence available to the judge. Judge Pinney, in sentencing Mae Woodman, stated that, having been found guilty, it became his duty to pass sentence; that while his sympathy as well as that of the community went out to her, being a woman, his duty as a magistrate prevented him from allowing it to warp his judgement or stand in the way of justice. The judge informed Mae that her term in the penitentiary could be best utilized by preparing for a higher and better life.

While still in jail, Mae attempted to take her own life. She had been given a mixture of chloride hydrate and morphine each evening to help her sleep. Instead of taking the opiate, she carefully saved it up until she had enough that she thought it would kill her. Dr. Goodfellow, of Tombstone, was called and saved her life.

The citizens of Tombstone were shocked at the severe sentence given to the woman and immediately began to circulate petitions to have her pardoned. By August her mother, Mrs. McIntyre, was in Prescott presenting the governor with a petition signed "by most of the county and city officials at Tombstone, by the best class of citizens, by the most of the jurors who tried Mae Woodman, by attorneys at law and by the editors and proprietors of all the city papers as well as the reporters on the same—and generally by a class of people who are law abiding and are interested in repressing crime than giving license to it" requesting that the governor pardon Mae Woodman.

On the 15th of March, 1884, Mae was released from the prison with the admonition that she leave the territory and never return. She left on the first train to California.

Almost without exception Mae has been accused by recent writers who have related her story as the woman who killed her lover over a joke in the newspaper. The writers missed two important factors of her story. First was her comment about Bill's abuse, repeated in the newspaper.

The most telling evidence of her true motivation for killing Bill is from a letter which is in the archives of the Yuma Territorial Prison. The letter is from Dr. Goodfellow, the attending physician in Tombstone, and was included with the packet of letters which Mrs. McIntyre, Mae's mother, presented to the governor (bold print by author).

Dr. Ainsmith (sic)   *Tombstone, A. T.*
Prescott, A. T.   *August 17th, 1883*

Dear Sir:

The bearer of this, Mrs. McIntyre, is the mother of Mae Woodman who is now in Yuma for the killing of her paramour. She goes to Prescott to attempt to secure a pardon for her daughter. The petition has, I believe, been generally signed for the majority of the community while deploring the murder seem generally to believe that **it was unpremeditated and provoked by the man's brutal treatment of her in her then pregnant condition.** *The evidence given shows this as well as the fact that she is of a neurotic temperament with a tendency to various nervous attacks upon the slightest excitement having been subject to epileptic fits in her youth.* **The condition of pregnancy was not, I believe, proven upon the trial thru neglect; But I can assure you of that fact for I delivered her of the fetus at a four or five month's miscarriage while she was in jail.** *If the evidence is presented to you, a much fuller and better idea of the case can be had than from my letter. I take the liberty of giving Mrs. McIntyre this note to you in the belief that you will extend to her some slight aid in presenting her case* *favorably to the Governor, also to present to you my idea of her inespousible (sic) condition at the time the deed was committed, predicated upon a personal observation of her immediately succeeding the animal act and for some months afterward during her incarceration here.*

In conclusion I would state that my interest in the case is purely a professional one inspired by the belief that an unjustly severe sentence has been imposed upon the woman.

Very Respy.
G. E. Goodfellow

Mae was pregnant when the joke came out in the newspaper. She and Bill had a fight, as they often did, but this time Mae knew he had done real harm. When she realized, after the brutal beating, her baby had ceased to move, she got a gun and killed Bill. He had taken from her the one thing she really wanted. Feeling she had nothing to live for, she tried to end her life a short time later in jail.

For over one hundred years various writers have retold Mae Woodman's story, ignoring the letter from Doc Goodfellow. Preferring to tell that she killed Bill over the newspaper joke, they have perpetuated a wrong.

Now you know the truth.

You're welcome, Mae.

∽∽∽∽∽∽∽∽∽∽∽

The Yuma Territorial Prison is open to the public and is operated by the Arizona State Parks Department. Open daily from 8:00 a.m. to 5:00 p.m., there is a modest admission charge. For more information call (520) 783-4771.

Yuma Territorial Prison.

Judge George Washington Swain's Home

"This is a Regular Chokin' Machine."
1883

"Dad-gum-it, if Miz Cashman hadun-uv tore down the bleachers, we kud shore see a lot better."

Craning his neck, the cowboy hung off the fence of Judge Swain's home, next to the Tombstone Courthouse, hoping to see more of the grisly proceedings taking place in the crowded courtyard. A five-man hanging was unusual, even for the frontier days of the Arizona Territory.

The tragedy, known as the Bisbee Massacre, took place December 8th, 1883, in the early evening, about twilight, as Christmas shoppers were looking over the merchandise in the Goldwater & Castenada Mercantile. Five grim-faced men walked along the boardwalk toward the mercantile in Bisbee with a brace of six-shooters and a magazine rifle hidden beneath blanket-lined thick overcoats. Approaching the store, three of the men raised their neckerchiefs over their noses and stalked into the store. Pulling their guns, they quickly lowered the shade covering the front window. Two of the gunmen were left outside to stand watch.

The three inside, James "Tex" Howard, Omar "Red" Sample, and Daniel "Mick" Kelly ordered the customers to throw up their hands. Howard forced Joe Goldwater to open the safe. The contents, odd pieces of jewelry and an engraved gold watch, were quickly stuffed into a barley sack.

During the robbery, the other two bandits, Daniel "Big Dan" Dowd and W. E. "Bill" Delaney, guarded the outside door. As citizens happened to come that way, they were immediately ordered to enter the store. One unfortunate man, J. C. Tappenier, panicked. As he bolted and ran, the two robbers shot him down with a burst from their .45's.

At the sound of shots, there was a rush of Bisbee citizens into the streets to see what was happening. Unable to control their own nervousness, the two bandits began to shoot indiscriminately.

The operator of a nearby boardinghouse, Mrs. Annie Roberts, who was pregnant, stepped to the front door of her home just as a bullet smashed through the glass, killing her and her unborn baby.

D. T. Smith, a deputy sheriff visiting from New Mexico, attempted to stop the killing. He ordered the bandits to surrender. Not about to give up without a fight, they shot and killed Smith.

Albert Nolly, innocently standing with his team of horses and trying to quiet them in the midst of the flying bullets, was caught in the hail of gunfire and dropped to the dirt, dead.

Four innocent people were left dying in the street as the five bandits jumped on their horses and wildly galloped out of town, firing their guns in every direction. Deputy Sheriff Daniel of Bisbee ran out and opened fire on the gang as they went by, wounding Sample. The cost in lives was high for such puny loot. The bandits thought the Copper Queen Mine payroll was in the safe. It wasn't there.

Quickly two posses were formed. Deputy Sheriff Bob Hatch gathered a group of men. In addition, Deputy Sheriff Daniel headed out with another group which included a recent resident of Bisbee, John Heath. Heath convinced the posse that he would quickly lead them to the bad guys. He vehemently swore to track them down and hang them to the nearest tree.

Soon many of the men in the posse with John Heath, all expert trackers themselves, began to suspect that Heath was deliberately throwing them off the track. When several days of searching yielded them nothing, they returned to Bisbee and promptly hauled Heath off to jail.

Reward posters written in both Spanish and English were sent to every town in the Southwest and northern Mexico. The entire territory was infuriated at the atrocity of the murders. It was generally felt that the robbery could easily have taken place without murdering innocent citizens, especially a pregnant woman.

The capture of the murderers took place within a month and a half. Daniel Kelly, looking like a hobo, was arrested while sitting in a barber's chair in Deming, New Mexico. Unable to be discreet about their haul, Red Sample and Tex Howard made the mistake of giving some of their stolen jewelry to a talkative saloon girl in Clifton. They were promptly arrested.

Deputy Sheriff Daniel found out that Big Dan Dowd and Bill Delaney had headed for Mexico. Sheriff Daniel followed them and soon found Dowd in Corralitas, Chihuahua. Soon afterwards he ran down Bill Delaney in Minas Prietas, Sonora, and finally had the entire gang behind bars.

The trial in Judge George Washington Swain's courtroom drew huge crowds. As the *Tombstone Epitaph* reported,

> *To say that the courtroom was crowded at the ap-*
> *pointed hour would but idly convey the idea. It was*
> *literally packed to suffocation, the crowd even pressing*

on the dias leading to the judge's seat. The prisoner's dock was croded with ladies and large delegations were also present upon the main floor inside the rail. Many of those present were also representatives of the wealth, beauty, and culture of this city, and it is but fair to presume that a desire to hear the eloquence of Messrs. Herring and Smith, was the motive prompting attendance, and not that of morbid curiosty to see five unfortunate victims of their own evil passions sentenced to die an ignominious death on the scaffold.

The trial went quickly. The jury was in no mood to be lenient. The five men pleaded not guilty. The jury didn't see it their way and sentenced them all to hang for first-degree murder.

John Heath, arrested earlier, demanded a separate trial from the robbers. During the Heath trial, witnesses testified that while the holdup at the mercantile was going on, John Heath was dancing a jig in the dance hall across the street, celebrating each shot.

The two trial lawyers became media darlings as the two trials were reported. Again, the *Tombstone Epitaph* recounted:

Col. Herring resumed his argument for the defense in the Health case, occupying a little more than an hour in addition to the time taken up by him in the morning. At the conclusion merited applause greeted the distinguished advocate, for the very skillful manner in which he had made the worse appear the better cause. It was evident that his cunning sophistries and ingeniously spun themes had made more than a passing impression on some of the jury, and all the efforts of District Attorney Smith, who followed him, were brought to play to disabuse the minds of that body. For the space of an hour he hurled the weight of his logic, satire, invective and legal eloquence at the legal barriers erected by Colonel Herring in his client's defense, and carried his audience with him as he pictured in glowing colors the depth of depravity into which he claimed Heath had fallen.

Perhaps because of his "cunning sophistries and ingeniously spun themes," Col. Herring's client was only found guilty of second degree murder.

There were howls of anger at the jury's decision. The compromise verdict was met with universal rage by the citizens of the territory. John Heath was either guilty of first degree murder or not guilty at all, they felt. The jury had only been able to reach their verdict after balloting six for murder in the first degree, four for acquittal and two for murder in the second degree. The compromise was the best they could do.

When word reached Bisbee that Heath had been convicted of man-slaughter and sentenced to life imprisonment, outraged men poured into the streets with justice on their minds—their brand of justice. The quickly formed "Vigilance Committee" decided the mines would be shut down for twenty hours and all citizens who could secure horses were to meet in Tombstone by daylight.

One can only wonder what the citizens of Tombstone thought as they heard one hundred horsemen ride into their town that early morning and stop at the sheriff's office. Facing one hundred armed men, the sheriff was quickly unarmed and shoved aside.

"I suppose you want me, gentlemen," John Heath coolly greeted his executioners.

The crowd, now sizeably larger as the angry men of Tombstone joined the Bisbee vigilantes, roped Heath and walked him down the street to a large telegraph pole.

"Have you anything to say?" an anonymous leader shouted to Heath as the noose was placed around his neck. A silk scarf was tied around his eyes and his legs were roped together.

"Gentlemen, you are hanging an innocent man, but I am not afraid to die," Heath calmly said. "I have two requests to make. Promise me

The Lynching of John Heath.

not to shoot into my body when I am strangling and give me a decent burial. I am ready."

Health's body was left to hang from the pole for a while with a note attached which read, "John Heath was hanged to this pole by the citizens of Cochise County for participation as a known accessory in the Bisbee Massacre, at 8:20 a.m. Feb. 22, 1884." Heath was 32 years old.

Most of the vigilance committee were leading citizens of Bisbee and Tombstone. To avoid legal complications, Doc Goodfellow ruled that Heath "came to his death from emphysema of the lungs, which might have been and probably was caused by strangulation, self-inflicted, or otherwise." No further testimony was necessary.

The remaining five robbers were sentenced by Judge Swain to hang on March 28, 1884. An enterprising carpenter named Constable decided to make a quick buck off of the impending air dance.

Sheriff Ward had issued over 500 tickets of admission to the jail yard to witness the execution. The small courtyard couldn't possibly hold that many people. Mr. Constable proceeded to erect a grandstand across from the courtyard to hold the overflow and, at the same time, line his own pockets. The charge for the extra seating was $1.50 each.

The story is told that when Nellie Cashman, owner of a local boarding house, got wind of the impending carnival surrounding the executions, she decided to put a stop to the frivolity. Two of the doomed men, Kelly and Delaney, were good Irish lads, and Nellie felt it was wrong for the bleachers to allow hundreds to gawk and joke about the death of the men, guilty or not. Known as the "Angel of Tombstone," Nellie talked about 20 men into taking axes to the bleachers the night before the hangings. That put an end to the ticket selling and bleacher seats.

The five men ate a last supper which included fried oysters and other delicacies. They reported they didn't sleep very well, which they attributed to the oysters rather than their fate the following day.

The morning of the 28th, the men were given a free haircut and shave, courtesy of the sheriff's office, and were issued black suits to wear for their hanging. It's unknown whether they were buried in them or had to give them back when they no longer needed them. The *Tombstone Epitaph* stated that "as they were being attired in grave clothes an occasional grim joke at the appearance of some of their comrades was indulged in by the bandits. The local priests and Miss Nellie Cashman were in constant attendance and the forenoon gradually wore away, the prisoners bearing up bravely, and conversing upon ordinary topics with greatest nonchalance."

A estimated crowd of more than 2,000 had gathered to see justice done. As the men mounted the thirteen steps to the scaffold, they noticed spectators perching on top of the stone wall of the courtyard and on surrounding rooftops. Gawkers lined the rooftop on Judge Swain's home, next door to the Courthouse. As the prisoners saw familiar faces, they each would shout out "Goodby," almost cheerily.

"This is a regular chokin' machine," Dowd joked as the noose was pulled over his head and tightened around his neck.

Each man's last words were to claim his innocence and request a Christian burial. Through his black hood Kelly shouted out, "Let 'er go!" The boards of the scaffold creaked as it took the weight of the five bodies dropped through the traps.

Nellie Cashman, fearful the bodies might be molested in some way, hired guards to watch over the five graves in Boot Hill Cemetery for several nights, until the height of the anger had receded.

The *Arizona Gazette* reported, "The five men walked fearlessly to the halter, and unflinchingly met the Mosaic decree of 'a life for a life,' which has been preserved by all civilized communities."

Judge George Washington Swain's stucco adobe home, located at 211 Toughnut Street in Tombstone, was built in 1880. Originally a boarding house, Judge Swain was one of the most famous residents to own the home. At one time the home was a gaming and "pleasure house" catering to the judges and attorneys at the courthouse. The restored home, now Victoria's Bed and Breakfast, features original hardwood ceilings and rose-etched and leaded glass windows. Call (520) 457-3677 for reservations, or write PO Box 37, Tombstone, Arizona 85638.

*Visit the Victoria's Bed and Breakfast Web Site at
http://members.gnn.com/cewarner/vicabb.htm
e-mail address vcbb@wow.com*

Colossal Cave

"They're Bound to Come Out Sometime."
1884

The old outlaw was never seen again.

In 1884 four bandits overpowered two heavily-armed Wells Fargo agents and robbed the Southern Pacific train at Pantano, getting away with $62,000 in gold coins. The money represented the payrolls for the Southern Pacific railroad and the U. S. Regiments then stationed at Fort Lowell.

The robbers rode to the Empire Ranch near Vail, a small town south-east of Tucson. There they forced a Negro named Crane to give them fresh horses. Before galloping off they told Crane that he could find his horses at "the hole in the ground."

As soon as the train reached Tucson, a posse was sent out to search for the bandits. The gang escaped the posse by hiding within the underground maze of caverns then simply called "the hole in the ground," today known as Colossal Cave. Sheriff Bob Leatherwood was unwilling to risk the lives of his men by sending them into the dark, subterranean passageway. He knew the crooks had to come out sometime, so they set up camp at the entrance to the cave. For two weeks the patient posse kept watch, even setting fires inside the entrance to try to smoke the four men out.

In the meantime, the bandits stashed their loot well within the cave and, finding a back exit, made a get-away. The weary posse found out about the escape when a cowboy rode up and told them the four robbers were in Willcox boasting about how they had escaped from being captured.

The bandits didn't taste freedom very long. Shortly after the escape from the cave, three of the men were killed in a gunfight in Willcox. The fourth was caught, convicted, and given twenty eight years at the Yuma Territorial Prison. By 1912, he had served his time and was released from prison.

Wells Fargo agents had a long memory, and since the stolen money had never been recovered, several of them trailed the ex-con after he left the prison. They followed him to Tucson and then to the mouth of Colossal Cave. Once again the outlaw slipped away from the agents. Twelve years passed before the avenue of escape was found with the discovery of a second entrance into the cave about a quarter of a mile distant. The old outlaw was never seen in Arizona again.

In 1924 Frank Schmitt, who had a permanent lease on the cave, took Prof. Hibbard of the University of Chicago and two other men on a tour of exploration in the seemingly endless series of passageways. The group took food for three days. They were gone seven days and six nights in the total darkness underground. They measured the distance they had traveled as 39 miles, and still had not found the end to the cave. They did find, however, a second exit which now bears the appropriate title of Robber's Exit. Bullet shell casings, blankets and utensils as well as the empty Wells Fargo bags were later found in the back recesses of the caverns.

Colossal Cave is open daily. The hours the cave is open change seasonally. Call ahead for information. (520) 647-7275 There is an entrance fee. The cave is 22 miles east of downtown Tucson. Take I-10 east to Vail-Wentworth Exit 279, then go seven miles north.

The tour covers a half mile and includes a great deal of stair climbing. Tours leave every half-hour and last 45 - 50 minutes. There is a snack bar and gift shop.

Strawberry School House

80 Years Later a Mystery is Solved
1886

"There is a thief among us, and I must know who it is!"

For days the teacher at the school house in the tiny mountain burg of Strawberry had noticed that things had been disappearing from her desk.

Because Strawberry was isolated in the mountains on the Mogollon Rim, it was far from a supply store. The teacher hoarded her school supplies fiercely. Chalk was like gold; each precious stick was counted and used until it was too short to hold.

One day a piece of chalk disappeared from the chalk rail. Puzzled, the teacher decided to keep the chalk on her desk where she could keep an eye on it. The next day the second piece of chalk disappeared.

When the third piece of new chalk was missing, the teacher exploded in anger and frustration.

"Someone is stealing the chalk and I must know who's doing it!" The teacher confronted the class. "I expect whoever is taking the chalk to confess right now!"

Not one student moved. The teacher sadly locked the chalk away after each use and puzzled over how to catch the thief.

Next an eraser vanished.

"This will not be tolerated," the teacher admonished her class. "There is a thief among us, and everyone of you will be suspect until some-one confesses."

The children sat wide-eyed and silent. There was not a clue to the thefts.

Several days went by with nothing new missing. Relaxing her guard, the teacher left her gold watch on her desk after timing a test for the older students. That afternoon, after returning from lunch recess, she noticed that her prized watch was gone.

"This is just too much!" she stormed. "That watch was very valuable and meant a great deal to me. I am so distressed to think that one of you would be so bold and so dishonest as to take my own watch!"

Furious, the teacher kept the children in after school hours in order to interrogate each one by one. One child at a time was summoned to her desk for a personal confrontation.

"Look me straight in the eye, young man, and tell me the truth," the teacher asked each one. "Are you the thief?" Knowing their personali-ties, she interrogated some more harshly than others. The oldest boy, the one who cut wood and made the fire each day for the school, caught the worst of her anger. He stood with his hands behind his back, red-faced with humiliation, as the teacher read the Ten Com-mandments. To the teacher's dismay, each and every child still denied any thievery.

Gossip began to target the usual suspects. Fingers surreptitiously pointed. To complete the shame, notes were sent home to the parents and the children were grilled at home. Some were even punished.

The school year ended with the crimes unsolved. The teacher packed up and moved on. Years went by and the children grew up. Several generations later school children began to take buses to bigger, newer schools.

The old school house was no longer used and began to deteriorate. The roof of the old building sagged and the walls were no longer straight.

In 1965, public-spirited citizens of the Rim country raised money to restore the old Strawberry School House. They planned to open it as a museum, a reminder of the pioneer teachers of days gone by.

The gray weathered logs were rechinked and straightened. Carpenters climbed into the attic to strip away the old rotten wood and prepare the building for a new roof. There, they solved a mystery which was still remembered 80 years later.

In the attic they found a pack rat's nest containing bits of shiny paper and glass, hairpins and coins, pieces of chalk and an eraser,...and a lady's gold watch.

Strawberry School House, the oldest standing school house in Arizona,
is located in the town of Strawberry, 19 miles north west of Payson.
It is open 10:00 a.m. to 2:00 p.m., Saturday and Sunday, May
through September. There is no charge but donations are
always welcome. The friendly folks at Strawberry Lodge
might be able to answer questions for you— (520) 476-3333.

Fairbank

The Good Ole Boy Trainrobbers
1889

"We don't know nothin' bout no trainrobbers.
We wuz playin' poker here all evenin."

Burt Alvord was called to the wild cowtown of Willcox to help tame the lawless element and clean up the town. Burt had just successfully brought the boom town of Pearce into a state of peace and serenity and the citizens of Willcox wanted the same.

Burt, their new town Marshall, was a bald-headed man with a big, toothy grin, an outgoing sense of humor and a love of practical jokes. Burt was popular with judges and merchants as well as cattle rustlers and gamblers. His formal education consisted of whatever he'd managed to pick up in the pool halls and saloons of Tombstone where he was raised. Burt was also fearless and deadly accurate with a gun.

Alvord's fractious crowd of cronies included Matt Burts, Three-Finger Jack Dunlap and Bravo Juan Yoas in addition to the deputy constable at Pearce, Billy Stiles. By far the scurviest of the bunch was a brute named Bill Downing. None of them appeared to have an IQ that would equal the temperature of a spring day, but they made up for being dumb by being mean.

A young Burt Alvord, all duded up in a bow tie and checkered pants for this photo looks one-armed due to damage to the original plate. He was, however, a two-fisted man in every sense of the word.

September 11, 1899, at about 11:30 p.m., the westbound Southern Pacific was pulling into the station at Cochise, just ten miles west of Willcox. Billy Stiles and Matt Burts climbed aboard. One of the robbers held his gun on the fireman and engineer as the other uncoupled the engine and express car from the rest of the train. They opened the express car and ordered the Wells Fargo messenger to vamoose.

Next they ordered the engineer to move the train down the track. After traveling a few miles, they ordered the train stopped. They jumped off, picked up a waiting box of dynamite and climbed into the express car. Piling the explosives around the safe, they lit the short fuse and took off running.

The huge blast shook the ground, blowing the express car to splinters. The door to the safe was blown open and the bandits quickly took what was there. Estimates at the time suggested anywhere from $3,000 to $300,000 was taken, but it was probably in the range of

$30,000. The robbers loaded the gold onto their waiting horses and galloped off into the night towards Willcox.

After the bandits left, the engineer recoupled his train and returned to Willcox. The town Marshal, Burt Alvord, was playing poker with his pals in the back room of Schwertner's saloon. Burt pinned a badge on sullen Bill Downing and they rode out. They returned to tell the town that they had found the trail of the robbers and had followed them into Willcox where the tracks were lost. Acting greatly grieved and frustrated, Alvord and Downing resumed their poker game.

The card game was actually a clever cover-up. During the evening Alvord and Downing climbed out the back window of the saloon to help with the train robbery. A bartender at Schwertner's had been bribed to take drinks to the room every so often and return with empty glasses, giving the illusion of a long-running poker game in progress. By the time the robbed train had returned to Willcox, Alvord and Downing had climbed back in the window and picked up their cards.

Burt, being only slightly brighter than the rest, decided to take all of the gold and bury it, lest the scruffy gang suspiciously begin to spend large amounts of money in celebration. He told no one where he'd hidden the gold. For a while good ole Burt got away with the perfect crime.

He didn't count on the perseverance of Wells Fargo detectives and an Arizona Ranger, Bert Grover. Perhaps Burt's acting abilities weren't as good as he thought, but Bert Grover suspected his innocent act from the beginning. Grover coaxed the bartender at Schwertner's into confessing his role in the alibi. But before Grover could press charges, the bartender decided to skedaddle for parts unknown.

Burt Alvord and his nefarious gang decided they had been so good at the first train robbery, they could easily do it again. Bravo Juan, Three-Finger Jack, Bob Brown and the Owens brothers were chosen to pull off the heist. This time, however, the express car was guarded by the legendary gunfighter, Jeff Milton.

When the train pulled into the Fairbank station, the would-be robbers were milling in the crowd, acting like they were drunk. Milton, not

Still readable 100 years later are the letters identifying the former Fairbank post office.

expecting trouble, stood in the open door of the baggage car. Suddenly the gang pulled out their lever-action Winchesters and opened fire. Jeff Milton caught a slug, shattering his left arm and severing an artery. In the chaos, as bystanders scattered for cover, Milton didn't return their fire for fear of hitting someone innocent.

The robbers charged through the frightened crowd and bolted toward the express car. Milton grabbed his shotgun with his good hand and blasted Three-Finger Jack. Bravo Juan, seeing Three-Finger Jack go down, turned to run and caught the full blast of the second barrel in his keister.

Milton abruptly slammed the door shut to the express car and threw the keys to the strong box into a dark corner behind some baggage. He quickly tore off a piece of his shirt and wrapped it around his nearly severed arm forming a tourniquet. Collapsing from loss of blood, he slipped down between two large trunks. Passing out probably saved his life because at that moment the remaining thieves riddled the car with rifle shots.

When there was no return fire, the outlaws opened the door to the honeycombed car and cautiously peered inside. Seeing Milton motionless in a large pool of blood, they figured he was dead. They quickly searched his body for the keys. Not finding them, the thought dawned on them that the robbery had taken a lot longer and gotten messier than they'd planned, so they'd better just take off. They

Arizona Walls

grabbed Three-Finger Jack, threw him on a horse, and galloped away empty-handed.

Along the route back to Willcox they decided that Three-Finger Jack was a gonner anyway, so they left him along the trail to die. This didn't sit very well with Jack. When the lawmen found him, he angrily spilled his guts and provided the sheriff with all the details of the two robberies.

Burt Alvord and his crooked *compadres* self-righteously proclaimed their innocence to all who would listen. Burt claimed he was being framed, and, being the likeable good ole boy that he was, had a large following who believed him. Others figured the whole gang didn't have enough gray matter between them to plan and execute the two robberies.

Meanwhile, the gang began to fight among themselves. Since Burt Alvord was the only one who knew where the gold was hidden, the rest were afraid they wouldn't get their fair share. Bill Downing, pugnacious and nasty-mean by nature, got along with no one. Finally under the pressure of questioning, Billy Stiles, a treacherous hooligan, confessed everything in exchange for his freedom.

The Alvord gang was immediately locked up in the county jail at Tombstone. On the morning of April 8, 1900, Billy Stiles burst into the jail. Shooting the jailer in the leg, he opened the cells of Burt Alvord and Bravo Juan. Stiles never had liked Bill Downing, so he left him in his cell. Downing roared curses, as the others ran from the jail to their waiting horses.

Burt Alvord and Billy Stiles headed to Mexico where they hid out for several years. Arizona Ranger Burt Mossman contacted them and talked them into helping to capture the infamous bandit Augustine Chacon. They agreed to help, then turn themselves over to the law and be given light sentences. In spite of the pending short jail terms, Alvord and Stiles once again broke out of the Tombstone jail. This time they dug their way out. Stiles was never caught. He changed his name to Larkin, moved to Colorado and got killed in a gunfight. Alvord was captured and taken to the Yuma Territorial Prison where he completed his sentence. Belligerent Bill Downing was also sent to the Yuma Territorial Prison.

Upon being released from the prison, Burt Alvord returned to Willcox for a few days, saying a fond *"Adios"* to his old buddies. After he left town he was never seen in the area again. His friends believed that he dug up the gold and, after moving to Honduras, found a wife and a new life.

Jeff Milton, the ex-Texas Ranger and one of the last of the old-time lawmen, recovered from the terrible wound to his arm received during the robbery at Fairbank. Milton enjoyed a long and illustrious career as a peace officer. He died with his boots off at the age of 85 in Tucson on May 7, 1947.

∽∽∽∽∽∽∽∽∽∽∽

Fairbank, the scene of the unsuccessful 2nd robbery, is now a ghost town. There are several interesting wooden buildings still standing. It is located on Highway 82, nine miles west of Tombstone. Periodically reunions are held for the former citizens to reminisce, swap tales and news.

Lowell Observatory

A True Aristocrat
1894

*Lowell believed there was life on Mars and that it was
Martians who dug the canals.*

It's quite surprising that an aristocrat like Percival Lowell ever considered the tiny mountain town of Flagstaff an appropriate place to establish his observatory. Lowell was the scion of two of the most distinguished families in Boston, the Lowells and the Lawrences. Both families enjoyed great wealth and social position. In addition they were admired for their public service and community achievements. A contemporary rhyme bandied about contended that:

In the land of the bean and the cod,
The Lowells speak only to the Cabots
And the Cabots speak only to God.

In 1894 Percival Lowell sent an emissary, Andrew Ellicott Douglass, out to search for the perfect place to build an observatory and set up a study of the heavens. Douglass chose Flagstaff, a frontier lumber and livestock village of fewer than 900 souls, located in the northern mountains of the untamed Territory of Arizona. Douglass assured Lowell that there were at least a few amenities in town, including a hotel sufficiently civilized that "ladies can stay." The main draw was the crystal clear mountain air.

Lowell had traveled extensively. At the age of nine, he had spent several years in a boarding school in Paris and became fluent in French. After school he traveled in the Middle East and Europe, and then worked as an executive in one of the family's big cotton mills. When he was 28 he traveled to Japan, learned the language and published four books on Japanese culture and religion. Although increasingly obsessed with astronomy, he continued an interest in botany as well as many other subjects. He read widely and was well-informed of national and international affairs.

As a result of his upbringing and station in life, Lowell displayed the social ease, self-assurance, impeccable manners and reserve to be expected of a wealthy aristocrat. The frontier people of Flagstaff accepted Percival Lowell as the Renaissance Man that he was. While not over-awed, they were always respectful. Years before he attained a doctoral degree, he was always "Dr. Lowell" and would tolerate no uninvited familiarities.

Andrew Douglass had searched eleven sites before he settled on Flagstaff. The hill west of town perched 330 feet above downtown Flagstaff, already 6,900 feet above sea level. The summer permitted incredibly clear nights with the distant stars brightly twinkling above in the crisp night air. Recognizing the advantages that an observatory might have for the small community, the local businessmen offered to buy the land for the observatory and cut a road up to the top.

When Percival first arrived, he occupied the Greenlaw home at 309 North Leroux, a lovely old home which still stands today. He adjusted to the relatively crude social activities that a frontier town had to offer. During his early days in Flagstaff he sardonically wrote to his brother Abbott:

There was a grand Republican party last night, and the young Flagstaff band that is learning to play in tune serenaded the speaker...under the hotel windows in fine style. When you knew the air (melody) beforehand you could follow it with enthusiasm.

The home that Lowell first rented still stands in Flagstaff.

Lowell's enthusiasm cooled in a few months when he realized he and Douglass had not taken into consideration the very cold winters of northern Arizona. Snow piled so deep in the winter of 1895 that Douglass had to use a ladder to enter the dome by crawling through the telescope opening in the roof.

By spring Lowell spent several months searching for an alternate site. After looking at the Andes of South America, New Mexico, Mexico City and the Sahara Desert, Lowell decided that Flagstaff, overall, suited him and his needs best. He reopened his small observatory and decided that he was in Flagstaff for good.

Stanley Sykes and his brother Godfrey, natives of London, England, owned a local machine shop where they sold and repaired bicycles. Lowell heard of their extraordinary mechanical skills and hired them to design the dome for his new 24-inch telescope. Edgar Whipple erected the dome. Now a National Historic Landmark and still located in its original dome of local ponderosa wood, the 30-ton telescope remains a workhorse for the observatory. In the 1960s, "The Clark" (from the famous refractor firm of Alvan Clark & Sons) gave the moon-bound astronauts a preliminary glimpse of their destination and provided valuable data for mapping the moon.

By March, 1895, the community fulfilled its offer by issuing a deed to Lowell for nine lots surrounding the newly erected dome for the payment of $1.

Mars was the object of Lowell's obsession and he became increasingly convinced that there had been, or perhaps still was, intelligent life on the red planet. Seeing the best he could through the telescopes of the day, he thought he saw canals on the planet which would have been dug by the inhabitants. His map of the canals was widely circulated and upheld the belief many had of Martians living on Mars. In honor of his favorite planet, he named the location of the observatory Mars Hill.

One of the first outer buildings was a shelter or "warm room" for observers, with a darkroom in a deep cellar. This early building was extended and became Lowell's home. The house grew to accommodate the constant flow of guests, some of whom stayed for weeks and even months. The residence eventually had 25 rooms, including seven bedrooms as well as servants' quarters. Lowell jokingly but accurately referred to it as the "Baronial Mansion."

The view of the San Francisco Peaks from Lowell's private sun porch was breathtaking. Lowell was so smitten with the view of the mountain peaks that he had openings cut into solid interior walls of the mansion in order to permit a view from otherwise viewless rooms. Eventually the original darkroom was moved and improved, and the cellar was well stocked with fine wines and spirits.

Soon after becoming established, Lowell brought Miss Louise "Wrexie" Leonard from the east to be his secretary. A diligent student, Wrexie became familiar with astronomy and was later elected member of the Societe Astronomique de France and honorary member of the Sociedad Astronomics de Mexico. She was also youthful, well-educated, sensitive and attractive. Observatory gossip had it that her relationship with Lowell was romantic as well as professional. Whatever their private relationship, they obviously shared many common interests. Wrexie was as interested as Lowell in the botany and zoology of the area, and they enjoyed picnics and outings to Oak Creek, Sycamore Canyon, the Indian country and other local areas. She was his confidant and close friend.

As Lowell advanced in age he became more unstable. He was diagnosed with an ailment known at that time as neurasthenia. The ailment, described in old medical dictionaries as a "debility of the nerves," would perhaps be what we would today call a nervous breakdown. His brother Abbott, in his biography of Lowell, described him as having attacks of illness leading to mental and emotional exhaustion. Neurasthenia was thought to be triggered by stress.

With an already tense situation perhaps exacerbated by his physical condition, Lowell had a terrible argument and split from his long time colleague and friend, Andrew E. Douglass. In the summer of 1901 the two parted with very hurt feelings on both sides. Douglass had sent a lengthy letter to Lowell's brother-in-law criticizing Lowell's research techniques and questioning some aspects of his theories about Mars. He expressed, in effect, that Lowell was not a true scientist. Douglass had unwisely thought the letter would be held confidential. When Lowell was shown the letter, Douglass's departure was inevitable.

At about this same time, Sykes overheard an angry and lengthy argument between Douglass and Lowell. Lowell accused Douglass of attempting to obtain information from his private valet regarding Lowell's personal relationship with Wrexie. Though rather tragic, since it spelled the end of a long friendship, the story was comical as told by Sykes. It seems that both sensitive gentlemen were subject to sudden bouts of diarrhea when emotionally upset. During the drawn-out dispute, they took turns politely excusing themselves. One would race to the bathroom while the other calmly cooled his heels. Each would return to the fray until the next sudden call.

Leaving the work with Lowell, Douglass eventually taught at the University of Arizona where he succeeded in establishing the Stewart Observatory. In addition, he became famous as founder of the science of dendrochronology—the dating of materials by tree rings. Douglass died at the age of 95 in 1962.

In 1908, at the age of 53, Percival Lowell, a confirmed bachelor, greatly surprised his friends by marrying Constance Savage Keith. Ms. Keith, 45, was a Bostonian, and longtime friend and neighbor of the family. After a large and well-reported wedding ceremony, Mrs. Lowell arrived in Flagstaff to take over management of the "Baronial Mansion." She graciously presided over many parties entertaining old friends and guests.

By 1912 Lowell had more frequent bouts with the nervous, emotional disorder that had disturbed his life ten years previous. Although usually courteous, he had always been demanding and impatient with servants and assistants. Now he became noticeably more so. W. H. Spaulding, who worked a few months on Mars Hill, wrote to Douglass for a job. He stated in his letter that Lowell had treated him with "abuse, brutality, arrogance, conceit and insolence." Lowell screamed orders, knocked things out of Spaulding's hands and once even shoved him over a stack of boxes.

After Spaulding refused to work further with Lowell, another employee named Hanway took the brunt of Lowell's sick temper. Once, enraged at the slowness of Hanway's response to an order, Lowell seized the switch-rope that operated the mechanism that turned the dome. He gave it a hard jerk, which locked the switch so tightly that it could not be turned off. The dome kept revolving for 20 minutes while the two men scrambled to keep chairs and other furniture out of the way of the large moving telescope. Finally another worker came to the rescue and shut off the main switch.

On Sunday, November 12, 1916, Percival Lowell died in his home of a cerebral hemorrhage. He was 61.

During his lifetime he had predicted the existence of another, yet unknown planet at the far reaches of the solar system. It wasn't until an amateur astronomer, a Kansas farm boy, Clyde Tombaugh, was hired on in 1929 that the planet was actually located. It was named Pluto, the first characters being "PL" in honor of Percival Lowell. Pluto was right where Lowell had predicted.

Mrs. Lowell died in 1954 at the age of 91. She had not used the Baronial Mansion for many years and it had been allowed to decay. Infested with pests and considered a fire danger, the directors of the observatory decided that money needed for an expensive restoration would be better spent on research. The lovely old home, site of so many elegant parties and intellectual guests, was torn down.

Wrexie Leonard, Lowell's longtime friend, secretary and companion, returned to New England after Lowell's death. She lovingly collected the notes and letters that she had received from Lowell over the many years of their relationship into a small book, *"Percival Lowell, An Afterglow."* She placed the following at the beginning of the book:

> **Preambient light**
> **Waning, lingers long**
> **Ere lost within.**
> **Just, kind, masterful**
> **Life's sweet constant,**
> **Farewell.**

～～～～～～～～～～～

*Lowell Observatory in Flagstaff is west on Santa Fe Avenue,
on top of Mars Hill. There is an interesting visitors' center.
Because of the danger of forest fires, smoking is not permitted
on Mars Hill. Also the road could be icy at times in the winter.*

*The observatory is open 9:00 a.m. to 5:00 p.m.
Monday through Saturday and from noon until 5:00 p.m. Sundays.
Modest admission fee. For information about lectures,
telescope viewing at night and other events,
call (520) 774-3358.*

Evans House

"James Told Me..."
1896

The brothers were very close.

John and James Evans both trained to be physicians. John decided to set up his medical practice at the edge of town in the growing farm community of Phoenix. His Victorian home, built in 1893, was large and comfortable compared to most of the other homes in the area at that time. The rooms upstairs were used for the medical practice. Brother James decided that he would make a better farmer than doctor, so he bought some land west of town near Buckeye. Although the two brothers chose to live different life styles, they were always close.

In 1896, James was tragically killed in a buggy accident in Buckeye. As fast as they could, riders from the farm saddled their horses and rode at a gallop into Phoenix to bring the sad news to his brother.

John came out on the porch as the winded riders rode up. He looked at them, and said quietly, "James is dead."

Stunned, the wranglers asked, "How did you know?"

"James told me," John said.

Yes, the brothers were close. They were very close. They were twins.

∽∽∽∽∽∽∽∽∽∽∽∽

There are six remaining Victorian style homes in the metropolitan area of Phoenix. Two homes have been restored as museums, one is a restaurant, one is a private home and one is a boardinghouse. The Evans house, located at 1100 W. Washington, presently houses an insurance office.

Arizona State Capitol

"Send Him to Siam.
He Can't Do Much Harm There."
1899

"I'm governor!"

"No, I'm governor!"

"Well, let's just see who can run the state!"

"If you won't leave the capitol, I'll have to set up my office at home!"

In 1916, Democratic incumbent George W. P. Hunt lost to Republican challenger Tom Campbell by only 30 votes. Hunt, convinced that there had been tampering with the votes, refused to concede. Both men took the oath of office in separate ceremonies on January 1, 1917. Hunt refused to give up his office in the Capitol building. Campbell set up office on his kitchen table at home.

The state treasurer, a Democrat, refused to honor checks written by Campbell. The post office was confused about where to deliver mail intended for the state governor.

Hunt took his case to the Superior Court and lost. Undaunted, he vacated the office in the State Capitol but appealed his case to the State Superior Court. The court found in Hunt's favor after discovering that while many voters had marked their ticket to vote straight Democrat, they had also voted for Campbell. The Democrats were sending a strong message to Hunt that they intended to vote for every Democrat except him. However, in voting twice for the same office, they invalidated their vote.

After serving unpaid for eleven months as governor, Campbell finally turned over the office to George W. P. Hunt. Campbell later served two terms as governor, so was able to fulfill his dream of governing.

George Wiley Paul Hunt was a clever, astute politician who served as governor seven terms altogether between 1912 and 1932. During World War I he knitted sweaters for the soldiers fighting overseas, after making sure the newspaper reporters were available to get his picture doing so. He often bought jams and jellies by the case, soaked off the labels, and presented them to voters and political pals as homemade gifts from the kitchen of his lovely wife, Duett.

On Valentines Day, 1912, Governor Hunt was to deliver his inaugural address from the second floor of the capitol building in Phoenix, as the first governor of the brand new state of Arizona. He almost didn't make it to Phoenix. Hunt had headquartered at the Ford Hotel in Globe, but planned to take a roundabout route on a train by way of Safford, Benson and Tucson in order to speak to the gathered, excited crowds.

Arriving in Tucson late in the afternoon the day before the inaugural address was to be given, he was met by perennial presidential candidate and famous speaker William Jennings Bryan. Unbeknownst to Hunt, an informal reception had been planned, not for Hunt, but in Bryan's honor. The proud governor-elect found himself in the curious role of introducer, and the long-winded Bryan wanted to be introduced to everybody on the train platform.

The festivities in Bryan's honor went on and on. Quickly the time for the train to depart arrived. The train slowly began to pull away from the station. Hunt looked in horror at his only transportation to Phoenix chugging away from him. Giving up all efforts at dignity, the rotund Hunt abruptly dropped Bryan and his introductions and chased after the back of the train. Arms flailing, loud curses carrying on the wind, Hunt barely managed to gain the attention of the rear end brakeman who noticed Hunt's breathless and sweaty efforts and signaled for the train to halt. By the next day Hunt had regained his composure and gave an excellent speech as the first governor of the new state of Arizona.

Governor Hunt helping to push his car out of the mud somewhere near San Miguel.

Hunt never mastered driving a car, but he worked for better roads and campaigned tirelessly over the roads that were available. In the days he was in office, the roads of Arizona were very rough and primitive. While traveling around the state campaigning, he sat in the back seat of the car and studied or updated his voluminous notes about the voters in the next town. When he arrived, he knew who had just gotten married, had a new baby, acquired new land, gotten elected to a local office and who were the wheeler-dealers that he wanted to befriend. "How's that new barn holding up?" he might ask of a rancher, referring to a discussion they'd had the last time he was in town. People were impressed to be remembered by such a wealthy and famous man, and it showed in the polls.

In 1919 word got around that Hunt planned to run for Democrat Mark Smith's Senate seat. Smith's friends in high places convinced President Woodrow Wilson to appoint Hunt to some position as far away from Arizona as possible. Those present reported that President Wilson spun the globe and his finger landed on Siam, a country directly opposite around the globe from Arizona. Hunt was subsequently appointed minister to Siam, present day Thailand.

Hunt made use of his free time while in Bangkok by making sure that the people of Arizona didn't forget him. Using his notes and large mailing list, he continuously mailed back gifts and postcards from exotic Siam. Upon his return, Hunt was elected to his seventh and last term as governor.

Easy to pick out in a crowd, Hunt was a colorful character. Large and rotund, he had a dome-like bald head and bushy walrus-style mustache. His friends began calling him "Old Roman". Those who liked him less referred to him as "King George VII."

∽∾∽∾∽∾∽∾∽∾∽

*The Arizona State Capitol Museum is located at
1700 W. Washington, Phoenix, AZ 85007. The museum is
located in the old capitol building, centerpiece of the
complex of state buildings. Open 8:00 a.m. to 5:00 p.m.
Monday through Friday. Closed all state and
federal holidays. Free entrance. Guided tours.
Call (602) 255-4675 for more information.*

The Palace Bar

There Was a Hot Time in the Old Town That Night.
1900

"Fire! Fire! Grab a bucket! Take that hose!"

Investigators later suspected that the Prescott fire started on a mild July 14th day when a miner jammed his sharp pointed candle holder into the wooden wall of the Scopel Hotel at the corner of Goodwin and Montezuma. Leaving the candle lit, he forgot about it. Soon the tinder dry walls of the hotel easily caught flame. The fire quickly spread to the other wooden buildings along the business and saloon district of Montezuma Street known as Whiskey Row.

The Prescott volunteer fire companies, self-named the Toughs, Dudes and O.K.s, arrived quickly, but soon found putting out the raging fire impossible due to the town's low water supply. They valiantly did the best they could to save a few furnishings.

Thanks to a group of loyal customers of the Palace Bar, the ornate cherry wood barfront, which came 'round the horn and then overland to Prescott, was saved. As the fire bore down on them, the patrons heaved the heavy bar, backbar and, of course, the bottles out of the blazing building. Going back in, they managed to get the piano and stool out before the building was lost.

Now safely across the street at the town plaza, the pianist played "There'll be a Hot Time in the Old Town Tonight," as the roulette wheels and faro tables continued to do business. A barber chair was carried across the street and set up in the bandstand where the barber clipped hair as he watched the flames rise above the nearby buildings. By 3 a.m. the fire had burned itself out.

As the morning sun peeked through the smoky haze, the town began to take inventory. Lost were at least 25 saloons, five of the town's largest hotels, and all of the red light district. The burnt buildings were still smouldering as the businessmen walked through their stores and saloons, searching for anything they could salvage. By mid-morning the saloon keepers had set up counters with "Business as Usual" signs on the sidewalks in front of the burned ruins.

Prescott recovered from the fire and quickly rebuilt Whiskey Row, including the Palace Bar. The lovely old cherry wood bar was re-installed and today the survivor of the fire of 1900 continues to serve patrons as well as stand as a centerpiece for historic downtown Prescott.

ᕦᕤᕦᕤᕦᕤᕦᕤᕦᕤᕦᕤ

The Palace on Montezuma Street, still known locally as Whiskey Row, in downtown Prescott and is now an upscale restaurant. Open for lunch and dinner. The splendid restored barfront is a showpiece of the antique-filled ambience. Call (520) 541-1996 for reservations.

Hotel St. Michael

Someone's Staring at Me...

1900

*"A building isn't truly grand unless it's four stories tall.
Anybody knows that."*

As the cowboy staggered out of one of the 20 saloons on Prescott's Whiskey Row and stumbled down the street, he had the eerie feeling that someone was staring at him. He kept looking around quickly, making his head spin even worse, trying to catch the stalker in the act. Shrugging his shoulders, he gave up the notion and entered the next bar along Montezuma Street.

If the cowboy had looked up high enough he would have seen the eyes that were staring down at him. They were the unseeing eyes of the gargoyles just below the roof top on the Hotel St. Michael. These gargoyles aren't like the monstrous mythical beasts that peer out from the roofs of cathedrals in Europe to ward away evil spirits. These gargoyles actually portray evil spirits—at least as far as the builder was concerned.

In 1900 a fire roared out of control along the streets of Prescott, engulfing most of Whiskey Row. Amidst the smoking ruins, local businessmen began their rebuilding plans. The owner of the lot at the corner of Gurley and Montezuma determined that his property would be an excellent place to build a grand hotel.

At that time the city codes limited buildings to three stories. It was the confirmed belief of the builder that a hotel was only grand if it was at least four stories high. He went to the county commissioners to request a waiver of the restriction. He argued his best, he pleaded and he discussed. He quibbled, he reasoned, he remonstrated and expostulated. He lost.

Work began on his now less-than-grand three-storied hotel. With each brick that was set, his resentment grew. Finally as the walls reached the limit of the three stories, the owner determined how he would seek his revenge on the short-sighted county commissioners. He would forever remind the population of Prescott of the mean-spirited bunch of yahoos who denied him his grand four stories.

Gargoyles on the Hotel St. Michael.

Each grimacing gargoyle glaring down from the three-storied Hotel St. Michael at the shoppers and tourists of Prescott represents a commissioner—whose names thankfully have been forgotten to all except the most avid of historians. If you want to continue the tradition of making fun of the long forgotten commissioners, stop in the gift shop and purchase a St. Michael T-shirt with a gargoyle on it. Revenge is sweet.

ᔕᔕᔕᔕᔕᔕᔕᔕᔕᔕ

The Hotel St. Michael is located in the center of Prescott at the corner of Gurley and Montezuma, across from the city square containing the historic Yavapai County Courthouse. The rooms are basic and inexpensive and do include a complimentary continental breakfast. Guests are within walking distance of most of Prescott's attractions, which is a real advantage as parking around the town square is limited.
Call (520) 776-1999, or 1-800-678-3757 for reservations.
(Fax (520) 776-7318) Call the Prescott Chamber of Commerce for information about festivals and events at 1-800-266-7534

Gargoyles or Commissioners.

South Canyon Ranch in House Rock Valley

C. J. "Buffalo" Jones and His Cattalo
1906

"Where'd all the buffalo go?
We couldn't have killed them all...could we?"

Between 1872 and 1874, settlers, professional hunters and Indians killed more than three and a half million buffalo. C. J. "Buffalo" Jones was one of the best of the professional buffalo hunters. He could kill, skin and butcher ten buffalo bulls a day. Selling the hide and meat brought him about $8 for each animal. It was dangerous, smelly, exhausting work but well paid. His $80 a day would equal about $300 by today's standards.

The building of the transcontinental railway made it easy to reach the buffalo herds on the Great Plains. In the early 1870's thousands of professional buffalo hunters like Jones swarmed into the area. Thousands of buffalo fell each day.

The railroad companies encouraged the slaughter. They advertised hunting expeditions where the brave men with rifles would wantonly kill as many buffalo as they could sight, all from the comfort of the lounge chair in their railroad car. Then the railroad would haul the meat, buffalo hides, even bones which were used for fertilizer, back to the Eastern cities. During the season of 1873, the Atchison, Topeka and Santa Fe Railroad moved a quarter of a million robes, each robe taking five buffalo hides to make.

The huge herds of buffalo seemed to provide an endless supply of food, money and entertainment. Soon reckless and greedy white hunters were killing thousands of buffalo for their tongues alone, leaving the rest of the carcass to rot, much to the dismay and bewilderment of the Indians who used every piece of the animal. Such senseless waste was unheard of in the Indian cultures.

In the spring of 1875 the party came to an abrupt end. The buffalo hunters outfitted themselves and rode out confidently to meet their shaggy paychecks. The massive beasts had vanished. The endless herds were no more.

"Buffalo" Jones, like the other hunters, cussed his rotten luck and turned his interests to other areas. He moved his family into Kansas and established the town of Garden City. But Jones, having been on the trail all of his adult years, didn't take to living in town. Thinking back on his days of buffalo hunting, he regretted somewhat being part of the reason for the near extinction of the beasts. He began to work on a plan to preserve the buffalo by breeding them in a safe environment.

Jones wrote in his journal:

"Often while hunting these animals as a business I fully realized the cruelty of slaying the poor creatures. Many times did I

swear off and fully determine I would break my gun over a wagonwheel when I arrived at camp, yet always hesitated to do so after several hours had elapsed. The next morning I would hear the guns of other hunters booming in all directions and make up my mind that even if I didn't kill any more, the buffalo would soon all be slain just the same. Again I would shoulder my rifle to repeat the previous day's experience. I am positive it was a wickedness committed in killing so many that has impelled me to take measures for perpetuating the race which I had almost helped destroy."

However, lest we think that Jones, ever the promoter and entrepreneur, was merely being sympathetic toward the buffalo, we should note that he made sure he built a profit into the scheme for himself.

Since it appeared that the time had past when he could make money killing buffalo in the wild, perhaps he could turn a profit by breeding them domestically. He began to make a mental list of the advantages of raising buffalo: the animals were adapted well to the high plains climate; they could withstand bitter winters; their sense of smell was so keen they could root out and find grass which was buried a foot under snow; and their thick fur protected them from snake bites. In addition, their meat was tender and lean, their milk was richer than a jersey cow's, their hide made excellent leather, and their fur could be woven into a light but warm fabric. He decided that the perfect domestic animal would be a hybrid of a cow and a buffalo.

Jones, knowing that trying to capture adult buffalo might be impossible, much less highly dangerous, decided to go after the calves in the remaining herd wandering the Texas Panhandle. The Panhandle was a hot, flat, featureless plain with very little firewood and sporadic water holes. It would be easy to get disoriented and lost in such desolate land, a dangerous position in which to get caught. All that remained of the six million buffalo which once roamed the Great Plains was a small herd somewhere in the vast traces of the Panhandle. "Buffalo" Jones set out with a small party of men and a vast load of determination.

After locating the small herd, they found they had to contend with the anger of the buffalo cow who was not about to let the white hunters take her calf. "More than once," Jones reported, "I or one of my assistants have managed to rope a calf only to find a mother buffalo, full of maternal wrath, eyes green and hair on end, bearing down on us. Occasionally we have managed to save the calf for ourselves; more often the mother wins."

Finally they attempted to catch the calves by chasing the herd and running them until exhausted. The younger calves would not be able to keep up and would eventually fall behind. The hunters would then rope them before the mother had a chance to look around and see she had been deceived.

From his first trip in the spring of 1886, Jones arrived home in Garden City, Kansas with 14 calves. On the trail he managed to feed them condensed milk until he could get them into a pen with his cattle who took over the nursing duties.

By the early 1890's he had caught more calves and was beginning to show some success with his breeding experiments. His cattalo were large and healthy. As he predicted, they produced tasty beef and good-looking hides.

Disaster struck when the economy took a downturn. Jones was always rich in dreams but short on cash. Helplessly, he stood by as his creditors took his precious stock, his home and his land. The final insult was the day his rifle was sold on the auction block for back debts.

Down, but never counted out, "Buffalo" Jones called upon his friend and fellow hunter, President Teddy Roosevelt. As a presidential appointee, Jones served as a game warden for Yellowstone National Park. There he was instrumental in establishing a buffalo herd before bailing out in the face of irritating bureaucracy.

By 1906 Jones had once again talked his buddy, President Roosevelt, into another favor. A true conservationist at heart, Roosevelt was enthusiastic about Jones' idea of establishing a national game preserve for buffalo. This would give Jones an opportunity to continue a little cattalo breeding as well.

President Roosevelt officially established the Grand Canyon National Game Preserve, located on the vast Kaibab Plateau between southern Utah and the north rim of the Grand Canyon. The government agreed to furnish the land and loan a few buffalo from the Yellowstone Park herd. Jones would furnish his expertise and the rest of the stock.

Problems persisted with the cattalo breeding. Unfortunately, buffalo bulls and domestic heifers did not have a natural affection for each other. In fact, they had to be coaxed to breed. Due to the buffalo hump, which would not seem to breed out, the cow had a difficult time with the birth of a cattalo. But worse, the male cattalo shot blanks—they were often sterile.

With not enough financial backing to see him through lean times, Jones again went bankrupt. Jimmy Owens, one of Jones' partners, wound up with the buffalo. He continued to keep the buffalo in House Rock Valley until 1926 when he sold the herd of 100 buffalo to the State of Arizona for $10,000. "Buffalo" Jones later became a side-kick of Zane Grey. Grey called Jones his mentor and included him in his book, *The Last of the Plainsmen.*

Today the Game and Fish Commission of the State of Arizona maintains a herd of about 100 buffalo on the Raymond Ranch and another herd of around 150 at the South Canyon Ranch in House Rock Valley.

∽∾∽∾∽∾∽∾∽∾∽

Both buffalo ranches are open to the public. Visitors should be aware, however, that the herds are small and the land is vast. Please call before making plans to visit either of the ranches. For further information, call Arizona State Game and Fish - (602) 942-3000, or North Kaibab Forest Service - (520) 774-5045.

South Canyon Ranch.

Groom Creek Ranch

How Not to Get Rid of Bossie
1915

"That's okay Bossie. It'll all be over real soon."

This old barn might be able to tell you, if only its walls could speak, about a local rancher with an incurably sick cow. He decided to put the cow down, but didn't have any ammunition on the ranch at the time, and didn't want to make a special trip into town. He did have several sticks of dynamite and an idea. He took the sick cow out into the field and tied her to a stake. He then tied the sticks of dynamite to her horns and lit the fuse. The hissing of the fuse was all the cow needed to realize that something was amiss. Suddenly desiring the comforts of home, she threw her head, pulled up the stake and headed for her warm barn. The rancher, not wanting to lose his barn as well as his cow, grabbed her tail and hung on for dear life. Bossy, being much stronger than the rancher, continued her headlong dash for the barn with the rancher making tracks in the mud with his boots all the way. Being only slightly smarter than the cow, the rancher let go just as the fuse burnt down. He took off running in the opposite direction. There was a huge explosion which wrecked the barn. The rancher's idea had worked only too well. His sick cow, indeed, was thoroughly dead. Unfortunately, she had taken two other cows with her in the explosion and another had suffered a broken back from the falling timbers.

∽∽∽∽∽∽∽∽∽∽∽

This old barn is on private property in central Arizona.

Luke Air Force Base
The Balloon Buster – Maverick and Hero
1918

When World War I ended, November 11, 1918, Americans were jubilant and there was dancing and celebration in the streets. But in Phoenix the celebration was dampened by worry about a handsome, young local hero. Twenty-one year old Frank Luke, Jr. , a daring pilot, was missing in action and feared dead.

Frank Luke, Jr. was one of nine children born to Frank Luke, a German immigrant. The elder Luke was a successful farmer and businessman in Phoenix. Frank Luke, Jr. graduated from Phoenix Union High School in 1916 and worked for a short time in the copper mines at Ajo.

Luke, Jr. joined the Aviation Section of the Army Signal Corps on September 25, 1917. About a year later he reported to the 27th Aero Squadron of the First Pursuit Group at Saints, France, near Chateau-Thierry.

Young Luke was a maverick, an intrepid warrior Hollywood would love. He was described as a "bad soldier but a good hero." Luke was a handsome, blue-eyed, blond-haired loner. He did not take well to discipline. From his actions it appeared that he planned to win the war single-handedly.

Frank Luke, Jr.

Luke's commander, Maj. H. E. Hartney, said of him, "No one had the sheer contemptuous courage that boy possessed. He was an excellent pilot and probably the best flying marksman on the Western Front. We had any number of expert pilots and there was no shortage of good shots, but the perfect combination, like the perfect specimen of anything in the world, was scarce. Frank Luke was the perfect combination."

Luke chose as his targets the deadly effective German observation balloons. In the present era of complex military technology, balloons sound insignificant. But in WWI's trench warfare environment they were critical. From the balloons, German soldiers could direct their artillery fire to greater accuracy. In attacking, a pilot had to fly close to the balloons, which exposed him to fire from the ground as well as from the nearby protective cover of German fighter planes. To attack the hydrogen-filled balloons, both expensive and of great military value, was practically suicide.

Luke shot down his first balloon September 12, 1918, and two days later downed two more. A few days later he was credited with shooting down three balloons and two German planes in one day.

Witnesses to the aerial dogfights confirmed that Luke downed 14 German balloons and three airplanes, but his fellow pilots said there undoubtedly were more unconfirmed kills. Some officers stated that the probable total in the 17 days Luke flew was closer to 21 kills.

On September 29, 1918, Luke took off for the last time. Before he left he told his officers that he was after three troublesome balloons along the Meuse River. Witnesses saw German planes firing at Luke's Spad XIII as he shot down the first balloon.

Either the plane or Luke was hit as he flew erratically, evading the German planes and managing to shoot down the second and third balloons in spite of incessant enemy fire.

Even though already wounded, he attacked one more observation balloon and the Frenchmen observing from below saw it burst into flames and plummet to the ground.

Luke descended to within 50 meters of the ground and opened fire on enemy troops, killing six and wounding as many more. Soon his wounds and the damage to his aircraft forced him to land. Luke's plane flew low and sputtered over the village of Murveaux, behind German lines, and landed in a meadow. The French villagers who watched later said they could tell that Luke had been wounded as he climbed out of his plane.

He struggled to make it to a nearby stream, but German soldiers appeared at the edge of the meadow. As he pulled his gun and fired, young Luke died in a ferocious hail of gunfire. The Germans took his shoes, leggings and wallet. Remarkably they left his Elgin wristwatch which the villagers later returned to his father.

Infuriated by the savagery of the American's final attack, the German commandant of the village refused to have straw placed in the cart that removed Luke's body. He also refused to allow the French women to shroud his body with a sheet. Witnesses reported he kicked Luke's body and snapped, "Get that thing out of my way as quickly as possible."

Two men from Murveaux, Cortlae Delbert and Voliner Nicolas, loaded the young Arizonan's body on a wagon and escorted him to the cemetery where they buried Luke in a shallow grave. For the short remainder of the war only the Germans and the villagers of Marveaux knew what had happened to the courageous young pilot. Two weeks after the war ended, on November 25, the International Red Cross confirmed his death and sent the sad news to his anxious parents by telegram.

Frank Luke, Jr., was awarded the Medal of Honor, the first aviator to receive the award posthumously. His other posthumous awards included the Distinguished Flying Cross, the Italian War Cross and the Aero Club Medal for Bravery.

When the Army Air Corps opened a base west of Phoenix in March, 1941, it was named Luke Air Force Base in honor of the young hero of an earlier "war to end all wars." Today Luke Air Force Base is the largest fighter pilot training base in the world.

Memorial of Frank Luke, Jr. stands in front of the Arizona State Capitol.

Though unmarried, Luke came from a large family. Many in the Valley of the Sun today proudly carry on the Luke family name.

〰〰〰〰〰〰

Luke Air Force Base, "Home of the Fighter Pilot," sprawls out in a huge complex 9 miles west of Phoenix. Each year the base sponsors an air show which is open to the public. In addition, you can tour the base if you call well ahead to make arrangements. You might be able to witness a mission briefing, tour the flight line, or talk to a pilot. They also allow visitors to eat in the Officers Club if you make advance arrangements. Call 856-7411 and ask for Public Affairs.

Tovrea Castle

The Wedding Cake House
1928

"Son, let's build us a castle."

Alissio Carraro didn't plan to build a landmark. When the Italian immigrant arrived in Arizona in 1928, he purchased 277 acres of open desert along the main highway from Phoenix to Tempe. Although considerably out of town from either direction, Carraro planned to build a subdivision which he would call Carraro Heights. The centerpiece of the housing development was to be a three-storied hotel.

A sketch of the hotel design was completed in November, 1928, by H. D. Frankfurt, but no detailed blueprints were ever prepared. Instead, Carraro began construction by himself with the help of his fifteen year old son. Carraro and his son cleared the land, excavated the basement and constructed the foundation. He soon hired carpenters, plasterers and electricians to join in the construction. Improvising as he built, Carraro modified the hotel's original design by adding a

Alissio Carraro and his son in front of Tovrea Castle under construction.

cupola, exterior walkways with crenellated battlements and other unusual features. Perhaps remembering the castles of his native Italy, Carraro built what turned out to be a small, stylized castle.

During construction, the Carraros landscaped the grounds with dozens of varieties of cactus from Mexico and the Southwest. The dense stand of saguaros is said to be one of the earliest and most successful attempts at transplanting cactus. Using smooth river rock from the nearby Salt River, they also built retaining walls, terraces, fountains, pools and benches. They transformed the knoll into a formal desert garden with smooth native rock-lined paths.

By late 1930, the hotel was completed. However, caught by the financial woes of the Great Depression, Carraro was forced to sell his dream. Edward and Della Tovrea lived nearby in a lovely home, but Edward had become fascinated by the castle on the hill as he watched it's construction. Tovrea was the founder of the Arizona Packing Co. and was a successful cattleman. The Tovreas purchased Carraro Heights in 1931 and moved into the eclectic castle where Edward could look out the windows and view his empire below, acres of pens filled with healthy cattle awaiting their shipment to eastern markets.

Soon afterward, Edward Tovrea died and left most of his fortune to Della who became a successful businesswoman and respected civic leader.

In 1936, Della married W. P. Stuart, owner of the *Prescott Courier* newspaper. The Stuarts summered in cool, mountainous Prescott and wintered in their castle in Phoenix. After W. P. Stuart retired in 1958 and passed away in 1960, Della lived in the cool, undivided basement of the castle until her death in 1969.

The property passed to the Tovrea heirs who became divided about what to do with the property. On April 25, 1991, an application to demolish was submitted to Phoenix by the Tovrea board of trustees. The board wanted to develop the land surrounding the nearly 60 year old castle. The trustees who administer the property for the heirs of Edward Tovrea must "maximize its value," they said.

Several of the heirs, however, were outspoken in favor of the preservation of the old castle. Philip Tovrea III, a great-grandson of Edward Ambrose Tovrea, said that the castle "has an intrinsic value you can't even use money to buy. It has value to society as a whole. It represents our heritage and the heritage of Arizona."

Philip, a construction worker and former mayor of Jerome, said he would like to see the city maintain the family castle, a job he lovingly has assumed for more than a decade. He has spent thousands of hours and dollars taking care of the old building, changing the hundreds of bulbs that light up the house and nighttime sky, and caring for the prize cactus that stud the land.

The castle had been given the designation of an Historic Landmark, but that didn't really protect the building. The Landmark status merely calls for a one year "cooling off" period before demolition can begin in order to allow alternative plans to be developed.

Five million dollars in bonds was overwhelmingly approved by the sometimes tight fisted voters in 1989 to purchase part of the property and hopefully ensure the castle's preservation. In May, 1992, after two years of turbulent negotiations, the city of Phoenix agreed to buy the historic Tovrea Castle for $1.74 million. Preliminary plans call for the castle to become a visitor center that would offer a bird's-eye view of the Valley. The purchase includes only 6.65 acres of the 43 saguaro-studded acres on which the castle sits. The city owned property will remain as a desert expanse and cactus garden. Long-range plans call for the city to use the castle as the centerpiece of a proposed tourism district that would link historical and community attractions in Phoenix, Tempe and Scottsdale. Among the properties proposed to be included are the Phoenix Zoo, the Desert Botanical Garden, the Hall of Flame Museum and the Salt River Project headquarters.

Phoenix officials said that the 36.35 acres of the property remaining with the trust would be developed under guidelines still to be outlined. In 1996 the city was able to acquire a little more of the land, bringing the city's ownership to 13.3 acres. The city is now trying to forestall any further deterioration by improving water lines to the building, restoring the cactus garden and repairing the walls and gate. Many of the old saguaros are in ill health and will need the attention of experts in order to survive. It will probably be a number of years before the building is ready to be open to the public.

Tovrea Castle, the "Wedding Cake House", is located at 50th Street and Van Buren, and its white lights can be seen at night from the 202 Loop.

Bill Wingfield Home

Oh, My Achin' Toe!
1924

"Be careful with that axe!"

One day Bill Wingfield was chopping wood on his ranch in the Verde Valley. The axe slipped and cut a gash in his boot. In great pain, Bill realized that he had been deeply wounded. He hobbled over to a large rock and propped against it, slowly taking off his boot. His foot was already covered in blood, and he realized, with some dismay, that he had completely severed his big toe. He upended his cowboy boot and shook it. Sure enough, out fell his big toe, right into the dust. Just at that moment, one of the ranch dogs rushed up, grabbed his toe and took off with it.

"You know," Bill said, "I never saw that dang toe again!"

~~~~~~~~~~~~~~~~~~~~

*Bill Wingfield's former home is a private residence
outside of Camp Verde.*

**The original Wingfield stone house has been enlarged and is now enclosed
in a screened front porch.**

Arizona Biltmore

The Jewel of the Desert
1929

"Let's build the very finest resort in the desert southwest."

$\mathbf{I}$n 1910 most people who came to Phoenix needed a good reason. Arizona was still two years away from being admitted to the Union, and the population of Phoenix was a mere 11,134 intrepid souls who lived and worked without the benefit of air-conditioning or even "swamp coolers." In 1910 twenty-year old Charlie McArthur came to Phoenix for his health.

While Charles came for his health, Warren, six years his senior, came three years later because he saw opportunity. Entrepreneurs to the core, Charles and Warren began a thriving mercantile business and then soon became the exclusive dealers for Dodge Brothers automobiles in Arizona.

Observing the influx of winter visitors even then—there were 3,000 winter tourists in 1913—the brothers formed the Arizona Hotel Company and optioned 100 acres of land "way out of town" as a site for a destination hotel and resort. With the advent of World War I, their financing fell through and the land they had optioned was purchased by the founders of the Phoenix Country Club. The "way out" land was at Seventh Street and Thomas, now very much in town.

Undaunted, the brothers McArthur continued to make the most of the opportunities at hand and to create new opportunities whenever plausible. In 1927 the brothers, in partnership with Bowman Biltmore Hotels, acquired 200 acres of citrus orchard at the foothills of Squaw Peak, a long, dusty eight miles from Phoenix. They called in another brother, Albert Chase McArthur who worked for Frank Lloyd Wright as a young draftsman and designer in Oak Park, Illinois.

Mr. and Mrs. Wright were at Taliesin East in Wisconsin when Albert McArthur wired Mr. Wright and asked him to come to Phoenix and assist in designing and building the hotel. The Wright family packed quickly and took the first train to Phoenix, then a picturesque desert town of some 39,000, with clear air and majestic views of the mountains from every street. The Wrights fell in love with the Valley of the Sun, and as a result, in 1937 they opened Taliesin West in the desert beyond Scottsdale as a winter home for their school of architecture.

In their optimism, Charles and Warren McArthur believed that the Arizona Biltmore could be built for $1 million. However, by the time it opened in February, 1929, the cost had escalated to $2.5 million. The majority of the funds had come from William Wrigley, Jr., chewing gum magnate and owner of the Chicago Cubs baseball team.

Less than three weeks after the opening of the 1929/30 winter tourist season, the October stock market crash spelled disaster for the McArthur brothers, and Mr. Wrigley became the owner of the Biltmore Resort.

Charles and Warren were financially ruined by the stock market crash and the dissolution of the company they had founded. Both left Phoenix for New York in 1930 where they subsequently built new businesses. Albert McArthur, the eldest of the brothers, who had been recruited to design the Arizona Biltmore and was its architect of record, moved to Los Angeles in 1931.

During the 44 years the Wrigley family operated the Arizona Biltmore, the resort gained fame as a luxury spot where tourists and executives could relax or conduct business during balmy Arizona winters. A brochure from the Arizona Biltmore states, "With elegance and style, the highest standards of gracious innkeeping were maintained at all times. The resort offered the best of service and finest of chefs to provide the utmost in hospitality and cuisine. Biltmore guests became a clientele that returned year after year to a place of beauty where they knew they would always receive careful attention to their every need."

Because it had a firm and formal policy of protecting the identity of its guests, (and still does) many came to the Biltmore to escape the spotlight. Others came because the Arizona Biltmore, known as the "Jewel of the Desert," was simply the best hotel in the desert southwest.

Ronald and Nancy Reagan spent their honeymoon at the Biltmore. Nancy's parents, Dr. and Mrs. Loyal Davis, lived in the Biltmore Estates at the time. Before and during his term of office, President Reagan often stayed at the Biltmore while visiting his in-laws. Those who lived in the Biltmore Estates at the time of one of his visits remember well the plethora of dark-suited, serious men with walkie-talkies who would invade the sedate lanes where the large homes of the wealthy are located. As can be imagined, housing a sitting President in a private home, even for one night, is a logistical nightmare.

Harpo Marx also honeymooned at the Biltmore, where he scandalized some guests with his lack of decorum and charmed others with his renditions on the harp. Harpo and his bride were known to hold hands and skip through the elegant, quiet Gold Room after meals. Harpo's behavior may have been less scandalous than that of his brother, Groucho, who would prowl the lobby patting female derrieres and making off-color comments.

Clark Gable was a frequent guest who loved to play golf. One day he lost his wedding ring on the course, resulting in a major search effort. The ultimate recovery, it is said, led to the largest tip ever offered at the resort. Gable loved to ride horses even though riding often triggered intense back pain. The stable master of the Biltmore, after learning of the actor's dilemma, always arranged to have Tennessee Walking horses—known for their gentle gait—available during Gable's stay.

Spencer Tracy was as popular with the Biltmore staff as he was with the movie-going public. He is remembered as a great tipper and a man who made a point of remembering the names of waitresses and bellhops.

Edna Ferber is purported to have written *Giant* and several other novels while staying at the Biltmore. Irving Berlin was such a regular guest at the resort that others timed their visits to coincide with his and vied to have the cabana closest to his at the pool. On one of his visits a young man named Alexander is said to have entertained him with an imitation of conducting a band.

In addition to Irving Berlin, many of the world's great musicians and singers have stayed at the Biltmore, often holding impromptu concerts in the Aztec lounge. Burt Bacharach, Carol Lawrence, Robert Goulet, Jascha Heifetz, Roberta Peters and Bing Crosby were all guests.

Johnny Carson, Jackie Gleason and Jack Benny were Biltmore guests. Bob Hope would often stay at the Biltmore when in town to play golf with his longtime friend Bob Goldwater, a Biltmore resident.

Joan Crawford stayed at the Biltmore, but, as the wife of the owner of Pepsi Cola, she refused to accept the Coke which was delivered to her room. It was said that she chased the abashed room service waiter off with a wire coathanger.

Edward, Duke of Windsor, and his wife Wallis Simpson motored to Arizona and stayed at the Biltmore to improve the health of their asthmatic dogs in the sunny Phoenix climate.

In June of 1973, the Wrigley family sold the Biltmore to Talley Industries. Closed for the summer season, the hotel underwent the installation of a sprinkler system to update the maturing grand dame.

Suddenly, on the afternoon of June 20th, a spark from a welding torch ignited insulation material in the ceiling. The roaring fire quickly spread through the roof and crawlspace above the fourth floor. While the fire was raging, Arizona was shocked with the possible loss of its distinguished landmark.

When the smoke cleared it was evident that the fourth floor was gone altogether, along with its beautiful copper roof, now grotesquely twisted and buckled. The floors below were so damaged by smoke and water that all furniture, fabrics, carpets and draperies had to be discarded. The hotel had to be completely rebuilt, redecorated, and refurbished. Outside on the steps of the entrance stood a sign—like some horrible prophecy—"HOTEL CLOSED FOR THE SUMMER. WILL REOPEN SEPTEMBER 20."

Mr. Franz Talley set that date as his goal, knowing that the seemingly impossible task would be a 24-hour job for all workers. The proud dowager, gutted to the core, would have her face lifted in a glorious manner.

The project was a combination of good old-fashioned Yankee ingenuity and the Southwestern spirit of cooperation and determination. The dedicated personnel of Talley Industries combined with the professional talents of the Frank Lloyd Wright Foundation brought together local craftsmen, artists, decorators, and specialists in all the building trades, pulling together to make it possible to complete the project in record time.

Blocks were cast from Arizona sand on the site just as a quarter million had been cast using the same molds as the original construction in 1929. Carl Lundine and Jim Oliger (who at age 29 had worked on the original hotel 44 years previous) taught 15 younger workers how to carefully apply more than 38,000 square feet of gold leaf to ceilings, allowing them to reflect the soft light.

Some of Frank Lloyd Wright's original drawings from early years were brought from the foundation's vault with the permission of Mrs. Wright. From this priceless collection, designs were chosen for new interiors and furnishings—translated into textiles, carpets, yarns, glass, wood and metals. The colors chosen represented the desert environment—sun, sand, rocks, cactus, desert flowers and foliage.

The entire reconstruction was completed with round-the-clock work in 82 days and the hotel reopened on September 29. Since that time the "Jewel of the Desert" has continued to provide the highest standards of gracious innkeeping with elegance and style, as always.

ᔓᔓᔓᔓᔓᔓᔓᔓᔓᔓᔓ

The Arizona Biltmore, a Mobil Five-Star, AAA Five-diamond resort is open year round. Located at 24th Street and Missouri in Phoenix. Phone (602) 955-6600.

Arizona Biltmore.

Wrigley Mansion

La Colina Solana - The Sunny Hill
1929

One of five Wrigley homes, a mere 20,000 square feet.

Impetuous William Wrigley, Jr. was an ambitious boy who started working in his father's soap factory. Starting at the lowliest and most unskilled jobs, he worked his way up to salesman. He hit on the idea of giving premiums to his customers to increase sales. When the new product of gum was introduced to the market, William thought that gum would be a perfect gift to include in the soap as a sales incentive. Soon complaints came back that the gum tasted like soap. Undaunted, William wrapped the gum in foil, the first to do so. In a short time William realized that the gum had more appeal than the soap, so he dumped the soap down the drain and kept the gum. Thus began the Wrigley Chewing Gum empire.

In 1926, the three MacArthur brothers began a project in the Valley of the Sun which was to be a one-of-a-kind facility, a retreat for the elite.

They purchased land in the desert nine miles outside of the city limits. They called their hotel the "Jewel of the Desert," the Arizona Biltmore Hotel. Unfortunately, when Wall Street crashed, the brothers had to let their dream go to one of their major investors, William Wrigley. Mr. Wrigley bought out the brothers, acquiring the resort and the surrounding land.

He looked up to the hill on the property and envisioned building a comfortable winter home for his family. William was married to Ada E. Foote and they had two children, Dorothy and Philip. They were a family who loved music, travel and horses.

Counting the Phoenix property, Mr. Wrigley owned five homes across the country. Since his business headquarters were in Chicago, they maintained a home there. In addition, they had a summer home in Lake Geneva, Wisconsin (Green Gables); a home on Millionaire's Row in Pasadena, California (now headquarters for the Rose Bowl Committee); La Colina Solana - the Sunny Hill, one of the smaller homes, at the Biltmore; and they owned the entire island of Santa Catalina off the coast of southern California.

The Wrigley family would hook their four private train cars to the next train headed west and travel in comfort. In the first car was the family, in the second were the nannies, servants, cooks and other hired help. In the third car was all the baggage plus Wrigley's six cars. Coming along in the fourth car were the dogs and horses.

Although William Wrigley, Jr. was never entirely comfortable with automobile travel, he maintained a fleet of six matching automobiles which he shipped from residence to residence by train. Why six? Apparently he believed that automobiles should not be used on successive days, and so he kept one for each day of the week. He was not about to push his luck by driving or riding on Sunday, so only six were required.

The Phoenix mansion was completed in late 1931. The entry rotunda with its hand carved and painted entry doors, sweeping circular staircase and 30 foot high ceiling decorated with hand-painting and gold leaf made a dramatic entrance to the 14,000 square foot main level. On the same level was the dining room and living room, each with hand painted ceilings, a pine paneled breakfast room, a full-service kitchen and library. The library was paneled with Philippine walnut which was imported in rough sheets and cut and fitted on-site. The main level also contains the "phone room" which was purported to have been wallpapered with sheets of chewing gum foil.

The 6,000 square feet of upper level contained two master bedrooms, two children's bedrooms, and living quarters for the upstairs maid and the head of the household staff. Each of the four family bedrooms had private bathrooms that were fully tiled with a different color of Santa Catalina tile. There were no guest bedrooms. The Wrigley's guests were housed in the Biltmore Hotel.

In addition to the family living quarters, there were eight bedrooms for household staff on the main level. Most of the staff traveled as part of the Wrigley entourage from home to home.

Not everyone approved of the 20,000 square foot residence on the Biltmore property. There was the reported pronouncement of Frank Lloyd Wright, who espoused low-profile architecture. "This house," the black-caped designer reportedly said as he took leave of the Wrigleys after a dinner party, "is an architect's desecration."

Wrigley's granddaughter, Dorothy Wrigley Rich Chauncey, remembers her famous forebear as "outgoing, genial, very awe-inspiring".

"He was stout. He smoked a big cigar and he was always in a hurry," she said. "When someone asked him how his golf game went, he said, 'I did it in 90 minutes,'" recalls Mrs. Chauncey, wife of television and radio executive Tom Chauncey.

Mr. Wrigley died shortly after the completion of his Biltmore home on January 26, 1932. After his death, the family continued to use the home as a 4 to 6 week stopover every year on their way to Catalina Island. The Wrigleys owned the Chicago Cubs baseball team and while the Cubbies were in Phoenix for their Spring Training, the family would stay at *La Colina Solana* for a few weeks. During those years a large American flag would fly from the flagpole, announcing to the city of Phoenix that the Wrigley family was in residence. The house was closed for the rest of the year and was maintained by Arizona Biltmore Hotel employees.

The family used the home sporadically until 1973 when they decided to sell the mansion and the resort. The Biltmore Resort, surrounding property and Wrigley Mansion were sold to Talley Industries which began developing the land around the hotel.

The Wrigley Mansion was used infrequently as overflow accommodations for the hotel. In 1979, the home was once again up for sale and was purchased by the Driggs brothers for $1.7 million.

By the time the Driggs purchased the Wrigley Mansion, it had been used hard for a number of years and was badly showing its age. The furniture had been well-used and was neglected over the years, leaving the new owners wondering if they had purchased nothing more than broken junk.

Tapping the talents of 73-year-old Hans Heinemann, a second-generation furniture restorer from Germany, Western Savings began the enormous task of reconditioning the furniture.

After eight months' work, Heinemann had restored about 60 of the 1930-era chairs to their original condition. In addition, he had beautifully restored four library tables, six chests, three wardrobes, several small tables and a bench. The centerpiece of his craftsmanship was a remarkable Steinway Grand self-reproducing player piano. The piano dominates one end of the living room. Made in New York by the Aeolian Duo-Art Co., it has a separate "remote control" mechanism that used to hold 10 rolls of music and would play after being programmed by pushing a button. There are reportedly only two of its kind in the world. The decision to buy the old "junk" and accept the refurbishing challenge was clearly a wise one.

During the restoration and preparation for painting, the door knobs, switch plates, hinges and other metal fixtures were taken down and put into a paper bag. Looking like black wrought-iron, they were kicked into a corner, half forgotten. One day a worker, earning the name "Brass Bob," began to polish one of the metal fixtures. He insured himself of a job for several weeks as he polished the entire lot. The black "wrought-iron" fixtures turned out to be ornate brass and solid sterling silver.

The Driggs brothers envisioned the use of the old home to be one of a private club and state-of-the-art conference center. A major challenge was the installation of a complete central heating and cooling system. No simple solutions, like rooftop units, were tolerated for aesthetic reasons.

The Wrigleys were prophetic in naming their home "*La Colina Solana*," the sunny hill , since about 98% of the mansion's

A solid sterling silver switch plate was among a blackened lot rescued from discard during the renovation.

heating and cooling energy needs now come from the sun through ten 8 X 40 foot solar collectors nestled in a "solar garden" at the base of the hill. Facing due south, the panels gain energy both by direct sunlight and reflection. They are motorized to track the seasonal angle of the sun, the area's most abundant natural resource.

For several years the Wrigley Mansion was used as a private club, conference center and popular location for weddings. When Western Savings collapsed in 1989, along with many other S&L's, the Wrigley Mansion closed and sat empty for a number of years.

A promotional piece describing the mansion at the time stated:

> "For $4 million you can have the most prestigious residence in Arizona, a superb view, landscaped gardens, courtyards, and

the huge adobe home—nearly 20,000 square feet—containing gold-leaf ceilings, pegged-oak floors, walnut paneling, six bedrooms, eight former bedrooms that have been converted to meeting rooms, two kitchens, seven fireplaces and 11 bathrooms. The price includes much of the original Wrigley furnishings, including a rare Steinway player piano, 60 chairs, several library and dining tables and Mrs. Wrigley's armoire."

Rescuing the mansion and once again opening it as a private club was George "Geordie" Hormel, owner of the McCune Mansion. In July, 1992, Hormel purchased *La Colina Solana*, his second mansion in the area, for the bargain price of $2.6 million. Western Savings had spent $10 to $12 million in the acquisition and renovations of the home. At that time, the cost of maintaining the building just sitting empty (utilities, maintenance, insurance, security, etc.) was estimated at $80,000 per month.

∽∽∽∽∽∽∽∽∽∽∽∽

The Wrigley Mansion is located atop a hill on the Biltmore Resort property. The entrance to the Biltmore is at 24th Street and Missouri in Phoenix. The Wrigley Mansion is operated as a private club and conference center, but is also open for public tours by reservation only. Call 955-4079 for information and reservations. Fee.

Mystery Castle

"Daddy, Build Me a Castle..."
1929

Commander in Chief of His Dreams.

"**W**elcome to my castle!" slim, silver-haired Mary Lou Gulley sings out to her guests. With a broad smile and obvious enthusiasm, Gulley leads each new group of visitors through her fanciful home in the foothills of South Mountain.

It is only natural that as the years pass, Mary Lou Gulley's memories of her father and his abandonment of his family seem to soften. Years ago, she told visitors how her father, Boyce Luther Gulley, left her and her mother when she was a small child in the late 1920's. He had tuberculosis and apparently left his home in Seattle to see if the dry, warm southwestern climate would help cure him. He left without a note or mentioning a reason to his wife and daughter. One day he just disappeared.

Two years passed before they heard from him. He wrote from Arizona and told them where he was, but that he didn't want them to come to him. He didn't mention his illness.

They didn't hear from him again. After a number of years passed, a lawyer contacted Mary Lou and her mother and informed them that Boyce Luther Gulley had died, having left them a castle in the desert of Arizona.

"It was like a second death," Mary Lou used to say. "We had given him up as dead years ago, and then to find out that he had been alive all that time without contacting us...well, it was very hard on my mother. She grieved again over his death."

More recently Mary Lou puts a softer spin on the tale by remembering when her father took her to the beach when she was a very little girl. She built herself a sand castle, and when the waves washed it away, she began to cry. "Don't worry, Mary Lou, I'll build you another castle someday which won't wash away," her father would console her.

"But unfortunately," Mary Lou tells, "he died before he could send for me."

Both stories are no doubt true, and perhaps Mary Lou tells the story whichever way her mood leads her at the moment.

Boyce Gulley studied architectural engineering at Texas A&M for two years. Without that foundation he probably never would have been able to build such a vast structure—particularly one that would hold up so well under the harsh southwestern climate. But Boyce was not a person to toe the line and create a textbook home. Not by a long shot.

Even from a distance, arriving guests can see that the castle defies being put into any category. One sees the influence of the pueblo Indians, miners' shacks and Spanish *haciendas* tied together with folk art whimsies. Boyce created a delightful hodge-podge of arches, beams, towers and columns, combining found river rock with tile, refrigerator glass windows, railroad ties and wrought iron. Bell towers poke into the sky, as do chimneys from the 13 fireplaces. Providing color and light are the ends of liquor bottles stuck into the outer walls.

Stairways, hallways, doors and even trapdoors connect the 18 rooms, each built on a different level.

Mary Lou proudly and graciously fills her role as heiress to the throne. Opening the door to her spacious, airy living room, she begins to point out the unusual features of her 18,000 square foot castle. The wall of windows in the living room were harvested from an old Sante Fe Railroad depot and frame the South Mountains, making them appear near enough to touch. Throughout the house Boyce tried to blend the outdoors with the indoors. The windowpanes open to admit a cool breeze, important to Boyce who began building long before air-conditioning was introduced to the valley.

Just a teenager when she and her mother arrived in Phoenix to claim their castle, Mary Lou has found her role in life as chief tour guide, caretaker and owner of one of the most unique homes in the state.

Mary Lou Gulley.

With a smile, Mary Lou tells visitors, "I had a free spirit for a father. He left me a castle when I was just 18, and I've been here ever since. Now how many young girls do you know who have a father that builds them a castle?"

Mary Lou seems to have inherited her father's whimsical sense of humor and the absurd. Set up against a photograph of her father, Boyce Gulley, is a rock with the words "Sea Gulley" printed on it and a rock painting of a sea gull. Living alone in the house, she's never lonely. Besides the constant stream of visitors, she shares her castle with a number of life-size dolls, including "Joy," the lady of the night, who provocatively perches on a red velvet love-seat used in a Jerome bordello.

"Joy" sits pertly on the loveseat from a bordello in Jerome.

"Sea Gulley."

The living room includes an intricate masonry candle shrine made of Mexican tiles and loaded with different size candles on each niche. Near the door is a drop-leaf table, nearly invisible as it blends into a pillar. Rock paintings line the hearth—large river rocks painted by an artist friend appear to be remarkably life-like bunnies, kittens and coyotes. Set into the castle floors are twisting rows of small rocks to depict snakes which, according to Indian legend, symbolize protection, wisdom and defiance.

Gulley spent 17 years building the castle almost single-handedly. To gain title to the land, he filed mining rights for gold and copper. The home now sits on eight acres, the rest belonging to South Mountain Park. The castle is silent testimony to Gulley's return to health, as the feat of building such a large structure of stone and concrete would exhaust any reasonably healthy man. He hauled water by hand from a canal two miles away and, by mixing it with sand, cement and goats' milk, he developed a hard enough mortar to create the huge castle which still stands as a monument to his free spirit and innovation. There was no running water or electricity until 1971 when Mary Lou installed the modern conveniences.

Frank Lloyd Wright coined the phrase "organic architecture," but Boyce Gulley practiced it long before Wright's time. He scavenged ruined, tossed out bricks called "clinkers" for his fireplaces. Each brick has melted, bubbled and oozed into an unusual shape. Once thrown away as useless, they are now quite expensive and used in many luxury homes. The entire castle is brimming with found objects. Whatever caught Boyce's eye as he roamed the desert might be included in the next room that he built.

Boyce made the castle as convenient and comfortable as he could for the times. The desert got cold in the winter, so he created the main bedroom to the back of the living room with the solid rock back of the living room fireplace taking up almost an entire wall of the bedroom. With no mess of an open fire, Mary Lou's mother slept in the bedroom comfortably with the heat from the living room fire radiating into her room at night.

Another convenience which would be greatly appreciated today is the grate which he built into the stone floor of the kitchen.

"To clean the kitchen floor all you have to do is turn the hose on it. Everything goes right down the drain. Now wouldn't you like that in your house?" Mary Lou asks with a smile.

In the wedding chapel is a round window made of thick glass refrigerator trays, forerunner to the use of glass block so popular today. The two-foot-thick rock walls make a comfortable window seat. An 1870's peddle organ adds to the chapel atmosphere.

Boyce Gulley, Commander in Chief of his Dreams.

Mary Lou's favorite room is a two level bedroom built around the skeleton of a massive saguaro cactus, now decorated with Christmas lights. Another clever innovation of Gulley's is the brass bed which he placed on tracks so it could be rolled into a niche in the wall, making more living space during the day. The wire wheel rims of a Stutz Bearcat create two round windows high up on the wall, letting in sunshine. Mary Lou laughingly says that due to the many pieces of a Stutz Bearcat she has discovered incorporated into the house, she wouldn't be surprised if the entire car is part of the house.

In one room is a painting of Boyce Gulley. On a flat rock leaning against the picture are the words, "COMMANDER IN CHIEF OF HIS DREAMS." Yes, he most certainly was.

Mystery Castle nestles in the foothills of South Mountain Park on the far south side of Phoenix. Take Seventh Street south to Mineral Road (two miles south of Baseline Road). Turn left and follow the sign. You'll be able to see the castle from there.

Tours are led Tuesday through Sunday, 11:00 a.m. to 4:00 p.m. Admission is charged. Flash photos are allowed inside the rooms.

For information write: Mary Lou Gulley, Mystery Castle, 800 E. Mineral Road, Phoenix, AZ 85040. Call (602) 268-1581.

Mesa Tribune

The Day They Killed Santa Claus
1932

"No one will ever know the difference."

Just as Arizona was still suffering the ravages of the Great Depression in 1932, the rural community of Mesa was going through its own hard times. As the Christmas season approached, the local merchants were feeling the pinch. Receipts from early Christmas shopping were lackluster. Even the annual Christmas parade looked like it was going to be a disappointment.

John McPhee, the colorful editor of the *Mesa Tribune*, decided to take the matter in hand. McPhee was popular with the merchants and he loved promotional schemes. This time he had come up with a doozy. The brilliance of his plan positively dazzled the town merchants.

McPhee said, "Why not hire a parachutist to dress up like Santa? He'll jump from a plane, parachute to the start of the parade, and then lead the annual Christmas parade through town." Never before had Santa arrived by parachute.

Keep in mind that parachuting was not as common an occurrence as it is today. In fact, it was considered a dangerous stunt. Indeed, aviation was still new and adventurous. Lindbergh had just made his famous solo flight across the Atlantic only five years previous.

The town businessmen loved the idea. Their faces lit up with anticipation of a happy and successful start to the Christmas shopping season. They could almost hear jingle bells—or perhaps it was the jingle of cash registers and coins.

McPhee hired an itinerant stunt pilot to make the jump in a rented Santa suit. All was ready. But the day of the parade came, and Santa was nowhere to be found. A frantic search revealed the erstwhile Santa fortifying himself with liquid courage in the local bar. In fact, he was by now so courageous he couldn't walk.

"Fear not!" said the undaunted editor. "I'll just get a department store dummy Santa and have the pilot circle over the field. We'll push the dummy out the door and he'll float down pretty as you please. Then I'll appear in a Santa suit and lead the parade. No one will ever know the difference." Great idea, the merchants thought.

A large crowd had already gathered near an open field on the edge of town, and the local businessmen waited anxiously. Soon the sputtering of the small airplane's engine signaled Santa's arrival and the crowd gazed skyward expectantly.

Suddenly there he was! Those gathered below could see Santa standing in the doorway of the airplane as it circled the field. A great cheer went up from the crowd. The children were thrilled. Just think! Santa arriving by plane!

Then Santa, with parachute attached, was pushed out of the plane according to the plan and began his descent to earth.

He fell,...

and he fell,...

and he fell.

He tumbled pathetically end over end with the limp, unopened parachute streaming behind him like a wet handkerchief. Down came the department store Santa like a rock and he hit—kersplat—at the end of the field in front of hundreds of horrified onlookers.

Undismayed by the apparent death of the parachuting Santa, McPhee jumped up gleefully, resplendent in his Santa suit. He took his place at the head of the parade as if nothing had happened. But it just didn't work. The children had been traumatized; the adults were disgusted. The merchants were in a daze as they gazed around their empty stores in the following days.

McPhee, sensing he was about as welcome as a scorpion in a boot, wisely decided to leave town for a few days. He hoped that all would be forgotten, but it wasn't. He never shook the label of the "Man who killed Santa Claus." The incident was even a part of his obituary nearly forty years later.

∾∾∾∾∾∾∾∾∾∾∾∾

The Mesa Tribune buildings, at 120 W. 1st Ave., have been enlarged over the years. The oldest existing building, of gray cinder block, would have heard the voice of editor McPhee.

Hotel Congress

The Capture of Dillinger

1934

"I'm not leaving without my luggage."

The predawn hours of January 21, 1934, were chilly when a defective furnace in the basement of the Hotel Congress overheated, igniting the dry, old woodwork nearby. Flames quickly roared through the third floor of the fine old Tucson hotel. Firemen responded to the alarm and swept through the building, banging on the doors to awaken the still sleeping guests. People in a variety of thrown together outfits, mixing day clothes with nightclothes, hurried out of the smokey hotel and stood shivering in the dark, early morning chill.

One guest, however, acted reluctant to leave. He argued with the firefighters and told them that he wouldn't leave without his luggage. The problem was that his luggage was too heavy for him to handle alone in one trip. He even carried on after the firemen insisted he leave the building. Watching the flames leap higher and higher, the man was so agitated he finally persuaded two firemen to return to the burning building and retrieve several heavy, expensive-looking bags from his room.

Three days after the fire, the firemen who had carried the heavy bags out happened to be leafing through "The Lineup" section of the popular *True Detective Mysteries*. They thought they recognized the well-dressed man in the lineup.

The photo in "The Lineup" was of Russell Clark, a dangerous member of the notorious John Dillinger gang. He was wanted for murder and bank robbery. The name he had used to register at the Hotel Congress was Arthur Long, an alias. He claimed to be a tourist from Florida.

The Tucson police also remembered a report from some vacationing New Yorkers who had sat in the bar of the Hotel Congress with three men and three women the evening before the fire. One of the men fit the description of the well-dressed man with the heavy luggage. The New York couple had reported to the police that the man had made a peculiar statement boasting that it was easy to earn a living by robbing banks. The New York couple also remarked that each of the three men carried guns.

In checking identification records, the police realized that the three men were not the well-to-do Florida tourists that they claimed to be. They were Russell Clark, "Fat" Charlie Makley, and Harry Pierpont, all members of John Dillinger's gang and America's most wanted gangsters. Dillinger himself was not with the gang at the hotel, but the police figured that he was probably nearby.

Each man was a known killer. Pierpont presented the greatest risk. He was known to be a psychopath who killed for the pleasure of watching a man die.

The police watched for the men to reappear around town. "Fat" Charlie Makley was a surprisingly easy capture. Makley was seen in a radio-repair shop. The police entered and acted as if they didn't know who he was. They just coolly and congenially asked him to come to the station house with them to check the papers on his car. Knowing that his papers were in order, Makley confidently went to the police station. Once inside the building, the police finger-printed him, identified him and immediately arrested him.

Russell Clark was traced to a rented house on North Second Avenue near the University of Arizona. He was found with his girl-friend, Opal Love. Ms. Love, a bosomy red-head, was also called the "Mack Truck" by the affectionate gang. When Clark realized that the police had arrived, he put up a fight which resulted in a bloody cut on his scalp. Searching the house, the police found the heavy bags which had been hauled out of the burning Hotel Congress. They were filled with machine guns, pistols, bullet-proof vests and ammunition. Small wonder that the gang didn't want the flames to reach the luggage.

Harry Pierpont was spotted driving along South Sixth Avenue in the Armory Park neighborhood. Two officers pulled him over and used the same ploy about checking car registration papers they had used on Makley. Unaware that his fellow gang members were now under arrest, Pierpont agreed to go to the station house to have the paperwork checked on his out-of-state car. A nervous officer rode with him in the back seat, stealthily holding his gun between his legs where Pierpont wouldn't see it. Just inside the police station, Pierpont saw the gang's stockpile of weapons which had just been taken out of the suitcases. Pierpont began to put up a fight in an attempt to escape, but he was immediately overpowered by several officers. After subduing Pierpont, the officers checked him for weapons. Among others, they found a pistol dangling down his back on a string.

With the gang members now in custody, the police focused their search on the illusive Dillinger himself. Confident he would soon show up at the gang headquarters on North Second Avenue, the small house was placed under constant surveillance.

On the evening of January 25, 1934, Dillinger and his lady friend, Evelyn Frechette, who was traveling with him, drove up to the small bungalow. Parking his newly acquired brown Hudson boldly in front, Dillinger and Frechette started toward the house.

The three policemen sprang up from the bushes where they had been hiding and shouted, "Stick 'em up!" One officer, evidently a fan of Dick Tracy, remembers shouting, "Reach for the moon or I'll cut you in two!"

Caught completely off guard, Dillinger was apprehended without incident. As he was cuffed, he remarked quietly, "Well, I'll be damned."

**This small bungalow which was Dillinger's hideout
on North Second avenue is a private home.**

*The Hotel Congress is open to the public as an economy class hotel.
Located at 311 E. Congress, Tucson, Arizona, 85701.
Call (520) 622-8848 for reservations.*

*(Note to Dillinger buffs: The Tucson capture was largely ignored
by Hollywood writers in creating screenplays about Dillinger's life.
He was extradited to Indiana where he escaped a month after his
arrival from the "escape-proof" Lake County jail. He resumed his
life of crime. Finally on July 22, 1934, Dillinger was shot and
killed outside the Biograph Theatre on Chicago's North Side after
police were alerted by the famous and mysterious Lady in Red.)*

Goulding's Trading Post

"Roll em!"
1938

"Mike, I want to go where I can look for 100 miles and not see a single second lieutenant."

T all, lanky Harry Goulding was leaning back in his chair, dreaming about the future with his wife, Leone, whom he'd nicknamed Mike. Although underage, he'd managed to sign up for the army and had served as a mule sergeant in the 7th Engineers during World War I. He soon discovered that the military was not his favorite lifestyle. Born in Durango, Colorado, in 1897, Harry was from a family of sheepmen, and he ran sheep as a youth in Colorado and New Mexico.

A short time after his conversation with his wife, Harry packed into the area beyond the Lukachukai mountains with his friend, John Stevens, in the isolated north-eastern plateau of Arizona. There they saw land so majestic it took their breath away. At that time, in 1919, part of the area was Paiute Indian Reservation and not available for private ownership, but Harry longed for that desolate, magnificent land for the next several years. In 1923, Utah swapped the Paiutes for some fertile land, and the area became available for homesteading. Harry and his young bride, Mike, immediately laid claim to 640 acres at the base of Tsay-Kissi Mesa (Big Rock Door Mesa). The land cost them $320.

Harry set up a make-shift counter for this first trading post, and he and Mike lived in a tent. The Navajo named Harry "T'pay-eh-nez" (Long Sheep) because he was over six feet tall and herded sheep.

Mike and Harry Goulding.

He was not immediately welcomed by the suspicious Navajo. Many members of the tribe remembered the killing of Paiute leader, Posey, by white settlers. In addition, there were continuing battles with Anglo stockmen over grazing rights for cattle. The Native Americans saw the influx of white men as a threat. Eventually Mike and Harry became trusted and beloved traders with a reputation for fairness throughout the reservation.

After living in tents for five years, the Gouldings finally built a solid trading post building made of the local red rock. The trading area was on the ground floor. The Gouldings lived on the second floor of the same building in a small apartment. Over the next few years they added a few stone cabins.

By the late 1930's the Navajo were desperately poor and struggling to recover from the Great Depression which still gripped the western United States. Indian rugs and crafts sold for a few pennies when they sold at all. There was very little tourism.

Harry Goulding heard about a western film produced by United Artists that was going to be shot on location. Although commonly done now, this would be the first such movie not filmed in a studio. Harry and Mike felt the filming of a Hollywood motion-picture could be a great economic boost to the area, and they knew they had the perfect location. Gathering together all the money they could put their hands on, they set out with $60 and a dream. In addition, Harry had a fist full of outstanding photographs of Monument Valley taken by renown photographer Josef Muench.

Upon arriving in Tinsel Town, Harry left his wife Mike with her brother. Gathering up his photographs, a Navajo blanket and the remainder of his courage, he entered the imposing main doors of United Artists. It didn't take long for Harry to discover that the friendliness of the west stopped at the desk of the receptionist. Despite his colorful descriptions of beautiful Monument Valley, Harry began to understand unless you had an appointment or knew someone important, you would not be invited into the inner sanctum.

"Surely I can talk with someone," Harry pleaded.

Another call to an inner phone by the receptionist brought another rejection.

"Well, " Harry smiled with resignation, "back on the reservation we always have plenty of time for a new friend. I'm sure they'll want to meet me eventually. I'll just make myself at home and wait." Spreading out his Indian blanket on the floor, he began to make himself comfortable.

Flustered and not knowing what to do with this lanky western stranger, the receptionist put in another frantic call to the inner parts of United Artist. Soon a location director came bursting through the doors intent on telling this hick from the sticks that only really important people are allowed to enter the hallowed doors of United Artist. The lull in the action had given Harry a few minutes to spread out his pictures of Monument Valley.

The short, important location director, having already formed his best "polite rejection" thoughts, was taken aback when his eyes fell on the stunning photos.

"What are these pictures of?" he asked.

"They're of Monument Valley,...where I live." Harry replied.

The Mittens at Monument Valley.

Harry spent an hour with the location director and soon John Ford was called. Mr. Ford was working on a picture called *Stagecoach*, starring two unknown B-grade actors, John Wayne and Ward Bond. Ford had been thinking about filming the movie in the "real west," beyond the Hollywood sound stages. Harry was finally asked if he could—in three days—be ready to service the cast and at least 100 technicians who would show up in the valley to shoot certain portions of the film.

John Ford filming in Monument Valley.

Harry, knowing he was penniless but sensing a defining moment, smiled confidently and said, "Of course."

Three days later dynamic John Ford and his crew were walking through Monument Valley for the first time, thrilled at the possibilities for backgrounds for the film. United Artists had wired money to Flagstaff to pay for food and housing for the influx of film makers, and Goulding's was on its way to becoming a center for film making as well as tourism for Monument Valley.

The motion picture, *Stagecoach,* launched the long, successful career of John Wayne. But another star was born in that picture—Monument Valley. John Ford, fondly nicknamed "Natani Nez" (Tall Leader) by the Navajo, would return to direct nine more movies. Such John Ford classics as *My Darling Clementine, Fort Apache, She Wore a Yellow Ribbon,* and *The Searchers* created such a strong image of the west that Monument Valley became a symbol of the western frontier known any-place in the world where television is available.

The Gouldings built a lodge and dining room for the influx of tourists and the intermittent film crews that came to visit. Harry continued to promote Monument Valley until he was forced to retire by ill health in 1962. Harry died in 1981 in Page. Mike returned to Monument Valley shortly before her death in 1992.

Today the property is owned by two self-called "trading-post brats," Gerald and Roland LaFont. The LaFont brothers added new sleeping rooms and a dining room. Before her death, Mike was pleased to see the old trading post turned into a museum, housing her personal photos, guest books, Anasazi artifacts and Indian art as well as motion-picture memorabilia.

John Ford was quoted in an interview with Cosmopolitan magazine, March, 1964, "I think you can say that the real star of my Westerns has always been the land.... My favorite location is Monument Valley; it has rivers, mountains, plains, desert...I feel at peace there. I have been all over the world, but I consider this the most complete, beautiful, and peaceful place on Earth."

ຑຉຑຉຑຉຑຉຑຉຑ

Goulding's Lodge, wisely built so every room faces Monument Valley with a private balcony, is open year round. Located just north of the Arizona/Utah border, the rates are lower in the winter months. The museum is open April through October. For reservations or further information write: PO Box 360001, Monument Valley, UT 84536. Phone (801) 727-3231. FAX: (801) 727-3344.
It is wise to make reservations for the tours when making your reservations for your accommodations. Half-day tour is of Monument Valley. The all day tour includes Mystery Valley and a lunch cooked out-of-doors by your Navajo guide.

Papago Park POW Camp

The Great Escape
1944

"How could there be such a thing as a river with no water?"

The frigid weather across the United States was as chilling as the bad news from the war front in those last few days before Christmas, 1944. A cold wave sent temperatures to 34 degrees below zero in parts of the Northeast, snow was falling across the northern plains and a cold drizzle was soaking Phoenix.

The bright hopes of an early victory over invading Germany had dimmed. The Battle of the Bulge had begun in Belgium. Newspapers and radio news announcers told of American troops being overrun by the advancing German army.

At a large encampment in Papago Park, east of Phoenix, approximately 1,700 German prisoners of war cheered as they heard broadcasts telling of German victories. The prisoners didn't believe the stories about American victories, thinking they were just propaganda. There was a general celebration and hell-raising in the camp at the first news of the Battle of the Bulge. The celebration on the evening of December 23, however, was a carefully planned ruse to cover the escape of a group of German navy officers and enlisted men.

The German POWs later shared strong memories of the heat and of sand drifting through the screened windows, covering their beds, clothing, and furniture with grit.

The Geneva Convention states that prisoners of war have a duty to try to escape. Submarine Capt. Jurgen Wattenberg, then 43, took his duty very seriously. The Papago Prisoner Of War Camp was so isolated in the desert that the American guards considered escape all but impossible. They were certain that the rocky, caleche ground was too hard for any attempt to escape by tunneling out. But that was just what the Germans did.

Wattenberg estimated later that digging began sometime in September, 1944. Prior to the digging, the officers had scoured the camp grounds for two areas which would be in blind spots, places where the guards couldn't readily see them. The entrance and exit to the tunnel were out of view of the two guard towers on the east side of the compound.

The German prisoners asked their guards for permission to create a volleyball courtyard. Innocently obliging, the guards provided them with digging tools. From that point on, two men were digging at all times during night hours. A cart was rigged up to travel along tracks to take the dirt out. The men stuffed the dirt in their pants pockets which had holes in the bottoms, and they shuffled the dirt out along the ground as they walked around. In addition, they flushed a huge amount of dirt down the toilets. They labeled their escape route *Der Faustball Tunnel* (The Volleyball Tunnel).

They dug a 178 foot tunnel with a diameter of 3 feet. The tunnel went 8 to 14 feet beneath the surface, under the two prison camp fences, a drainage ditch and a road. The exit was near a power pole in a clump of brush about 15 feet from the Cross Cut Canal. To disguise their plans, the men built a square box, filled it with dirt and planted native weeds in it for the lid to cover the exit. When the lid was on the tunnel exit, the area looked like undisturbed desert.

Wattenberg ordered the men in an adjacent compound to throw a noisy party the evening of December 23, 1944. They weren't told why, but many of them guessed and silently wished their comrades luck. Besides, they were happy to celebrate the good news of Hitler's final offensive, the Battle of the Bulge.

Beginning at about 9:00 p.m. on December 23, prisoners started crawling out along the tunnel in teams of two or three men. Next door their German buddies were singing, breaking bottles, waving flags and generally making the biggest hullabaloo they could. Each escapee carried clothing, food, forged papers, cigarettes and medical supplies, plus anything else they had been able to save up in the past several months. Wattenberg had managed to procure the names and addresses of people in Mexico who might help them get back to Germany.

The plan was to float down the Cross Cut Canal, then to the Salt River, to the Gila River and on to the Colorado River which would take them into Mexico. Three of the men had constructed a canoe which could be taken apart and carried in three parts. They had blocked up the drains in the shower room to test it for water-tightness. It never occurred to the Germans that in dry Arizona a blue line marked "river" on a map might be filled with water only occasionally. The three men with the canoe were disappointed to find the Salt River bed merely a mud bog from recent rains. Not to be discouraged, they carried their canoe pieces several miles to the confluence with the Gila River, only to find it a series of large puddles. They sat on the river bank, put their heads in their hands and cried out their frustration.

By 2:30 a.m., December 24, all twelve officers and thirteen enlisted German submarine men were on their way. Their efforts have been described as the largest POW escape in the United States. The POW camp's security officer, the late Army Maj. Cecil Parshall, insisted in 1978 that 60 Germans actually escaped that night. He stated that the only reason 25 prisoners were counted as escapees was because that's how many were eventually caught and returned to the camp. The rest were ignored in a government cover-up. Wattenberg, however, has said only 25 escaped. Wattenberg stated later that few of the men had high hopes of actually escaping from the United States and returning to Germany. But once they conceived of the tunnel plan, they were enthusiastic about trying it anyway. Two escapees eventually made their way to Mexico where they were about to be shot as spies when they were rescued by American authorities.

Although the men left in the wee hours of Christmas Eve, the camp officials were blissfully unaware of anything amiss until the escapees began to show up that evening. The first to return was an enlisted man, Herbert Fuchs, who decided he had been cold, wet and hungry long enough by Christmas Eve evening. Thinking about his dry, warm bed and hot meal that the men in the prison camp were enjoying, he decided his attempt at freedom had come to an end. The 22-year old U-boat crewman hitched a ride on East Van Buren Street and asked the driver to take him to the sheriff's office where he surrendered. Much to the surprise of the officers at the camp, the sheriff called and told them he had a prisoner who wanted to return to camp.

Shortly after the sheriff's call, a Tempe woman called in to tell them two prisoners had knocked on her door and surrendered to her. The phone rang again, this time from a Tempe man who said he had two escaped prisoners to be picked up.

The highest ranking officer, U-boat Commander Jurgen Wattenberg and two of his U-boat crewmen, Walter Kozur and Johann Kremer, crawled through the dark tunnel together and slipped into the cold waist-deep canal. They were the fifth of ten teams to leave the tunnel that night. They grinned at each other as they heard the ruckus being raised on their behalf by the noncommissioned officers' compound, diverting the guards' attention. Rising silently from the water, they took a generous snort from their schnapps, homemade hooch made from distilling potatoes and citrus.

They hurriedly settled their gear on their backs and set off north-west through the desert. By 2:00 a.m. they were huddled, dripping and cold, in a citrus grove where they breakfasted on grapefruit. They settled down to try to sleep in the continuing drizzle.

They found a dilapidated shack by sunrise the next morning and spent the day taking turns sleeping and guarding. By evening Kremer remarked, "It's Christmas Eve." He took out his harmonica and softly played, "*Stille Nacht*,"—"Silent Night."

By evening they enjoyed a dinner of canned meat and milk, dried bread crumbs, and chocolate bars hoarded from the daily rations in camp. They talked of their loved ones, and of their other comrades. They spoke of how proud they were of their escape and how well it had all gone so far. Then each sat silent in his own thoughts.

By dawn they had reached an area that today would be along Stanford Drive, between 32nd and 44th streets. They hid out in the gullies, concealed throughout the day and exploring the mountains to the north after dark.

The American guards back at the POW camp were not having a merry Christmas at all. They had been called back from holiday leave to beef up the guard at the camp, certainly a rather late effort. In addition, personnel at the Ninth Service Command, Fort Douglas, Utah; the Provost Marshal General's office in Washington, D. C.; the Federal Bureau of Investigation; and other governmental agencies were arriving for intensive investigation.

Several days passed before American Army Private First Class Lawrence Jorgensen, on a search detail, discovered the camouflaged escape hatch and solved the mystery of how the POW's escaped.

In their reconnaissance of the area, the three German escapees finally found a jagged channel that numerous cloudbursts and gully washers had carved into a slope near the Squaw Peak area. One of the many eroded alcoves had an overhang of six or seven feet. Desert weeds on top of the ravine helped to conceal the shallow cave. They rolled a few large boulders across the opening. Then they cut brush and propped it in front of the cave to obscure their activities. Kremer scooped out a pit for a fire and their first pot of coffee was brewing by sunrise.

For the next two nights Wattenberg and his two men scouted their environs. On the second night they went to the area east of the Arizona Biltmore resort. Creeping through a citrus grove they heard voices and a dog began to bark. They stopped and crouched low. Finding an irrigation pipe, they filled their canteens, returning to their camp with citrus and fresh water.

By the end of the first week of January, 1945, the three men resolved to find out what had happened to their fellow escapees. Kremer and Kozur slipped into Phoenix at nightfall. As the eastern sky was turning pink the two men returned with their bounty, one sack of fruit and another full of newspapers. They had hoped to find a map, but no luck.

The headlines screamed, "WHOLESALE NAZI ESCAPE SCREENS BIG SHOT'S FLIGHT." Wattenberg was amused at being labeled a "big shot." Previous to this his description had been "the chief troublemaker."

Another newspaper read, "TWO NAZIS APPREHENDED AT MEXI-CAN BORDER," referring to the capture and near shooting of Reinhard Mark, a midshipman, and Heinrich Palmer, a petty officer, south of Sells, Arizona.

By the end of their month-long outing, Wattenberg and his men became bolder. Prior to the escape, Wattenberg had informed one of the men who was not in the escape party of his intention to remain in the mountains to the north until he could manage to escape further. He had drawn a sketch of the landscape and marked an area for a possible food drop when the group was outside the camp on a work gang.

On January 18 or 19, Wattenberg gave Kremer a note thanking their comrades for the supplies. After dark, Kremer went to the agreed-upon place, an abandoned, dismantled vehicle. He left the note and returned with fruit and several packs of cigarettes. Their remaining food supply was by now depleted.

Kremer decided on an exceptionally bold plan. He decided to sneak back into camp by infiltrating one of the work details. There he could get the news of the other escapees, as well as procure more food before slipping away from another work detail the next day. He was only half successful. He made it back into camp. But during a surprise inspection on the afternoon of Tuesday, January 23, Kremer was caught and discovered. He had been in the camp undetected for three days.

The next day Walter Kozur came down a hill after sundown and was met by three soldiers. Soon Wattenberg realized that he, alone, was still free.

As Saturday dawned, Wattenberg decided that he would go into Phoenix and perhaps get a job as a dishwasher. He also considered hopping a freight train, hoping to arrive at some faraway place that hadn't heard of the POW escape; perhaps a farm where he might get a job. He again looked through the newspapers from which he had clipped articles about the escape. His attention was drawn to some church notices. Perhaps he could get help from a Catholic priest, while being protected by the privacy of confession. He cut out the section of church addresses and folded them neatly, adding them to the collection of clippings in his rucksack.

After sundown he walked for nearly two hours to East Van Buren. No one seemed to notice him as the cars moved along the busy thoroughfare. He passed numerous motels where Americans in uniform were spending the weekend on passes. He ducked his head and quickly passed the crowds of soldiers.

Walking into the central business district of Phoenix, Wattenberg stepped into the American Kitchen restaurant. In a voice as devoid of accent as he could manage, he ordered noodle soup with beef, washed down with a cold beer, a meal familiar to a German.

Wattenberg then went to several small hotels and asked about a room for the night. They were all full. He entered the Hotel Adams. The front desk clerk told him they were full for the night, but a room would probably open up in the morning after check-out. Wattenberg, tired and discouraged, noticed a vacant chair in the lobby. He sank into the soft cushions and opened a newspaper which had been discarded. Within minutes he was sleeping soundly.

About an hour later, the escapee awoke and noticed that the bellhop was watching him with more than passing interest. Wattenberg suddenly wondered if his picture had appeared in the newspapers. He also felt very conscious of his brown U.S. Army issue trousers dyed blue. He decided to leave. The bellhop, Ken Vance, reported later that Wattenberg left the hotel at 1:30 a.m., Sunday, January 28.

Wattenberg left the Hotel Adams and headed north. At Central and Van Buren, he stopped Clarence V. Cherry, a City of Phoenix street foreman, and, in heavily accented English, asked for directions to the railroad station. By this time, perhaps he was willing to be caught, but just didn't want to surrender.

When Wattenberg turned to walk on down the street, Cherry caught the attention of Sgt. Gilbert Brady of the Phoenix Police Department. He told the policeman that the tall man in the yellow checkered shirt had just spoken to him in a heavy German accent. Brady caught up with Wattenberg at Third Avenue and Van Buren.

"Sir, could I see your Selective Service registration?" the police officer asked.

"I left it at home."

"Where is home?" Brady asked.

"Glendale."

"Glendale, Arizona, or Glendale, California?" Brady asked again.

"Glendale—uh, Glendale, back east," Wattenberg replied.

"You'll have to come with me to the police station," Brady ordered. Brady offered his fugitive a cigarette.

Wattenberg lit the cigarette, took a deep drag, and exhaled with force and resignation. "The game's up, and I lost," he admitted quietly.

At the police station the police found that Wattenberg had with him 50 cents in coins, a blank notebook, and several newspaper clippings—some about the escape, others of restaurant and nightclub advertisements, and the Saturday directory of churches.

When Wattenberg was returned to the Papago Pow Camp he was taken to the hospital where he was served a Sunday dinner of beef broth, roasted chicken, vegetables and ice cream. It had to last him awhile, since his punishment for the escape was bread and water rations for fourteen days.

By March, 1946, the last of the Papago Park POWs were sent back to their home countries. On June 16, 1946, Wattenberg was reunited with his wife and two sons at Neustadt, Holstein, a German seaport village on the Baltic Sea.

EPILOGUE

On January 5, 1985, the Papago Park Prisoner of War Camp Commission held a commemorative observance at the campsite. The festivities were attended by mayors of Phoenix, Scottsdale and Tempe. One of the special guests of honor was 85 year old U-boat Commander Jurgen Wattenberg. Looking back on his stay in Arizona, Wattenberg remarked how much he had enjoyed the SPAM dinners.

A banner over the camp meeting declared, "TO RENEW IN FRIEND-SHIP AN ASSOCIATION COMMENCED IN ANGUISH."

∽∽∽∽∽∽∽∽∽∽∽

Today a residential subdivision, a Saturn dealership and a baseball field cover most of what was once the Papago Park POW Camp. The only remaining building which would have heard the voices of the German POWs is now used as a Lions Club.

The Rex Allen Arizona Cowboy Museum

The Last of the Silver Screen Cowboys
1950's

"As I walked out on the streets of Laredo..."

The sounds of Rex Allen's clear baritone voice can be heard on the street as you approach the white-washed adobe building. All the songs are so very familiar—"Streets of Laredo," "The Last Roundup," "Arizona Waltz."

Rex was born on a ranch in the Willcox area. He was a handsome little boy, but with one detracting feature—his eyes were crossed. His family earned a marginal living on the ranch and couldn't afford the necessary surgery, plus the expenses of a trip. The small town of Willcox stepped in to help the young boy who was already showing signs of real talent. A group of local friends, spearheaded by the Rotary Club, took up a collection and held fund raisers to send Rex back east for the surgery. His life was forever changed.

Rex went on to a 35 year career recording cowboy songs for Decca Records as well as starring in 19 movies for Republic Pictures. Handsome, with a crystal clear voice and an effortless three octave range, Rex was also one of the few Hollywood cowboys to be a real cowboy, comfortable on a horse, wearing jeans, chaps and spurs. Rex never forgot the kindness of his Willcox friends. Every year since 1951 he has returned to Willcox to head the parade for the Rex Allen Days, held the first weekend in October.

Rex Allen.

The people of Willcox are rightly proud of their native son and have created a museum in his honor in one of their oldest commercial buildings. Constructed in the early 1890's of adobe, it operated as the Schley Saloon from 1897 to 1919. Prohibition shut down the saloon, so it was converted to a grocery store. In 1989 the town of Willcox realized a long-time dream with the opening of the Rex Allen Arizona Cowboy Museum, honoring its favorite local-boy-done-good, as well as other well-known ranchers of the area. The front of the Rex Allen Museum has been restored to resemble the original saloon store front. Displayed in the museum is the following:

Minimum Requirements to be a Cowboy:

A wide-brimmed hat and a pair of tight pants, and
twenty-dollar boots from a discount store.

At least two head of livestock—preferably
cattle—one male, one female.

An air-conditioned pickup with automatic
transmission, power steering and trailer hitch.

A gun rack for the rear window of the pickup big
enough to hold a walking stick and rope.

Two dogs to ride in the back of the pickup.

A forty dollar horse and a three hundred dollar saddle.

A goose-neck horse trailer small enough to park
in front of a cafe or bar.

A place to keep the cows, on land too poor to grow grass.

A spool of barb ware, three fence posts, and a bale of hay to haul
around in the back of the truck all day.

Credit at the bank.

Credit at the feed store.

Credit from your father-in-law.

A good neighbor to feed the dogs and cattle
when you are away.

A pair of silver spurs to wear when you dress up.

A cushion to sit on for hours at the livestock auction every Thursday.

A wife that believes your lies and has a good job.

The Rex Allen Arizona Cowboy Museum is located at 150 N. Railroad Avenue in Willcox. Open from 10:00 a.m. to 4:00 p.m. daily, except Thanksgiving, Christmas and New Year's Day. Phone (520) 384-4583 for more information.

Rex Allen.

McCune Mansion
53,000 Square Feet of Home Sweet Home
1965

"Okay then, I'll just take my 5 million and build us a home."

The original builder, Walker McCune was known as a town character. Although he lived the life of a very rich man, he usually dressed as if he were fresh from the corral. His family had made a fortune in oil and McCune lived off of a very generous trust account. He married a waitress from the Pink Pony restaurant in Scottsdale. His wife was a former actress who appeared under the name Carole Donne in fifteen movies as a contract player for Warner Bros.

In 1965 Walker McCune offered to give $5 million to Arizona State University in Tempe to start a medical school. One of his restrictions was that the medical school was to be named after himself. The Board of Regents turned him and his money down. In addition to not liking the restrictions on the money, a medical school was being built at the University of Arizona in Tucson.

So Walker McCune decided to take his $5 million and build a house for his bride.

Sadly, he and his wife disagreed from the beginning about various aspects of designing and building the house. They never lived together in the main house. McCune lived in the guest house, which was as large as the average home at 2,400 square feet. Eventually tiring of it all, his wife ran off with the chauffeur. When Walker McCune died from a heart attack sometime later, some of his friends stated that he died of a broken heart.

The huge house went into bankruptcy and was purchased by a Mormon multimillionaire, Gordon Hall. The 90 room home was Hall's for a mere $2 million. The 32 year-old real estate tycoon and owner of 24 Hour Nautilus set out to make the already immense house the largest single family dwelling in the world. He enlarged it to the present 52,800 square feet.

The following is a list of rooms as outlined by Realty Executives:

LOWER LEVEL
Wine cellar
Workout Room
Billiard Room
Video Game Room (w Bathroom)
Therapy Room
Photography Room
Ice Rink (indoor)
Wrestling Room (indoor)
Children's Theatre (indoor)
Laundry Room
Fan Room
Water Softener Room

14 Car Garage complete with gas pumps, both unleaded and diesel
Climate Controlled Kennel
Refrigeration Room
Men's Dressing Room w Locker Room
Women's Dressing Room w Locker Room
Servants' Bathroom

MAIN LEVEL

Living Room
Dining Room
Main Kitchen
Three Bedrooms
Lounge
Bath
Caretaker's Suite (self contained)
Maids' Quarters w 2 Bathrooms
Foyer

Dining Room
Entry
Library
Ballroom
Drawing Room
Two Men's Restrooms
Two Women's Restrooms
Servants' Bathroom

UPPER LEVEL

Master Suite - 9,000 square feet
Boudoir
Theatre w 15' by 20' Movie Screen
Private Dining Room
Bathtub Room
Dressing Room
Family Room
Family Dining Room
Children's Playroom

Sauna
Spa
Steam Room
Four Children's Bedrooms
Kitchen (in Governess' Suite)
Governess' Suite
Study
Children's Study

EXTERIOR

Guard House
Racquetball Court w Kitchen and
    Viewing Area
Tennis Court
Tennis Room
Jacuzzi - Seats 35 people
Olympic sized Pool w Waterfall
    and Gazebo

Pool House
Locker Rooms
Hair Salon
Dining Area
Industrial Kitchen
Playground
Elevator Room

GUEST HOUSE

Entry
Office
Two Bedrooms
Gallery
Dining Room

Living Room
Basement
Kitchen
Four Bathrooms
Laundry Room

Fourteen fireplaces, unneeded for heat, were added for atmosphere. The home has its own power sources. In case of power failure, its own generators switch on to keep the house secure and running properly. And to protect it all, are a million dollar James Bondish set of 49 cameras with infra-red detectors and two and one-half ton remote control entry gates.

Remote controlled entry gates said to be strong enough to stop a tank.

Lest anyone should wonder, Hall placed a 44 foot wide black sign on the roof declaring, GORDON HALL MANSION. He said simply, "I want people to know who lives here."

No matter how big the home was, it was too small to house his ambitions. Hall said that he planned to be a billionaire by 1990 and a trillionaire by 2012. And, oh yes, he also planned to be world body-building champion. "I say to myself, 'The biggest and the best.' That's what I'm here to do," Hall explained.

Unfortunately, Hall's dreams didn't materialize. His chain of spas, 24 Hour Nautilus, failed and Gordon Hall went bankrupt. Hall had put $13 million into the house on Sugarloaf Mountain.

The huge house sat unoccupied for several years. From time to time the neighbors would hear unsettling rumors of unsuitable potential buyers. Word was out at one time that the Moonies were buying it.

The McCune Mansion went up for public auction in 1988. The insurance replacement value was at that time $30 million. The brochure about the property said it had been reduced for quick sale for the unbelievably low price of only $9,850,000. The bank did not receive a bid for anything over $1 million so the house was taken off the market again and it sat empty for two more years.

It sold at auction in 1990 to a young California businessman, Bruce Jennings. He purchased it for $3.05 million. The house was in disrepair when he bought it and he worked to renovate it. Jennings was able to get some of the recreational facilities, including the indoor ice-skating rink, operating again. His wife, AnnaLeah, redecorated the servants' quarters where the family stayed while they worked on the rest of the house.

Their initial plan was to completely remodel the entire house, but they changed their minds shortly after the purchase. Realizing that their plan for turning the monstrous house into a family home was beyond their reach, they put the home back on the market.

The most interesting and eccentric of all of the home's owners, George A. Hormel II, purchased the home for $3.75 million in March of 1991. Hormel is an heir to one of the nation's largest meatpacking fortunes. The Hormel company is a leading meat processor that specializes in pork products and is known for its canned meats, stews and chilis. Some of its trademarks are the Hormel, Dinty Moore, Spam, Little Sizzlers, Top Shelf and Kids' Kitchen brands. The home was immediately dubbed, "The House that Spam Bought."

Hormel owns eight homes, including one around the corner from Arnold Schwarzenegger's in Los Angeles. But Geordie, as he prefers to be called, is not your typical tycoon. One of his best friends says, "If you saw him on the street, you would want to give him a buck."

Hormel's long, scraggly grey hair hangs limply past his shoulders. His missing front teeth are only somewhat covered by his bushy mustache and full grey beard. Too rich to wear uncomfortable clothes, he is usually seen in jogging suits. Due to painful feet, he goes most places in big soft moon boots. He has filled the mansion with used furniture. The complex is dotted with a variety of hand-lettered notes and signs, such as "Please don't use electricity between 5 and 9 am and pm unless you really have to,"—understandable since the electricity bill is said to be as high as $8,000.

In spite of being born to luxury, Geordie has not taken an easy, straight path in life. He was named after his grandfather, the founder of the Geo. A. Hormel & Co. Meatpacking empire. His father, Jay C. Hormel, developed the well-known little blue tin of processed pork, Spam.

Typical of Midwestern "old money" millionaires, the family was not ostentatious. He and his two younger brothers were instilled with a sense of social responsibility and admonished to set an example for others, Hormel recalled. The brothers continue to be involved in social and charitable causes, especially environmental preservation.

"I was brought up to be a butcher," Hormel said. "Up until my father died, that was the only option I knew I had."

When Geordie Hormel was a young man back in the 1950's, the meatpacking business wasn't so profitable. So the self-taught jazz pianist went off to California after a stint with the Coast Guard.

He traveled to Las Vegas to marry popular French actress, Leslie Caron, in 1951 while he was in the service. Caron starred in *Gigi, Fanny* and *An American in Paris*. They divorced in 1954. In 1956, Hormel again was married in Las Vegas, this time to Texas beauty Mary Lou Wadsworth. Sammy Davis Jr. was the best man.

Hormel had a commission in the Army Reserves, but classmates from military school were being killed in the Korean War. Hormel didn't like the killing part. "So I joined the Coast Guard thinking that they guarded the coast," he said, chuckling at his own naivete. "I didn't know they cleared the beaches for the Marines." Instead of clearing beaches, he helped establish a Coast Guard band. He also promoted a couple of Coast Guard Welfare Fund concerts, one featuring his former boss, Lawrence Welk. After his discharge, Hormel went back to playing the piano with Los Angeles area jazz and be-bop bands.

Hormel started his first recording studio, which was not successful, and then composed a musical score for a movie that was never produced. He had the music recorded, but since he had no formal music training, he ended up with a library of various sounds. He rented out a portion of this pre-recorded original music for a Playhouse 90 television show and discovered the lucrative market of performance royalties. By 1956 he had music on at least half of all the shows on TV, so he made his money back which he had lost with the recording studio.

With money in his pocket, he went back to Minnesota and bought the family estate, turning it into a hotel-restaurant-conference center.

"That was very successful until I got a divorce," Hormel said. "The lawyers cut the house in half, so I had to sell it in about 1960."

Broke again, he ended up in a piano bar in Portland, Oregon. From there, he traveled the country, playing in concerts and nightclubs, finally ending up again in Los Angeles. Hormel got a bank loan and started his Village Recorder studio. He also got married for the third time, in 1968, to Nancy Friedman. That lasted six years.

During the 1970's, Village Recorder was the place to cut a record. Frank Sinatra, Barbra Streisand, Bob Dylan, the Rolling Stones, and Frank Zappa, among others, recorded there.

Fleetwood Mac sort of lived there for a year while recording an album.

After ten years of sixteen hour days, Hormel said he took a break from the studio. The last ten years before moving to Phoenix Geordie worked on various ecological projects.

He decided he could afford the 52,000 square foot McCune Mansion shortly after his mother died and he discovered she had left behind $40 million.

"I didn't know my mother had money," Hormel said. "I was paying for her servants and her household expenses and stuff like that because she was always selling carpets and things. I thought she was house poor."

He intended to transform the 30 year old house on Sugarloaf Mountain into a think tank where executives could share ideas on environmental technology. But money can't buy everything, such as a zoning variance in a luxurious residential area of Paradise Valley.

"When I came here, I didn't intend to move here," Hormel said to *Arizona Republic* reporter Phyllis Gillespie. "I had never been to Phoenix. I only knew about this house. When I learned I couldn't do anything with it, I could have left, but all of a sudden, I discovered that I loved it here. I don't like the desert, but the people are just wonderful. I just love the people here. I've never been anywhere where I've met so many nice, wonderful people."

So, he and his fourth wife, Jamie, 26, and their entourage of friends and family retainers loaded themselves into Hormel's touring bus and moved into the 20 bedroom, 26 bathroom mansion.

The place is always full. Hormel's youngest daughter, five year old Geri, lives there and has a nanny. Then, there's the cook, the driver, the security guards, the cleaning people, recording technicians and their families. Two engineers look after the air-conditioning system.

Hormel's adult children—a son and two daughters—and five grandchildren are frequent visitors, as are friends and musicians from California.

"Having lived in hotels so much, I really like this atmosphere," he said. "I think it's really criminal to take a place like this and say only one family can live in it."

Hormel and his wife use the servants' quarters while the 3,000 square-foot master suite has become somewhat of a dormitory with six beds sprinkled around it. All the furniture in the house was purchased used from Terri's Consignment World.

Arizonans who have met Hormel generally like him, too. At first, people wondered about him because of his long hair, but now he's accepted into the Valley's high society, said Kathy Shocket, who writes society news for *The Arizona Republic*. "His name on an invitation is a prestigious sign now," Shocket said in an article in the *Arizona Republic*. "People want to say, 'We have the Hormels coming.' It's very in. People will ask me how they can meet him. And a lot of people will ask, 'How can we get him to donate to our cause?' because he's a new face in town with a lot of dollars."

Hormel has been generous with his money, Shocket said, but neighbors especially are taking a genuine shine to the couple.

Maybe it's Hormel's irreverent sense of humor which is most likely to make himself the butt of a joke. "I guess I'll just keep calling this place the McCune Mansion," he likes to jest. "I would love to call it the Hormel House and put a sign on the roof and then have someone shoot out the m-e-l, but the town of Paradise Valley wouldn't go for that."

Some of Hormel's favorite neighbors are former U. S. Senator Barry Goldwater and his wife, Susan.

"His wife is just wonderful," Hormel said. "She put me in shoes. My feet were such that I couldn't wear shoes. I wear these (moon boots) all the time. She actually got me to face some painful things in my old age. She's a wonderful person."

Hormel endeared himself to Arizona preservationists when he rescued the Wrigley Mansion from possible destruction. Hormel bought the Wrigley Mansion, which already had been a money-losing club, against the advice of his lawyers. He went through three managers in a short period of time. It was reported in 1993 that the private club was losing $200,000 a month.

Some members of the private Mansion Club felt that perhaps the prestigious image of the club was slipping. One woman called to complain about an old long-haired guy hanging around the dining room. Classic Lesson: Don't judge a book by it's cover.

∽∽∽∽∽∽∽∽∽∽∽

The McCune Mansion is a private home located in Paradise Valley

McCune Mansion.

Maricopa County Courthouse

"You Have the Right to Remain Silent..."
1966

Nearly every TV cops and robbers story contains the lines,
"You have the right to remain silent. If you give up that right,
anything you say can and will be used against you in a court
of law. You have the right to an attorney. . ."

Ernesto Arturo Miranda's name has become well known thanks to a
U.S. Supreme Court ruling thirty years ago that greatly expanded consti-
tutional protections against self-incrimination and created sweeping
restrictions on how police can question suspects in custody.

Of course, it was his lawyers, not Miranda, who were responsible for
the June 13, 1966, ruling that requires police to tell arrested suspects
that they have certain rights. The Supreme Court's *Miranda* decision

actually involved appeals from four defendants across the country, all challenging the legality of how police got confessions. Because the name Miranda alphabetically preceded those of the other defendants (Stewart, Vignera and Westover), the ruling has come to be known as the *Miranda* decision.

Barry Silverman, a U.S. Magistrate, who as a student interviewed Miranda said, "He was a guy who was a troublemaker in school, a troublemaker in the service, and a troublemaker in prison. He was not a very appealing human being. Then this happened. The role he played in it affected him, and he sort of had to live up to it. It seemed like he wanted to be deserving of having made legal history."

Miranda was arrested in March, 1963, in Phoenix and admitted to kidnaping and raping an 18 year old woman. His signed confession ended with a statement saying that his confession was "made voluntarily...and with full knowledge of my legal rights." Based on his confession, Miranda was convicted and sentenced to 20 to 30 years in prison.

But the Supreme Court ordered a new trial. The Court ruled that suspects in police custody specifically must be told of their right to remain silent and to have a lawyer with them during questioning before answering any police questions.

FCI LOMPOC, CALIF
1119 - LC
5-26-60

Ernesto Miranda.

Miranda went to court again in 1967. Without his confession as evidence, he was once again convicted and sentenced to 20 to 30 years in prison. After his parole in 1973, Miranda became a street celebrity. He managed to make a few bucks by charging for his autograph on Miranda-warning cards.

His notoriety led Maricopa County Superior Court Judge Philip Marquardt to sequester the jury when Miranda was retried for a 1962 robbery/kidnaping. The judge even referred to Miranda by a pseudonym, Jose Gomez. The jurors were told of his real identity after convicting him.

Miranda's troubled life ended on an ironic note. In January, 1976, he was stabbed to death in a Phoenix bar during a fight over money. He was 34 years old. His suspected killer was "Mirandized" when he was arrested. Taking the advice of the arresting officers, he refused to talk. There was never a conviction and Miranda's killer walked away free.

∽∽∽∽∽∽∽∽∽∽∽∽

The Maricopa County Courthouse is a public building in downtown Phoenix. In 1990 the old building underwent a $1.8 million restoration. The fifth floor jail, where Ernesto Miranda was held, has been left intact, a chilling reminder of old style lockups. The building is open to the public from 8:00 a.m. to 5:00 p.m. Monday through Friday for self-guided tours. For more information call (602) 261-8699.

Camelback Castle

From Medieval Castle to Yee Haw
1970's

"Every night I come home...and say...'Thank you, Lord'"

Dr. Mort Copenhaver spent twelve long years building his very own 8,000 square-foot castle by hand, stone by stone. Every day he was at the building site, slowly watching the walls rise on his castle, his dream home. Overlooking the city, 1,200 feet above the street, Copenhaver's castle was built on eight levels and has seventeen rooms including five bedrooms, a dining hall, living room, family room...called a great room, billiard room, library, study and maid's quarters, plus seven bathrooms. Adding whimsy and intrigue to his castle are secret passageways, countless nooks and crannies, and even a dungeon which doubles for the bar.

Copenhaver would slave away on his castle every morning. Around noon he would shower, change clothes, and work in his orthodontist office all afternoon and into the early evening. Back home after work he would be up until two or three a.m. at his drawing board, dreaming up new additions and modifications to his castle. He remembers that he never slept more than two or three hours a night during those years. In the evenings he was reading up on architecture and building, problem-solving by picking people's brains, and keeping up with all the new building code changes.

Dr. Copenhaver has remarked that ever since he was a child he wanted to build a castle. After he grew up and established himself in his profession, he started looking for a lot on which he could make his dream come true.

In 1966 Copenhaver found a perfect two-acre parcel of land high up on the side of Camelback Mountain. It wouldn't have looked so perfect to most people because there wasn't a flat space to be seen. The land sloped up at a dauntingly sharp angle. At 2,500 feet above the valley floor, his castle home would become the highest home by elevation in the entire area. There will never be any homes built higher either, since the rest of the mountains in the area have now been protected from further development.

Having grown up on a Colorado ranch, he was filled with the assurance that he could do things himself. He was right. The first thing he had to do was build a 350 foot road up the steep incline to the level that he had chosen as his building site. Using a bulldozer and old mining equipment, he gained the experience building the road that he would need to perform his greatest feat of all: cutting the stones for his castle directly from the mountain on which the castle would stand.

The first year he built 18 inches of road. Legal battles with a neighbor, as well as the city of Phoenix, plus a near death accident slowed him down. One day while Copenhaver was working on his road the bulldozer exploded and he was severely burned. "I drove myself to the hospital," he said. "I was in the hospital for over a month."

Copenhaver won't say how much the house cost to build, but he has admitted the road up to the house cost around one-half million dollars. In addition to money, it has been said the castle cost him one wife and two live-in girlfriends.

Copenhaver could be described as a maverick, a wild young thing who liked to make his own way in the world. By the time he was 18, he was married and a father. Graduating from the University of Kansas City's dental school, he set up a private practice in Phoenix and soon divorced the wife who saw him through school. Widely known as a "man about town," he has competed in ski and speedboat races. Adding to his reputation for social adventure, he only vaguely remembers a Las Vegas marriage to a legal secretary that lasted all of three days, according to a 1978 article from People Magazine.

Copenhaver's own hard work plus his ability to barter helped his dream house become a reality. He made a deal with Mexican laborers for minimal wages plus board to do some of the labor on the stone house. He traded his professional services with an electrician and a plumber who needed dental work. He operated his own tractors and learned the art of stone cutting.

"It's amazing how, if you hit a rock with a sledgehammer just right, it breaks the way you want," said Copenhaver. "It's sort of a knack you learn."

"The stone was very hard granite," he said. "It's very tough on your hands. A lot of my friends were worried that I'd lose a finger or do permanent damage to my hands...which would have been disastrous for a dentist." Undaunted, Copenhaver used no machinery to lift his stones into place. Each stone was cut small enough for him to handle and he laid every one in position by hand. He figured each stone weighed about 100 pounds. Because the rock was blasted and cut directly from Camelback Mountain, it blends in with the mountain and becomes one with the scenery. Copenhaver's carefully kept records show that he used nearly 50,000 bags of cement, mixed in a proportion of six parts sand and rock to one part cement.

In addition to bartering, Copenhaver fine tuned his bargain hunting skills. Some of the iron balconies were salvaged from the old Fox Movie Theatre before it was demolished to build the city bus station. The bar was constructed of brick obtained from an old hacienda in south Phoenix. The entrance doors to the castle and all of the bedroom doors were constructed from wood originally part of the Santa Fe stockyards in Flagstaff. The stockyards were built at the turn of the century and were torn down only a few years ago.

As a guest descends the stairs to the lower levels (there are ten different levels throughout the castle), he notices a wall of white mineral rock on his left. The rocks were collected by Dr. Copenhaver over the years and each has a personal memory and story attached to it. This particular wall is estimated to weigh one and one half tons.

In contrast to its medieval appearance, the castle has all of the most modern conveniences. An up-to-date kitchen is adjacent to the dining area. The great room features a Jacuzzi to seat twenty with a roof that retracts to view the night sky. With eighteen inch thick rock walls, the castle stays comfortable year round with very little help from the solar heating and cooling systems.

In 1979, twelve years after turning over the first shovel of dirt, Dr. Copenhaver moved into his dream home. He hosted lavish parties in his castle and was a shooting star on the Phoenix social scene. He lost it all less than ten years later.

Copenhaver had taken out a second mortgage on the castle to pay off creditors of his company, DentaHealth, which advertised and sold dental franchises. DentaHealth's expansion exceeded its reach, and it went into bankruptcy in 1987. Seeing troubled waters ahead, Copenhaver put his castle up for sale in March, 1985, for $7 million. That summer, he rejected an offer from a group of Nevada doctors for $5.8 million. By July, 1987, the U. S. Bankruptcy Court listed the asking price as $2.5 million. In June, 1989, Copenhaver Castle was sold to Jerry Mitchell, owner of Krazy Horse Ranch, for $985,000.

"I played polo with Mort (Copenhaver), and he was my friend, so there's a lot of sentimentality tied up in this," Jerry said. "I think that him losing the castle hurt me almost worse than him."

Mitchell said he was a frequent guest at the large parties at the castle and enjoyed the dramatic view of the city below.

"And I always loved the place, but I never thought that one day I would own it." Jerry said. "I stole it for a fraction of what it's worth. It took a lot of bulldogging, but I finally got it done."

Jerry Mitchell enjoys purchasing the unusual. Mitchell, with a partner, Jim Paul, built Rawhide, a Western town located in north Scottsdale. They envisioned it as a place where visitors could step back 100 years and feel what it was like to live on the frontier in the Arizona Territory.

Jerry also recently enjoyed fixing up a ranch in Branson, Missouri, which he turned into a summertime, western-style tourist attraction. The resort was built in two sections with a lake in the middle. Guests could visit the two separate parts of the resort by either a stagecoach ride, or a train ride. He purchased the entire train system which was used in the movie, *The Blue and The Gray*, and moved it to Branson for his resort visitors. After fixing up the resort, Mitchell sold it to investors who promptly turned it into a gravel pit. Jerry still owns the train and is contemplating what he'll do with it.

Jerry enjoys life and especially enjoys life in Arizona. He says, with his pretty girlfriend, Jennifer, standing by his side, "If I didn't live here, I'd move here." Growing up in west Texas, he is glad to be away from that part of the country that boasts severe winters, muggy summers and lots of mosquitoes.

At his Krazy Horse Ranch in Scottsdale he rents horses for trail rides, breakfast rides and overnighters. Jerry owns about six or seven ranches in Arizona, New Mexico and Texas. He claims to own around 150 to 200 cowboy boots, but he says he's lost count now. He keeps around 150 at the castle, and then each ranch is equipped with clothes and boots so he can travel light.

Seemingly fearless, Mitchell lives high and drives fast. He loves to compete. He has owned a dragstrip, raced funny cars, snow-skied, water-skied and enjoys hang gliding and flying Ultralights. His dare-devil nature has beat up his body over the years. He has crash-landed airplanes, broken his leg in four places playing polo, broken his back several times and fractured a few ribs.

"I've had 150 broken bones, and I've broken each one of my arms five times and each one of my legs five times," Mitchell said.

Jerry says that he likes anything that is different or original. The castle appealed to him because of its unique nature. Before Jerry took possession, the bank held an auction and stripped the castle of all of the medieval furnishings which Mort had so lovingly collected. Gone were the oversized, ornate chairs, armor, and torture instruments. Gone were the doors, lamp posts and light fixtures. Jerry purchased the castle stripped to the rock walls. Because Jerry had collected western art and furnishings all of his life, and the cowboy life is what he has lived, the once medieval castle has been turned into a cowboy castle. Surprisingly, it works.

Walking through the heavy wooden doors, the visitor enters at the highest level of the house and sees a breathtaking view of the lower family room/living room areas and out through the two-storied arched windows to the city below. To the left is the 20 person Jacuzzi tucked into the far edge of the family room on the lower level. The blue-tiled, still water looks invitingly like a reflecting pond. Along with taking out a wall at the entrance level, he created a white marble floored balcony where the guests can pause and enjoy the view of the rooms below. The balcony now successfully hides the pool motor and equipment for the Jacuzzi which formerly sat out in the room.

Directly in front of the entry is a perfect place to display Jerry's many trophies, awards and memorabilia...trophy saddles, polo awards, belt-buckles from Rawhide and other mementos which reflect his taste and hobbies.

Hanging above the trophy display is a huge, stuffed head of an African water buffalo which serves as a hat rack. Jerry loves to tell the story of his African safari adventure and his encounter with the 2,400 pound water buffalo. The huge beast went on a rampage and attacked several of the jeeps. Snorting loudly, the animal tore off a fender of one jeep and completely turned over the other one.

Wryly, Jerry says, "Just before pulling the trigger I said, 'He wasn't on my list, but now he is.' "

Thinking back on the days when he first moved into the castle and remodeled, Jerry does a perfect imitation of Snagglepuss, the cartoon cat, when he quotes himself as saying to the workers, "Slow the forward motion.... Like maybe even stop." By the time he had managed to slow the forward motion, he had spent another $550,000 inside the castle painting and adding white marble floors.

Painting the former brown walls and ceilings white adds a lightness to the rock house and also provides a pleasing backdrop to the exquisite western artwork which Jerry proudly displays throughout his home. Western bronzes, authentic Indian rugs, Russells and Remingtons are displayed on antique furniture pieces next to the works of well known local artists and Jerry's chaps. Adding to the western flavor is a 2" diameter rope trim at the windows.

At the base of the stairs in the living room is a 100 year-old craps table from the Stockman's Hotel in Elk Horn, Nevada. The old hotel burned down shortly after Jerry rescued the gaming table. Another purchase which pleases Jerry is the 100 year-old billiard table located in its own room down a half flight of stairs from the living room. Off the billiard room is the famous dungeon, no longer spooky with torture instruments, but a solid rock, windowless room, lit by red lights, western sconces, and colorful neon beer signs. It's whimsical, it's fun, and it's a party waiting to happen.

Born and raised in West Texas, Jerry's fundamental Christian roots define the man today. He could be described as an entrepreneur, a champion polo-player, a rancher, an investor, an art-collector, a wheeler - dealer, and a developer of the unusual. Typical of his heritage, Jerry often quotes one of his parents. "M' Mama always tol' me..." His mama is a wise woman who steered him right, too. In addition, he has a winning, likeable manner of putting a guest at ease and making each new acquaintance feel like an old friend.

One suspects that lurking in back of all that Texas-good-ole-boy exterior is the mind of a very shrewd businessman. Driven by a strict inner code of business ethics, he has a strong sense of when "a deal" is good, and when to back off.

"When you get up in the morning and look out the windows from up here, if you don't have inspiration, then you don't have any," Jerry says, "and I'm an Inspiration Boy. I run on inspiration. If a deal is…if I don't like it, or don't enjoy doing it, then I just don't do it. And I don't want anybody hurt. If I've got a business deal and somebody's getting hurt in it somewhere, then it's no good. But where you have a deal where everybody gains, everybody does good, then that's the kind of deals you want."

Jerry is driven by fun. Life is fun for him and Jennifer. They show off the three guest rooms with pride and obviously delighted in decorating them. Each room has its own theme. First is the Ranch Room with its cowboy decor. The next guest room is the Polo Room, announced by the polo mallets hung on the door. The third room is the Jungle Room with stuffed lions on the bed and a giraffe shower curtain.

Jennifer doesn't seem to know that she has captured the heart of a very wealthy man. Seeing a picture of a kitchen in a decorating magazine, she asked Jerry to buy her some hunter green paint so she could paint the kitchen cupboards. So far she has painted five coats herself. Living in a castle hasn't seemed to convince her that she could hire that done. Taking pride in the castle and making it their home, she loves doing these things herself. She loves turning her dream of a hunter green and white pine kitchen into a reality.

Jerry Mitchell and Jennifer Tuzzolino in their kitchen.

True to his enjoyment of buying the unusual, Jerry's latest project has been the purchase and remodeling of an old stage stop and dude ranch. Located in New River, the Wrangler's Roost has been a relatively unknown dude ranch where Teddy Roosevelt as well as the Kennedys have enjoyed the western life. The rooms have been remodeled and there is a western steak house soon to be open to the public. Wrangler's Roost offers trail rides and overnights on the desert to its guests. "I'm really excited about this," Jerry says. "It's the West's most authentic dude ranch. It was the original stagestop between Prescott and Phoenix."

When asked what he likes best about living in a castle, Jerry replied, "The good Lord gave it to me. Every night I come home and look up here at the castle and say, 'Why me, Lord? Thank you, Lord, but why me? What did I ever do?' I never get used to it. Every night when I drive up and it's all lit up...I just appreciate it everyday."

∽∽∽∽∽∽∽∽∽∽∽

Camelback Castle is a private residence on the side of Camelback Mountain.

For more information about Wrangler's Roost Dude Ranch and Restaurant, call (602) 465-9559.

Camelback Castle.

Arcosanti

The Utopian Dream of a Visionary
1970

"As urban architecture, Arcosanti is probably the most important experiment undertaken in our lifetime." Newsweek

The soft clanging of bronze wind bells moved by the gentle warm breeze of the high Arizona mesa and the innovative structures clinging to the edge of the cliff above a dry arroyo all create an atmosphere of...what? A futuristic city? The dream world of a kook? An extraordinary place where one man's vision is ever so slowly becoming a reality?

Paolo Soleri's concept of a better society, Arcosanti, is gradually being created amidst the prickly pear cactus in central Arizona. Twenty years ago the project was described as a "slumbering dream," but not anymore. Stop by any day during the winter months when the project is really humming and you will see architectural students working on the buildings, Elderhostel participants attending classes, music and dance students preparing for concerts as well as some of the over 60,000 visitors a year who tour the facility.

Paolo Soleri was born in Turin, Italy, where he received his doctor of architecture degree with highest honors from the Torino Polytechnico in 1946. He studied with Frank Lloyd Wright in the late 1940's. Soleri's dream began to take form in the early 1970's when he and a group of dedicated apprentices began to build avant-garde structures in the high desert near Cordes Junction, 65 miles north of Phoenix. The complex is to eventually be a self-sustaining town of 7,000 people in a series of densely populated structures on a scant 15 acres of ground. One structure is to be 25 stories high.

Dr. Paolo Soleri.

For a short time in the 1970's and 80's the work slowed to a crawl. It was tough to get support due to the wall of scepticism and even ridicule over Soleri's blueprints for a futuristic new kind of city.

Today Arcosanti stands only 3% completed. The resident population can get as high as 150 during the height of the summer, including workers, students and apprentices. Soleri would like to have seen 1,000 workers by now.

The annual construction budget for materials alone, not including labor or overhead, runs an average of $200,000. One third of the income is produced by selling the bronze and ceramic wind bells which have become world renown. Individually designed and cast, the bells are an attractive and popular addition to thousands of homes. The bells are priced from $20 for a small single bell, to tens of thousands of dollars for the large, ornate, one of a kind art pieces. The bells are sold at Arcosanti, and Cosanti, Soleri's first unique structure in Paradise Valley, as well as 300 retail outlets around the world.

It has been estimated that the Arcosanti as envisioned would cost as much as $1.5 billion to complete, but any grouping of buildings being built at the rate of 3% per 25 years is difficult to cost out. Lack of funding has been the major factor in the slow growth of the project. In addition to the income from the wind bells, the construction of Arcosanti is supported by donations and tuition from the educational programs.

For Soleri, the ideal city would be one without cars, where people would not perceive a need for four-bedroom suburban homes surrounded by their own turf. Soleri sees the desire for single family homes as the root of many of society's problems. He says that "once you have a big house, you have an avalanche of goodies to put into it." You end up with "unlimited consumption and environmental mediocrity." Instead, Soleri sees Americans happily living and working in one vast, dense, beehive-like structure, of which Arcosanti is only a tiny model.

"Arcology" is the term used by Paolo Soleri to describe the concept of architecture and ecology coherently working as one integral process. Arcosanti is a prototype of Soleri arcology. Arcology suggests that cities be designed to maximize the interaction and accessibility associated with an urban environment; minimize the use of energy, raw materials and land, reducing waste and environmental pollution; and allow interaction with the surrounding natural environment.

Soleri envisions a city called Novanoah I—a floating city shaped like a snowflake, home for 400,000 people all dedicated to studying the seas. Also picture Hexahedron—two pyramids mated together for 170,000 people. The population density would be 1,200 per acre. The density of New York City is 33 people per acre.

A future project for Arcosanti includes Via Deliziosa, a paved and ever-changing road designed and painted by artists which will connect Arcosanti to its surrounding communities. Via Deliziosa has been awarded a planning grant from the National Endowment for the Arts. It is one of the largest environmental projects on the theme of endangered species. The Arcosanti Foundation is seeking additional funding to begin actual construction on the roadway.

Soleri has now gained not only acceptance within the architectural community, but has achieved the status of an honored elder states-man. Architects, academicians and leaders in a variety of fields visit Paolo Soleri and Arcosanti each year. Soleri is invited to speak at and present designs to international forums dealing with architecture and the environment, and is invited by faculty and students around the world to speak at universities. He has been awarded three honorary doctorates and in 1996 became an honorary Fellow of the British Royal Institute of Architects. Many of his ideas about archology, once dismissed as futuristic babble, are now routinely incorporated into urban planning and architectural dialogue. Today density, multi-use facilities, conservation and recycling are concepts which are taken for granted as necessary components of good city design.

Soleri dislikes the terms "utopian," "dreamer" and "visionary" being applied to his work. He prefers to be called a realist. "I'm suggesting the American dream needs to be revised," Soleri states. "It can't go very far. If we begin to export that dream as good democrats, it will offer disaster for the whole planet."

$$\sim\sim\sim\sim\sim\sim\sim\sim\sim\sim$$

Arcosanti is located 65 miles north of Phoenix at Cordes Junction on I17. The Visitor Center is open seven days a week from 9:00 a.m. to 5:00 p.m. Tours are on the hour from 10:00 a.m. to 5:00 p.m. Admission fee for tours is by donation. There is a bakery open from 8:30 a.m. to 4:00 p.m. In addition to the breads, cookies, brownies, etc., heartier fare is often available between noon and closing (home made mini-pizzas, rolls stuffed with meats and cheeses, etc.) The bakery also offers a variety of beverages. Call (520)632-7135 for information. Call from Phoenix 254-5309.

Shungopavi -
Second Mesa

The Theft Which Was a Murder
1977

*"You cannot become a man in the eyes of the tribe
now,...perhaps never."*

On that warm summer night in 1977, Jimmy Lee Hinton and Randy Morris thought they were merely stealing Hopi religious relics. According to an article in the *Arizona Republic*, ransacking sacred Hopi burial plots was something they had done since they were teenagers and they evidently thought nothing of it. Stealing from the Hopi was simply a way to make an easy buck to them. But this evening was special. This evening, in the eyes of the Hopi, they were committing murder.

The relationship of the Hopi to the Anglo has been marred by a constant chipping away of the Hopi way of life and religion. The

Spanish came to the Hopi villages, high atop windy, lonely mesas, seeking gold which was not there. The Hopi religion predicts the return of a long-lost white brother named Pahana, and so they welcomed their white conquerors.

The Spanish soon found that the Indian cultures were nearly impossible to conquer since they did not build large cities to overrun, nor did they have a president or commander with whom to make a treaty. The best way to conquer the native tribes would be to assimilate them and make Catholics of them. The Spanish immediately sent priests to stamp out the Hopi religion.

During the Great Missionary Period in the early 1680's, the Spanish *padres* traveled extensively throughout the southwest bringing a great deal of good to the Indian tribes.

They taught them animal husbandry and brought them cattle and horses. They also expected them to provide a labor force for Spanish settlements. The Hopi were able to accept the new religion of the *padres* as long as they were able to continue their own ceremonies and beliefs. The *padres* could not accept this. The practice of their native religion was strictly forbidden and the Hopi religious leaders were imprisoned or killed. Soldiers intruded into sacred kivas and destroyed religious articles.

In 1680 the Pueblo Indians of what is now northern New Mexico and Arizona revolted from this oppression in the greatest Indian revolt in American history. In one day, the great pueblos rose up against their padres and slaughtered them. Father Garces, one of the great *padres* of southern Arizona said, "We have failed. It is not because we haven't tried. It is because we have not understood." His words ring true to this day.

The first anthropologists to study the Hopi people described them as gentle, patient people. The Hopi, their name meaning "peace," believe that their mission as a people is to pray for the peace and well-being of all mankind. They still pray for peace even as the assault on their faith continues. Not since the Spanish invasion had so much damage been done to the Hopi people until two cowboys from

Safford went sneaking around the base of Second Mesa, upon which the Hopi village of Shungopavi rests.

Hinton and Morris, young cowboys in their early twenties were good at digging up rare Indian pottery and were looking for more that July day in 1977. They had been out most of the day, and Hinton wore a headband, helping him to pass for Hopi. As the setting sun highlighted a cave in front of them, the two young men tossed the rocks aside to investigate. Inside the small cave were four crudely carved wooden objects, club shaped characters, lying on a bed of feathers.

The three foot-long carvings were Corn Maiden, one of the most sacred and fundamental of all Hopi gods, her husband and their daughter, all looking as if they were asleep on the soft bed of feathers and prayer sticks. Their heads rested on a log pillow. In addition was a root, twisted into a figure eight who was Dawn Woman, resting upright against the wall of the cave, as if she were looking after the other three. They had been gently placed in the cave to rest for four years by the religious leaders of Shungopavi.

Hinton, who had passed time as a teenager breaking up ancient Indian pottery shards with a slingshot, called Morris over to see what a great find they'd stumbled onto. They decided to come back the next evening.

The two young men skulked back after dark with the light of small penlights to guide them. Morris crept into the cave and handed the carved figures out to Hinton.

Fearful of being caught, they dashed back down the side of the mesa. They stashed the deities like so much cordwood under a bush along the dirt road and walked back to their car. Knowing they were guilty of a crime, they hid behind rocks and bushes whenever headlights approached.

Driving back to the site where they had left the idols, they began to load them into the back of the car, trying to hide them under their gear. They were suddenly startled by a Hopi game warden who drove up. Hinton and Morris lied and convinced the warden they were out of brake fluid. Generously, he gave them some and they made their way across the dusty reservation roads to Winslow. Later they discovered that they had left the smallest of the four *taalawtumsi*, Corn Maiden's child, beneath the bush.

Pueblo village.

Hinton and Morris suspected that they had stolen some kind of old kachina doll. What they didn't realize was they had stolen the heart of the Hopi religion. The presence of the *taalawtumsi* (pronounced tah-LAO-toom-see) is a requirement at the secret rite of Astotokya. It is during this ceremony that the young men of the Hopi tribe become adults in the mysterious Night of the Washing of the Hair. This ceremony, held the winter before, was only performed every four years. Without the vital *taalawtumsi*, the ceremony couldn't be performed at all. Without the ceremony there would be no more young men entered into the Hopi way.

Consider the outcry if there would be no more bar mitzvahs allowed. Or consider the impact on the Christian churches if no more baptisms could be held.

This theft struck at the very core of the Hopi existence. Without being initiated into the Hopi way, a young man is unable to participate in ceremonies heralding the planting of corn and the request for rain. Without initiated Hopi men, the Hopi way of life, the core of their identity, would die.

Upon discovering the theft, the Hopi leaders struggled for six months with the devastating, brutal effects. The *taalawtumsi* were too sacred even to tell the white police about. They had never been spoken of outside of the sacred ceremonies. They finally chose to speak to former Tribal Chairman Ivan Sidney, who was then Hopi Chief of Police.

Sidney, who is a Christian, felt torn between two religions. He also knew the future of the Hopi people was at stake. He knew Shungopavi was the last village holding all of the yearly religious ceremonies, and if this was gone, their religion would be gone forever.

Sidney remarked to *Arizona Republic* reporter Richard Robertson, "I was afraid. I had to pray a lot. In Hopi religion there is a penalty for misuse of these idols...death; a prolonged, real painful death."

Hinton and Morris were unaware of their penalty. They were joined by Hinton's best friend, Stanley Olsen, and together they visited the galleries of Scottsdale trying to sell their goods. They have remarked that not once were they asked if the idols were stolen. Not one of the gallery owners felt it was appropriate to alert authorities that two Safford cowboys were trying to peddle Indian artifacts for $50,000.

By the end of 1978 they showed the objects to a well known photographer who has had many of his photographs of Indians and their culture printed in the *Arizona Highways*. He took pictures of the objects, the only ones in existence, but told the two men that he really didn't recognize the wooden clubs as anything he'd seen before. He promised to send copies of the pictures to other experts to see if they could be identified. They were not recognized by others because they were too sacred to ever be seen or even described to anyone outside of the initiated elders of Shungopavi.

Not only were the two thieves unable to identify what they had, but they weren't even able to peddle them. As the months went by, unaware of the penalty for disturbing the sacred objects, the three began to suffer setbacks. Morris was struck by a car while riding his motorcycle and nearly killed. He recovered but will never regain the use of his arm and leg. Hinton began suffering kidney, liver and gallbladder failure. Olsen went to prison three times for theft, illegal Indian-site excavation and endangerment.

After talking to a Chicago gallery owner, Hinton was told of the penalty attached to the figures and began to see a connection between his problems and the stolen objects. The men wrapped the centuries old *taalawtumsi* in a plastic garbage bag, stuffed them into an old refrigerator and buried them in the dirt of a chicken coop in Morris' back yard.

Word of the find got around the Indian-artifacts black market. Arthur Neblett, living in Ramah, New Mexico, told fellow collector Eugene Pyle about them. Pyle got in touch with Hinton and they agreed to meet behind a store near Safford in August, 1979. There Pyle paid $1,600 for the three *taalawtumsi*. Pyle later stated he thought they were probably just old kachina dolls.

Meanwhile, Hopi Police Chief Sidney decided to draw the FBI into the case. Sidney, being a man who straddled both worlds, was the perfect person to try to explain the sensitivity of the case to the Anglo agents of the FBI. At first, to the FBI, it appeared to be a case no more important than the theft of a television. They soon understood the devastation to the Hopi. In the grief of the disaster, traditional Hopi pointed their fingers at non-traditional Hopi, even accusing them of helping the thieves.

In late 1979 two young men who were caught digging for pottery in Hopi ruins offered information about one of the *taalawtumsi*. Under interrogation the man offered to take the authorities to one of the sacred objects in exchange for being released. The authorities summoned a medicine man to accompany them to the location. They walked about 10 feet from the dirt road and found Corn Maiden's Daughter under the bush where it had been left. The medicine man went straight to the bush and then started sobbing.

The elder kept repeating, "Quaqua, quaqua" (thank you, thank you). Upon returning to Shungopavi, he promptly called the elders of the village and took the sacred object back to its home in the kiva.

The young man didn't reveal to Sidney why he knew where the Corn Maiden's Daughter was. He didn't tell that his brother-in-law, Jimmy Lee Hinton, had drawn a map for him and asked him to go look for the idol.

The FBI pursued every lead, making inquiries of gallery owners, collectors, Indian experts and anyone else who might hear of the sale of the objects.

"I wasn't that worried in the beginning, but I kept hearing that people were out there trying to find them," Pyle said. He soon became afraid to have them. He was afraid to try to sell them, afraid of getting caught with them, and even more afraid of trying to give them back.

Sometime in late 1980 or early 1981, feeling that he was in "a mess of trouble," Pyle chopped the centuries old sacred objects into pieces with an ax and burned them in his wood stove. He remembers that the largest, the Husband of Corn Maiden, burned the hottest.

During the next two years, Morris, still on crutches from his motorcycle accident, was arrested on federal charges for illegal pot-hunting. Olsen and Hinton, who was recovering from gallbladder surgery, were sent to the Arizona state prison on drug charges. Neblett crashed his car and died after several months in a coma.

The FBI had run out of leads by the time Hinton was released from prison in 1981. Hinton decided to make another pot-hunting run to the Hopi mesas with two friends. They were digging at night when they got separated.

All at once, Hinton said he saw lights and heard all kinds of strange sounds. He said he was "a blubbering idiot" by the next morning. When the three men found each other they discovered that they had all had the same experience.

Hinton decided that he was cursed and that the only way to relieve himself from the curse was to go to the FBI and confess his part in the theft. Hinton, however, didn't know who had purchased the *taalawtumsi*.

The case stayed open for the next seven years, with no new leads. In the spring of 1990, the name of Eugene "Jinx" Pyle came up during an investigation of an unrelated case. It was soon thought that Pyle might have the missing objects.

Three years earlier Pyle had moved from Arizona to Oregon where he was raising Texas longhorn cattle on Pantera Ranch. Pyle admitted that he had been in possession of the Hopi gods, but he had chopped them up and burned them.

The FBI agent remarked, "Under our laws we were dealing with a theft, but to the Hopi it was tantamount to murder." To the Hopi they were more than just objects. To the Hopi the *taalawtumsi* hurt, they feel, they share human emotions. White man's laws do not adequately cover something many Hopi still regard as a homicide.

The FBI agents conferred with the Hopi leaders before deciding whether or not to press charges against Pyle. The meeting was terribly painful to all involved. Some of the religious leaders insisted that the *taalawtumsi* were not gone—they could still hear them crying and sighing. They felt Pyle was covering up their sale.

The FBI felt it would be difficult, if not impossible to attain a conviction. There was no proof that Pyle had ever been in possession of the objects, and the statute of limitations had run out long ago. However, the officials told Pyle they would not prosecute if he cooperated with the investigation and agreed to a polygraph test. He also agreed to tell what he knew to the Hopi tribal elders in hopes of achieving a "spiritual reconciliation."

After passing the polygraph test, arrangements were made for Pyle and the FBI agents to have a meeting on Second Mesa. The March day dawned cold, cloudy and windy as the men arrived at the Hopi Cultural Center, near Shungopavi, for breakfast. One of the tribal leaders approached their table and remarked, "You guys have a lot of nerve coming up here. You ever hear of Custer?"

After breakfast the three men approached the crowded Shungopavi meeting hall. The rock building, built of the stones of the mesa itself, was filled with adult Hopi males who had waited years to be able to call themselves men.

Pyle spoke with great remorse. He told the gathering that he had no idea at the time the importance of the *taalawtumsi* to the Hopi people. He greatly regretted that he had destroyed them. Gradually, as the meeting progressed, Pyle understood why the FBI insisted that he meet with the Hopi. It was the only way for them to begin to understand that their sacred *taalawtumsi* were gone forever.

Eight months later Randy Morris also traveled to Shungopavi to apologize. He was under no threat of prosecution like Pyle had been. He felt strongly that he needed to try to make amends. Even in prison Jimmy Lee Hinton felt the need to tell Indian inmates, though they were non-Hopi, about the theft. At first the Indians were so angry that Hinton thought they were going to attack him. But later, as their talks continued, they were able to forgive and even gave Hinton an amulet of peace. In addition, they invited him to their sweat lodge and made him an assistant pipe bearer in the native American Church, which is considered an honor.

In the intervening time the elders of Shungopavi agonized over the tough decision before them. Their choice was to either lose their religion completely, or go ahead with the initiation ceremony with just the Corn Maiden's Daughter. One driving factor was that the key priest was already 95 years old and soon knowledge of how to conduct the ceremony would be lost forever. The decision was made after much anguished discussion to resume the ceremonies. Many parents were eager to have their sons initiated into full manhood with the tribe. Some elders still felt the missing *taalawtumsi* were still alive and should be there. They said they felt the three *taalawtumsi* crying in the wind, crying to come home.

Sixty-three men, some in their thirties, were finally initiated into Hopi adulthood in November, 1992. In the ceremony they have the whole purpose of being Hopi given to them. It is like a book being opened up. Some of the men had waited to be called by their adult names for fifteen years.

Jimmy Lee Hinton says that it never occurred to him that his thieving was harming living Indian cultures or that it ruined sites that professional archeologists might want to document. He says he saw the light when he learned that his theft of the *taalawtumsi* almost destroyed the Hopi religion. Hinton says that even 17 years after the crime strange things still happen to him. Owls appearing, shadows, twinkling stars, unusual sounds at night, strange dreams—all are evidence to him that the Hopi gods have not forgiven.

"Hopi law is simple: Do a wrong against someone, and you will eventually pay for it."

No one was ever brought to a law court for the theft of the Hopi *taalawtumsi* or for their destruction.

Jimmy Lee Hinton said his health began to deteriorate a few months after he and Randy Morris stole the sacred objects. He served three prison terms on drug and burglary charges between 1981 and 1988. Hinton says that he is trying to purge himself of the curse which he is convinced has plagued his life.

Randy Morris was seriously injured in an accident when a car hit his motorcycle shortly after the theft. He suffered permanent damage to an arm and leg. He later was arrested for digging in an Indian ruin, but the charges were dismissed. Morris met with the Hopi leaders in 1991 to apologize for the theft.

Stanley Olsen helped Hinton and Morris look for buyers for the idols, carrying the *taalawtumsi* to various Scottsdale galleries. Olsen went to prison three times for theft, illegal excavation of an Indian site and endangerment between 1981 and 1992. He died in a traffic accident in 1992.

Don Stephenson helped Hinton, Morris and Olsen find buyers for various artifacts. Don says the Hopi themselves are to blame for the black market in Indian goods because they are willing to part with their works. Stephenson suffered a heart attack in 1993, and his wife was recovering from cancer.

Arthur Neblett found a buyer for the *taalawtumsi* in 1979. Neblett died in July 1983 at the age of 40 when he drove off a road in New Mexico.

Eugene "Jinx" Pyle destroyed the *taalawtumsi*. Pyle feels that the misfortunes which have happened to the others involved in the theft are merely coincidental.

ᘒᘒᘒᘒᘒᘒᘒᘒᘒᘒᘒᘒ

*The village of Shungopavi is located on 2nd Hopi mesa.
It is home to the most traditional of the Hopi clans.
The tribal leaders request no pictures be taken on the
entire Hopi homeland. The photographs in
this story were taken approximately
70 to 80 years ago.*

Helmsley Home

The "Queen of Mean" or Just Misunderstood?
1988

*The papers screamed for her head. The IRS wanted her in jail.
Disgruntled former employees couldn't wait to dump the dirt
on her in the tabloids. The year was 1988 and Leona Helmsley,
the self-appointed Queen of the Helmsley Hotels, was in trouble.*

Leona's husband, Harry Helmsley, personally created a dynasty in real estate. Harry was known as a shrewd but honest businessman. His world of holdings, which eventually included 27 luxury hotels, 50,000 apartments and controlling interest in the Empire State Building, created a net worth of $1.7 billion, according to *Forbes* magazine in 1996.

Harry was the son of a dry-goods buyer, born in 1909. Harry never attended college. His first job was as an office boy at age 16 at the real-estate company he eventually came to head, now known as Helmsley-Spear, Inc.

His first purchase, a run-down office building, cost $1,000 in 1936. Ten years later he sold it for $165,000.

The *Arizona Republic* quoted his longtime friend and employee Howard J. Rubenstein about Harry: "His ethical standard was really high. He always returned his phone calls, always would meet with people who wanted to see him. He wasn't pompous. He was very modest. He didn't have the trappings of wealth."

Leona began working for Harry as a successful real-estate broker in 1971. She was immediately drawn to him. Leona and Harry married in 1971. Leona took control of the six luxurious Helmsley hotels in New York and the Harley chain of hotels based in Cleveland. Ads featured Leona, dressed to the nines, stating that the quality would be of the best, because at a Helmsley "the Queen is in residence."

Leona and Harry lived a fairy tale life for the first years of their marriage. In 1988 Leona looked for another spot for a get-away for herself and Harry. She told her Phoenix real-estate broker, Ellie Shapiro, that she wanted to be up high and have a view. Her house in Connecticut was on a hill. In addition, the Helmsleys lived on the top floor of their hotel in New York. Leona loved having a view.

At first Ellie took Leona to the Walker McCune mansion in Paradise Valley which was for sale at that time for $30 million. Leona took one look and turned away, refusing to get out of the car. "Too ostentatious," she said.

Leona finally settled on a 26,000 square foot, three storied mansion located on a ridge of Mummy Mountain. It is said in Phoenix that if you are wealthy enough, you can live in the "tummy of the mummy." The house sits on 48 acres of prime land.

Leona ordered $2 million worth of changes to make the house suit herself and Harry. Wooden floors were ripped out and replaced by marble. The tennis court was taken out and a second swimming pool, indoors, was added.

The large first floor had been used by the previous owner as a garage for his boat, RV and other vehicles. Leona changed the former garage to four bedrooms, a kitchen and a living room for servants' quarters, still leaving room for a four-car garage. She put in an elevator, six feet by six feet, taking guests from the garage to the third floor. This was a necessity in order for the Helmsleys to live in a multi-storied home since Harry's health had begun to fail.

Their joy in their new home was short lived. In 1989 the IRS turned their magnifying glass on the Helmsley fortune. The IRS charged that the Helmsleys billed personal expenses for renovations to their home in Greenwich, Connecticut, as business expenses. When told they owed more in taxes, having already paid millions for that year, Harry got out a blank check and said, "How much do they need?" Rather than allow Harry to pay the back taxes owed, the IRS insisted on settling the matter in court.

Although the case regarded the improper use of deductions on their tax statement, soon Leona's personality was also on trial. Several unhappy former employees took the witness stand to finally have their chance to tell their stories about Leona. Her title bequeathed by the newspapers became the "Queen of Mean." Harry, in declining health at 83, was considered unfit to stand trial. He was fragile and totally dependent on Leona. Their friends felt Harry would not survive if Leona were taken away.

During that time Leona appeared on television in an interview with Barbara Walters. Leona had been sentenced to four years in prison, fined $7.1 million, and ordered to pay $1.7 million in back taxes for income-tax evasion. In addition she was ordered to do 750 hours of community service.

Leona, in an emotional visit, explained to Barbara Walters that she had no idea what was used as an income tax deduction on their statements and what wasn't. One can only imagine the complexity of the tax statement for an empire such as the Helmsleys. Leona said that she would be handed a large stack of tax papers and told where to sign. She trusted their accountants to handle their tax preparation in a legal and ethical way. Looking vulnerable and helpless, she appeared on TV in a pink bathrobe with almost no makeup.

According to reporter Tom Fitzpatrick of *New Times*, the IRS had an opportunity to show Mr. Every Day Citizen what happens when you try to get around their tax laws. The Helmsley case was as high profile as it gets. The message became clear…don't mess with the IRS. No matter how rich you are, no matter how powerful you are, no matter how mean you are, we will get you and we will take you down. Leona Helmsley, the Queen of Mean,entered the gates of the federal prison on April 15th, 1989. The date could hardly be coincidental.

The sentence was later reduced to 30 months. With good behavior she was released in 18 months. The fines were paid. Whether or not the required community service was fulfilled seems to be in question. Leona reported that she performed her community service by working at St. Joseph's Hospital and Medical Center in Phoenix. However, a hospital spokeswoman said that Leona was not listed as a volunteer and no one was aware of any community-service that she had done.

Harry did survive the imprisonment of his beloved Leona, but continued to become increasingly fragile and incompetent. During the last five years of their lives together, Leona didn't leave their home on the hill in Paradise Valley. She adored Harry to the end.

Harry died on Saturday, January 4, 1997. He was 87.

Through tears Leona said, "I lived a magical life with Harry. My fairy tale is over."

ɷɷɷɷɷɷɷɷɷɷɷ

The Helmsley home is a private residence in Paradise Valley

Paul Harvey's Home

A Real Cowboy
1990

"Well, it's a darn shame we don't dress western anymore."

While Paul Harvey, famous TV and radio commentator, lives most of the time in suburban Chicago, he and his wife also maintain a large home in the Biltmore Estates area of Phoenix.

Escaping a Chicago winter, they sought a reprieve at their home in Phoenix. One cool, cloudless day Paul's wife went shopping in Scottsdale. While she was gone, Paul began lamenting to himself about how people in Arizona don't really dress western anymore. He decided to remedy the situation.

Donning his best western shirt, bola tie and white cowboy hat, he was gussied up to meet his wife for a post-shopping lunch. Harvey was waiting for her along the sidewalk outside the store, when a tourist couple approached. "May we take a picture of you?" the lady excitedly asked.

Thinking he was recognized for his "...and now you know the rest of the story" commentaries, he kicked the sidewalk a little with an "Oh, garsh,...me?" demeanor.

The tourist's next comment brought him back down to earth.

Looking him over, she smiled and said, "We've been here two weeks and you're the first real cowboy we've seen!"

~~~~~~~~~~~~

The Paul Harvey home is a private residence in Phoenix.

Sky Harbor Airport

"You Have Huevos All Over Your Face."
1992

How do you say "embarrassed" in Español? You might have asked the officials in charge of the new English/Spanish signs at Sky Harbor Airport, but be sure to speak English, because their Spanish is not so bueno.

There was some discussion of a run for the border after the airport officials realized that the new Spanish language signs intended to help the Mexican visitors were threatening them with death instead.

The signs were posted throughout the airport in May of 1992 in preparation of the new service that America West Airlines was initiating to Mexico City.

One of the signs intended to request all visitors to declare all plants, fruits, vegetables, meats and birds. The last line of the sign was stated a little strongly: *Violadores serán finados.* Translation is—VIOLA-TORS WILL BE DECEASED.

Airport spokesman Rick Martinez said that they would make every effort to let the Mexican visitors know that they will not really be shot if all the procedures are not followed. Martinez, with his Hispanic sur-name, had a hard time living down the infamy of the death signs. But, he explained, in spite of his Spanish name he does not read or write Spanish, so relied on others for the translation.

Part of the problem stems from the differences in dialects. Although the word *violadores* means violators in some parts of Mexico, in other parts it means a rapist. In addition to other signs with embarrassingly wrong translations, misspellings and garbled tenses, one sign was pointed out as perhaps causing the most blushes. On one sign the tilde was left off above the "n" for the word año. Instead of meaning year, the word now meant,...well,...a personal part of the human anatomy better discussed with a proctologist.

೧೮೧೮೧೮೧೮೧೮೧೮

Sky Harbor Airport is a public building in Phoenix.

Barrow Neurological Institute

"Except for You, Dr. Sonntag."
1994

"We would like to see you right away in Paris."

Dr. Volker Sonntag received the unusual call while he was speaking to a group in Cartegeña, Colombia, in October, 1994. Could he come at once to Paris to consult on the illness of the wife of King Fahd of Saudi Arabia? Dr. Sonntag tried to beg off, but the royal family was very insistent. On a Friday, the day after his speaking obligations were over, he flew to Paris.

A private limousine met him at the airport and took him to the palace of King Fahd. There he found himself auditioning with four other internationally known neurosurgeons and orthopedists.

Sonntag laughingly said, "We were known as the Final Five."

The first wife of the king of Saudi Arabia (only westerners who don't know better refer to her as the Queen) was nearly a quadriplegic because of general health problems and an injured spinal cord. Only 68 years old, her body was so stiff it took several helpers to get her out of a chair.

The five physicians were shown the matriarch's medical records. Each physician made his recommendation. The Saudi royal physicians and family conferred and then returned to the room to tell the doctors they could all leave. Just as Sonntag reached the door they said, "Except for you, Dr. Sonntag."

Mixed emotions flooded through Dr. Sonntag. He was proud to be selected but also wondered what lay ahead for the frail, but very important and wealthy patient.

Dr. Sonntag suggested that the surgery take place in two weeks. The Saudis insisted that she fly to Phoenix the following Monday for tests and then undergo the surgery on Wednesday.

Because her spinal cord was so severely damaged from an accident, there was great concern about her traveling. It was thought that any sudden jerks or bounces during the flight might cause her to stop breathing. Barrow Neurological Institute quickly sent an anesthesiologist and a neurologist to Paris to accompany the patient on her flight to Phoenix.

With only two days' notice of the arrival of their royal patient, the hospital went into high gear. A few select hospital executives were briefed. For the sake of security, it was felt that the fewer who knew about the royal patient, the better. Patients from Barrow's seventh floor were quietly moved to other floors to make room for the royal party.

Over the weekend, representatives of the Saudi Embassy flew in from Washington to oversee the preparation of the seventh floor. The entire seventh floor was repainted and Persian carpets were laid out. Nurses attended etiquette classes. A chef from the Arizona Biltmore was hired to prepare the meals for the entourage, which at times numbered as many as 300. A satellite dish was installed to receive TV stations and other communications from Saudi Arabia. The appearance of the entire seventh floor began to take on a decidedly Arabian look.

Dr. Sonntag remembers that as he walked the corridors of the seventh floor, he felt like he was in a rose garden. The walls were lined with huge flower arrangements and plants, some as tall as 7 feet, which were sent from various heads of state and well-wishers. All of this was watched over by large, silent, square-shouldered men in dark suits and sunglasses.

During the five-hour surgery, Sonntag removed four compacted cervical discs. He then took bone from her left hip and carved it into four new discs. He fixed a plate to the discs to stabilize the spinal column. As with all surgery, Sonntag was extremely careful, knowing that one mishap might leave his royal patient paralyzed.

While the king's wife was recuperating at Barrow, the royal family settled in at the Biltmore and the Phoenician resorts, renting floors of rooms. The private Biltmore chef made daily runs to the hospital with food suited to the royal palates.

The two five-star resorts, world-renown for their amenities and service, made every effort to make their royal guests comfortable. A full-time private butler was assigned to the family members at the Phoenician. Two Saudi television channels were added to the Phoenician's TV listing. In all, they were to rent almost 80 rooms at the Phoenician for nearly two years. Room rates at the Phoenician range from $505 for premium rooms to $1,500 per night for 2 bedroom casitas. At the Biltmore, 30 rooms were taken for two years.

The Saudis would often reward service generously. Their money clips seemed to be stuffed with $100 bills which they would often offer as tips. Word of their generosity spread quickly through the resorts and the hospital. One week after the royal matriarch left Barrow, a Saudi family member dispersed envelopes with money to the hospital staff, from nurses to janitors, wishing to thank all who had cared for the royal wife. Hospital administrators, however, disapproved and told the employees to return the money.

At the resorts there were $100 tips given for the delivery of bottled water. One Saudi asked a member of the staff to make dinner reservations for him. After noticing that her watch was a fairly inexpensive make, the next day he purchased a new watch for her.

A Saudi from the entourage was eating at Aldo Baldo Ristorante in Scottsdale and asked for a $100 bottle of champagne. Within a short amount of time he had asked for two $150 bottles of champagne. He drank only a glass or two from each one, deciding that he didn't want any more once the chill had gone off the bottle.

The king's wife responded well to the surgery and, after recuperating at Barrow for almost four weeks, she was ready to leave the hospital. But an MRI showed that the plate had moved and that her bones were not healing together.

She had to undergo a second surgery and wear a "halo," a metal head piece to keep her neck straight for the remaining recovery. Her questions to the doctor indicated that she was not so much concerned about the surgery itself as a possible loss of dignity from the "halo." She was assured that her dignity would be maintained.

She recovered quickly from the second surgery, but was set back by another complication when her abdomen began to swell. Gastroenterologists were flown in. Then her liver started to fail and liver specialists were called in. After recovering from her third surgery, she and her entourage left Barrow and stayed in rented homes in Paradise Valley. They had taken up 28 rooms of the hospital for more than three months.

Dr. Sonntag made daily house calls. Her Saudi physicians stayed with her throughout her time in Phoenix.

The family rented six houses near Lincoln Drive and Invergordon Road ranging from 5,000 square feet to 7,000 square feet. Real-estate agents said the Saudis rented the homes for $30,000 to $50,000 a month per home. At first neighbors resented the Saudi security guards asking the business of people driving through the region. Before long, the security guards memorized the license plates of area regulars. The neighbors began to realize they now had the safest neighborhood in town.

Whenever a royal family member went for a stroll, she would have to be accompanied by a companion and a security guard, and often with a security van moving slowly along the street behind them.

Their homes were cleaned by housekeepers who were paid $16 to $20 per hour. Their shopping sprees became legendary. Shopkeepers' eyes would glow brightly when they saw a Saudi limo pull up in front of their store. One Saudi woman bought jewelry, paying $30,000 in cash, during a quick trip to Capriccio Fine Jewelry at the Borgata. At least two satellite dishes were purchased at Jerry's Audio for $4,000 each. Housekeepers have reported that every bedroom of each of the six houses contained a TV, with a 52 inch set in each family room.

For a taste of home, the Saudis stopped in at Sphinx Date Ranch in Scottsdale for large platters of gourmet dates and figs. They also picked up 24 five-gallon buckets of honey every six weeks from Crockett-Stewart Honey Co. Brian Nipper, the store manager, remarking about the weight of even one five-gallon bucket of honey said, "They'd stack it inside that mini-van so tight, I thought the whole thing was just going to pop."

Dr. Sonntag remembers the royal family as being very close and affectionate. "Family is very important to them," he said, "and they would always ask about yours."

During his wife's stay at Barrow, King Fahd had a stroke. Concerned for her husband, the royal wife slept with a portable phone beside her pillow to get the latest news. The Saudi women staying at the Phoenician slept quite a bit during the day so they could call home at night, catching up on the news of the country as well as the remaining family.

The Saudis would give elaborate birthday parties for their children which included clowns to entertain and ponies to ride. Children from the nearby homes in the Paradise Valley neighborhood were invited and were given $30 electronic games to take home as party favors.

Under a cloudy sky and a curtain of anonymity, Al-Anud Bint Musaid Bin Jilawi, first wife of King Fahd, left Arizona 22 months after her arrival. Once again the gleaming white jet emblazoned with the palm tree and crossed swords, insignia of Saudi Arabia, quietly ferried down a lesser-used runway at Sky harbor International Airport. Aids helped the frail lady buckle her 24-karat gold seat belt in preparation for her long flight home.

∽∽∽∽∽∽∽∽∽∽∽

Barrow Neurological Institute is a world re-known medical center located in the heart of Phoenix at the corner of 3rd Avenue and Thomas Road.

America West Arena

Sir Charles, Come Back. It Jest Ain't the Same!

1992

"When you step on the court and the crowd goes wild, you get energy you never knew you had."

Some say America West Arena is the house that Sir Charles built. There were sports reporters that even went so far as to say it was due to The Chuckster and the increased interest in sports in general that the huge, modern Bank One Ballpark was built in downtown Phoenix in 1997. Jerry Colangelo, Suns' President, says those plans were already in the works before Charles appeared on the scene. Perhaps we'll never know the full impact of his Fun House personality and heads-up basketball game, but we do know Charles Barkley gave the Suns' fans a heck of a four years.

In addition to his award-winning basketball skills, Barkley's side comments to the sports reporters became famous.

Comments to dapper Dan Majerle as he pointed to the less fashionable reporters:

"Dan, you look good. You're destroying my perceptions of how white people dress. I thought they all dressed like this bunch (pointing to the reporters). Man, media wages must be real bad."

About being a celebrity guest for the opening of Planet Hollywood in Phoenix:

"I got a feeling it could be a bad night for me tonight. I'm going to be hanging out with "Rocky" and "The Terminator" tonight. Jean Claude Van Damme, Arnold (Schwarzenegger), Sylvester (Stallone) and the Chuckster, all in the same place. I wish you were somebody so you could go, too."

As he announced his plans for a post-game meal at Majerle's Sports Grill, which had been investigated by the health department:

"Save me a table, Dan. He should save me a table. I'm one of the three people still alive after eating there."

His feelings on putting floodlights in Chicago's Wrigley Field:

"That was sacrilegious. I don't know what made them think the Cubs would ever win the World Series. Talk about a waste of the tax-payers' money."

During a game against San Antonio, he complained to a referee:

"I know women who don't hold me that tight."

His response to a fine for criticizing officials:

"This ain't about money....They (officials) were bad that night. I said it then. I say it now. You can't control me with money."

On whether he would ever return to play for the 76ers:

"I can be bought. If they paid me enough, I'd work for the Klan."

About the future of black children:

"I don't care about more black athletes. I want to see more black doctors and black lawyers and black Indian chiefs."

About the NHL's automatic suspension for coming off the bench to join a brawl on the court:

"That's crap. If they don't come off the bench to protect a teammate, I'm going to beat the crap out of them. It's stupid if your teammates don't protect you. Those guys don't throw real punches, anyway."

His feeling about young players with big money contracts and instant star status:

"I don't think they work as hard as the old players do. Every time they block a shot or dunk, they stand over you. I don't like that stuff. I liked the good old days, back when you worked hard for star status. The veterans would slap you upside the head if you did that."

His comparison of preseason to opening night:

"Preseason is just a way to screw fans out of money."

Asked whether he felt any pressure on the court:

"Pressure is when I get to the Pearly Gates and God says to me, 'Oops, sorry, you're going to hell.'"

After he was traded in 1996, the Chuckster wrote an open goodbye letter to the Phoenix fans, published in *The Arizona Republic* newspaper, which read in part:

To the Fans:

From Day One, four years ago, these friends of mine, 19,023 (the seating capacity of America West Arena) and the rest of Arizona, have shown me nothing but great loyalty and love. I was skeptical in the beginning (remember, I came from Phila-delphia), but four years later I wish every professional athlete could experience this kind of support.

I don't think fans truly understand what great support does for a team. There are many times during the season when you are physically tired and it's hard to get motivated. But when you step on the court and the crowd goes wild, you get energy you never knew you had.

So many people have touched me in four years. Thanks to the police force for doing you know what, but 55 is still too slow.

Thanks to all the restaurants who never made me wait.

Thanks to all the older people who I got a chance to meet, especially the little old ladies.

Thanks to all the Hispanics, I learned a lot about your culture. Keep pride always.

I truly in my heart believe you are the best fans in the world. One day you will get a championship because you deserve it.

You will always have a special place in No. 4's heart, I couldn't get No. 34 because some other guy (Hakeem Olajuwon) had it. I can't believe it either.

Thanks,

Charles Barkley

∽∾∽∾∽∾∽∾∽∾∽

America West Arena is located at 201 E. Jefferson.
For tickets and event information, call (602) 379-7800.

Bisbee Library

The Bats that Raised a Stink
1993

It was hard to check out a book and hold your nose at the same time.

No one really minded the bats. They had probably been roosting in the attic of the Bisbee Library since the three-storied landmark was built in 1907.

But the smell. Wheeooooeee!

And when workers disturbed the bats in the attic by removing nearly 200 pounds of bat guano, about twenty bats moved downstairs with the humans. That was a bit too much.

"During a meeting of an arts advisory group at the library Tuesday night, the bats were flying around, so we ended the meeting," city recreation director, Jeri Dustir, was quoted in the *Arizona Republic.*

Dustir estimated about 200 Mexican free-tailed bats called the library home. There was still about 100 pounds of guano left to be removed.

Bisbee Library

The twenty bats who had relocated to the downstairs part of the library were removed during the day while they slept. As the bats huddled sleepily together, it was easy to gather them up and place them in a box. They were then taken out of town and set free.

Usually in September the bats would leave the library and fly south. As long as they stayed in the attic during their summer sojourn in Bisbee they weren't a problem. But over the years so much guano had accumulated that the smell was a bit powerful. It was said the bat guano could be smelled even from outside of the building.

The city applied for a $5,500 grant from the state Historic Preservation Office to seal exterior cracks the bats used to enter the attic.

Meanwhile, there may be an added benefit to the guano cleanup other than sweeter smelling air.

"Hopefully, we'll be able to sell it," Dustir explained. "It makes great fertilizer."

*The Bisbee Library is a public building in the heart of
the oldest section of Bisbee.*

Carefree

Meet Me at the Corner of Ho and Hum
1996

If only the walls of Carefree could speak,…well, they probably wouldn't.

Being discrete, low key and unobtrusive is what Carefree is all about. The wealthy residents come to live in the village of Carefree for the natural desert, the vibrant sunsets, the desert wildlife which still surrounds them, and the quiet.

Carefree has no streetlights and many streets are deliberately left unpaved. Sidewalks are scarce, with the residents preferring paths through the desert. There is no nightlife, no trendy bars, not even a movie theater. A movie theater is considered vulgar. Nightlife for Carefree residents consists of watching the javalina, coyotes, rabbits, fox and deer wander about at the edge of their property in the evenings.

A few famous people have found their way to this rock strewn covey of large homes. John Denver is sometimes seen about town. Paul

Harvey, the radio announcer, is a regular. Jane Russell has been a resident for many years.

Perhaps the best known resident is Hugh Downs, commentator for ABC's "20-20." He loves living in Carefree and feels that his commute weekly to New York is not too high a price for living here. Downs tells that a recent visitor to his home remarked, "Well, this is all very nice, but where's the action?" Downs replied, "The action is in New York. That's why I'm here."

But the majority of Carefree residents aren't household names. They are mostly the captains of industry, such as:

*   Rusty Lyon, the founder of Westcor, which manages the Valley's largest shopping centers.
*   John Carley, past president of Albertson's food stores
*   Fred Langhammer, president and chief operating officer of cosmetics giant Estee Lauder.
*   J. Orin Edson, founder of the company who makes Bayliner yachts
*   A member of the U-Haul Shoen family

Houses generally start at $300,000 and quickly soar to several million dollars. Realtors report that most Carefree residents pay cash for their houses. The lots alone go for $1 million to $2 million. Spec homes are built for $4 million and quickly sold.

Carefree has evolved into exactly what the two original planners had envisioned. Over a business lunch in Phoenix one day in 1946, Tom Darlington, a corporate manager, said to K. T. Palmer, a lawyer, "Someday I would like to plan and build a town from scratch." Palmer nodded, "So would I."

In 1955 they had the opportunity to purchase the original 2,200 acres which included an old ranch. At a cocktail party the town planners and their friends picked the whimsical street names. Winding through the desert community you'll find Languid Lane, Leisure Lane, Meander and Rocking Chair Road. Of course, the bank is on Wampum Way. What retiree wouldn't love to live on Easy Street, or Never Mind Trail? The center of town is at the intersection of Ho and Hum.

Motivated by a desire for privacy, a love of serenity and respect for the beauty that surrounds them, the residents of Carefree build roads and homes which nestle amongst the boulders and straddle washes, curve around saguaros and lie low in the ravines. Roads are carefully plotted through the landscape forming graceful, easy curving paths.

One of the homes includes tunnels between rooms for a cat who never leaves the house. The tunnels include an entry to a special "kitty litter facility."

A number of homes are such an integral part of the desert that a huge boulder forms one wall of a living room or bedroom. Several have the original desert plants growing in the undisturbed crevices, watered only when it rains.

One home has the roof designed such that it is within 18 inches from the adjoining mountainside, with the opposite edge of the roof hanging over a massive pile of rocks and boulders. The homeowner was so familiar with his property when he built that he knew about a pack of coyotes who used a certain path in their nightly prowls, right through the area where he planned to build. Now the crown of his roof simply creates a higher path for the coyotes who jump from the mountain to the rooftop, pad along the crown of the roof and leap down from roof to boulder, disappearing into the shadows of night.

What serves as the center of town is a shopper's haven. Trendy boutiques selling candles, upscale clothing, Southwestern jewelry and other must-buy items tempt visitors from all over the world. Meet you at the corner of Ho and Hum.

While many of the largest homes are behind security gates
there are others which can be viewed from the road.
To reach Carefree, drive north on Scottsdale Road about
45 minutes. Located in downtown Carefree, you'll find
unique boutiques, art galleries and restaurants.
Most stores are open daily the year round. Check with
the Chamber of Commerce for special fiesta days.
Carefree-Cave Creek Chamber of Commerce,
Box 734, Carefree, AZ 85377;
(602) 488-3381.

The roof of this home continues to provide a path for the coyotes.

Mission San Xavier del Bac

The White Dove of the Desert
1997

Mission San Xavier del Bac,...a place of silence, a place of mystery, a place of miracles.

In the early morning hours the silence of the old mission is complete. A lone visitor can hear the *sotto voce* whispering of the candles, as if they are muttering to themselves. The spirits of the past seem to surround the supplicant with warmth and comfort. Mission San Xavier del Bac stands alone in the desert, a pristine monument to the faith of generations of Tohono O'Odham (formerly called Papago). In the deep silence a whispered prayer joins the hundreds of thousands of others which have been murmured within the centuries-old walls. Soon the silence will be broken by the footsteps of others.

As visitors step across the worn threshold, their voices naturally take on a hushed tone while they gaze at the dark interior of the old mission. A recorded voice tells about the history of San Xavier. As the tourists enter and quietly find a seat on an old bench, they look around, marveling at the ornate, Mexican baroque artwork of the old church. Then always their eyes go up, and up, and up to the highest point of the altar, just as the architect intended. Their eyes become a physical prayer.

Interior of Mission San Xavier del Bac.

Surrounded by the mystical, Our Lady of the Sorrows, Mary Immaculate, the Apostles, the Evangelists, the Virgin Martyrs, St. Joseph and St. Francis of Assisi all look down upon the worshipers in silent testimony of their faith. In the center of the main altar piece is San Francisco Xavier del Bac, patron saint of the mission. Above San Xavier is the Virgin of the Immaculate Conception and, high above all, stands God, the Father, Creator of Heaven and Earth and all things, mystery of mysteries.

Forever a part of San Xavier's history is Father Kino, the beloved Jesuit priest who established a series of missions in northern Mexico and southern Arizona. Planning his mission at Bac to be the center of his ministry, he began work here in 1692. Father Kino raised the subsistence level of survival for the Indians by bringing in horses, cattle, sheep, goats and wheat.

Although Father Kino began the work among the people of Bac, he died in 1711 after starting only the foundations for what he described as a "large and capacious" building. In 1767 the Jesuits were expelled from their global missions by the King and required to return to Spain. It was Father Juan Bautista Velderrain, a Franciscan, who built the church at Bac in 1783, which still stands today and is known throughout the world for its serene beauty and mystery. The mission was completed in 1797, celebrating it's 200th anniversary with a series of festivals and activities in 1997.

Some of the mysteries are voiced by the visitors who arrive daily. Why was one tower left unfinished? Some say a workman fell to his death and the tower was left as it stood as a monument to him. Others say the mission simply ran out of money. It is suspected the wise padres decided they didn't need a finished tower; once the building was completed they would have to begin paying taxes to Spain. If only these walls could speak, they would tell us.

As with many European cathedrals, Mission San Xavier del Bac has its own end-of-the-world story. High up on the sand-colored fretwork on the front of the church one can see two large, carved scrolls. On one perches a mouse and on the opposing scroll is a cat. The legend tells that when the cat catches the mouse, time will be no more. In other words, the church will stand until the end of time.

In addition to silence and mystery, the church is filled with miracles. The miracles are kept behind a counter at the gift shop. The box must contain at least a hundred of them, these *milagros*, as they are called in Spanish.

The *milagros* are tiny metal cutouts of arms and legs and hearts and hands. They are surprisingly light, almost light enough to be carried up and away into a breeze as they are carried into the chapel. Those who bring them to the chapel know they do fly upward, up to heaven. They represent heartfelt prayers.

Turning into the side chapel to the left of the altar, the prayerful bring the *milagros* to pin onto the coverlet that lies across the reclining statue of San Francisco Xavier. Each *milagro* is attached with a prayer, sometimes written, other times merely spoken in a whisper. They are also pinned on when a prayer has been answered, when the *milagro* has come to pass.

Other symbols of prayers are pinned to the coverlet: photographs, medical bracelets, ribbons and bouquets of flowers. The notes are perhaps the most wrenching. These prayers are written to reach the heart of heaven, but they touch the human heart as well.

"Protect my sons," the prayer reads, "wherever they may be."

"Please help us find the way," begs another.

Attached to a child's picture, a note reads, "Your soul will be with all of us always. We miss you."

There are prayers requesting strength and courage, honesty in a relationship, and protection. Some prayers simply ask for help in making it through each day. Surrounding the statue of San Francisco are the hundreds of prayer candles lit by the faithful.

Do they work? Are the prayers answered? Do miracles happen?

Here at San Xavier Mission are many stories of healings of both body and mind. Sometimes miracles are subtle. Father Michael Dallmeier, former pastor of the mission, tells of a visitor who wrote to him of his experience at San Xavier. The man had recently lost his wife and was continuing to live with deep depression and grief. Not a Catholic, he had little interest in the church and no desire to leave the tour bus. But something compelled him to get out and go into the old mission. While seated in that holy place, he began to feel that his wife was there, and everything would be all right. He received a calmness of spirit, and he left with a new sense of peace.

Father Michael has his own definition of a miracle. He finds a daily miracle in the strength of those who come here, those who write the notes, attach the *milagros*, endure the pain. He says, "In the face of overwhelming odds, they continue to walk with hope and dignity. That's a miracle."

Silence. Mystery. Miracles. The old mission invites you to come see for yourself.

～～～～～～～～～～～

The mission of San Xavier (pronounced locally as "san ha veer") has recently undergone an extensive $2 million restoration. Removing the centuries-old build-up of varnish, candle smoke, dirt and bird droppings, repairing the statues and regilding the altar have once again revealed the beautiful, vibrant original colors.

Mission San Xavier del Bac is three-fourths of a mile west of Interstate 19 about 10 miles south of downtown Tucson. There is a gift shop at the mission as well as a grouping of shops to the south across the parking lot. Often there are Tohono O'Odham women selling fresh Indian fry bread under the ramada near the front entrance. Indulge yourself. There is no admission charge to the mission, but a donation is gratefully accepted. Please remember that this is an active church. Visitors should act and dress accordingly.

The church is open to the public from 8:00 a.m. to 6:00 p.m. except during services. For times of services, call (520) 294-2624 or write to Mission San Xavier del Bac, 1950 West San Xavier Road, Tucson, AZ 85746.

ABOUT THE AUTHOR

Judy Martin, a native Arizonan, is proud of her home state and loves to show it off. Born in Phoenix, she received her BS Degree in Elementary Education, with honors, from Northern Arizona University. She met her husband, Dick, in high school and they married in 1965. Judy taught school in Flagstaff, Tucson and Chicago, helping put her husband through dental school. Dan, their son, is a jeweler who works in Scottsdale. Their daughter Debby is married to Mark and teaches first grade. When Dick isn't driving Judy around the state helping with research on her next book, he keeps an active dental practice going in Glendale. Judy worked as a travel agent for ten years before deciding to narrow her interests to Arizona tourists. She has worked as a storyteller and Arizona Tour Guide since 1990. Phasing out of her tour guiding activities, Judy spends the majority of her time researching and writing about Arizona.

Arizona Walls
If Only They Could Speak

Bibliography

Albano, Bob. *Wild West Series: Arizona Highways Days of Destiny*.
Phoenix: Arizona Highways, 1996.

Archives of Arizona Historical Society, Tucson

Archives of Arizona State Capitol Museum

Archives of Yuma Territorial Prison State Park

Arizona Highways Magazine

Arizona Republic Newspaper

Arizona State Capitol Times. Volume 94, Issue 7, February 17, 1993.

Brophy, Frank Cullen. *Arizona Sketch Book: Fifty Historical Sketches*.
Phoenix: AMPCO Press, 1952.

Caillou, Aliza, Editor. *Experience Jerome and the Verde Valley*
Legends and Legacies. Sedona: Thorne, 1990.

Chaput, Don. *Nellie Cashman and the North American Mining Frontier*.
Tucson: Westernlore Press, 1995.

Cline, Platt. *Mountain Town: Flagstaff's First Century*.
Flagstaff: Northland Publishing, 1994.

Heatwole, Thelma. *Ghost Towns and Historical Haunts in Arizona*.
Phoenix: Golden West Publishers, 1981.

Lauer, Charles. *Tales of Arizona Territory*.
Phoenix: Golden West Publishers, 1990.

Lockard, Peggy Hamilton. *This is Tucson: Guidebook to the Old Pueblo*.
Tucson: Pepper Publishing, 1988.

Martin, Douglas D. *Tombstone's Epitaph*.
Albuquerque: The University of New Mexico Press, 1951.

Murbarger, Nell. *Ghosts of the Adobe Walls*.
Tucson: Treasure Chest Publications, Inc., 1964.

Myers, John Myers. *Tombstone's Early Years*.
Lincoln: University of Nebraska Press, 1995.

Paplow, Bonnie and Ed. *Pioneer Stories of Arizona's Verde Valley*.
Verde Valley Pioneers Association, 1954.

Phoenix Gazette Newspaper

Rogers, W. Lane. *Crimes and Misdeeds: Headlines from Arizona's Past.*
Flagstaff: Northland Press, 1995.

Ruffner, Budge. *All Hell Needs is Water.*
Tucson: The University of Arizona Press, 1972.

Ruland-Thorne, Kate. *Experience Sedona Legends and Legacies.*
Sedona: Thorne, 1991.

Schweikart, Herman. *99 General Stories in Arizona.*
Provo: Community Press, 1971.

Sherman, Barbara, and James E. *Ghost Towns of Arizona.*
Norman: University of Oklahoma Press, 1969.

Stewart, Janet Ann. *Arizona Ranch Houses.*
Tucson: Arizona Historical Society, 1974.

The Cochise Quarterly, Volume 15, #4, Winter, 1985.

The Press of the Territorials Presents #15 of the Series. Two Guns.

Trimble, Marshall. *Arizona: A Cavalcade of History.*
Tucson: Treasure Chest Publications, 1989.

Trimble, Marshall. *Arizona Adventure.*
Phoenix: Golden West Publishers, 1982.

Trimble, Marshall. *In Old Arizona: True Tales of the Wild Frontier.*
Phoenix: Golden West Publishers, 1985.

Trimble, Marshall. *Roadside History of Arizona.*
Missoula: Mountain Press, 1986.

Traywick, Ben T. *The Chronicles of Tombstone.*
Tombstone: Red Marie's Bookstore, 1994.

Traywick, Ben T. *Tombstone Clippings.*
Tombstone: Red Marie's Bookstore, 1994.

Traywick, Ben T. *Legendary Characters of Southeast Arizona.*
Tombstone: Red Marie's Bookstore, 1994.

Varney, Philip. *Arizona's Best Ghost Towns.*
Flagstaff: Northland Press, 1980.

Varney, Philip. *Arizona Ghost Towns and Mining Camps.*
Phoenix: Arizona Highways, 1994.

Weir, Bill, and Blake, Robert. *Arizona Traveler's Handbook.*
Chico: Moon Publications, Inc., 1996.

INDEX

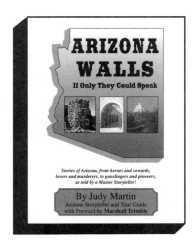

To order your copy of:

ARIZONA WALLS
If Only They Could Speak

by Judy Martin

MAIL YOUR ORDER TO:

5700 W. Olive, Ste. 102
Glendale, Arizona 85302

Retail price of each book is $14.95.

All prices in U.S. $
Add 7% sales tax for AZ residents ($1.04)

SEND MONEY ORDER, PERSONAL, OR CASHIERS CHECK
(U.S. FUNDS ONLY) PAYABLE TO: Judy Martin

Would You Like to See Your Arizona Story in Print?

Just contact Judy Martin at e-mail address: judes1@juno.com

THANK YOU FOR YOUR ORDER AND YOUR INTEREST.

(Please Print Only)

_____ BOOKS ORDERED
$14.95 X EACH = _____

SALES TAX _____

S/H $3.00 PER ORDER _____

DATE ____ / ____ / ____

TOTAL AMOUNT ENCLOSED $ _____

SHIP TO:

NAME _____ COMPANY _____

ADDRESS _____

CITY _____ STATE _____ ZIP _____

PHONE ( ) _____ FAX ( ) _____